Sarah Armstrong is the author of three previous novels, most recently *The Wolves of Leninsky Prospekt,* the first in the *Moscow Wolves* series. She teaches undergraduate and postgraduate creative writing with the Open University. Sarah lives in Colchester with her husband and four children.

THE
STARLINGS
OF
BUCHAREST

SARAH ARMSTRONG

SANDSTONE PRESS

... at Britain by
... ss Ltd
... 1
... rd

www.sandstonepress.com

Sandstone Press is committed to a sustainable future.
This book is made from Forest Stewardship Council ® certified paper.

ISBN: 978-1-913207-00-7
ISBNe: 978-1-913207-01-4

Cover design by Kidethic
Typeset by Iolaire, Newtonmore
Printed and bound by Severn, Gloucester

To Mark Armstrong –
historical adviser, fact checker, tyrant

They talk of a man betraying his country, his friends, his sweetheart. There must be a moral bond first. All a man can betray is his conscience.

Joseph Conrad

1975

BUCHAREST

CHAPTER 1

It made no difference whether I tried to sneak out by using the lift or the stairs. He was always waiting for me before I got outside.

'Ted!' Vasile managed to convey exactly the same amount of surprise each time. 'How are things for you today?'

'I'm still waiting to get to the studio.'

'I know, I know. Directors.' He tutted, and smiled in his wide, insincere way. 'I am going to sort that out, don't you worry.' He looked me up and down. 'Another pair of trousers?' He was obsessed with my clothes.

'No, I wore these on the first day.'

'Of course, of course.' He nodded, his hands open in front of him. 'Shall we get something to eat?'

'I was just going for a walk.'

'But how will they tell you when your car is available?'

They were never going to tell me when my car was available. I was never going to get to interview that film director, I would lose my job and my landlady would throw me out. I was never going to leave this hotel. My shoulders slumped.

'It's going to be fine.' He slapped my shoulder. 'Nici o problema.'

Nothing was ever a 'problema' for Vasile, but nothing was ever achieved either. Days of postponements were nothing

3

to him, but it wasn't as if there were daily flights back to London. My booked flight had already taken off, and the rearranged one was in two days' time.

Still, I looked at his hopeful face and agreed. He led me to the dining room.

'After I eat I'll go for a walk,' I said. 'They aren't going to send a car after three, are they?'

He looked at his watch. 'Maybe after three that will be safe, yes. I will check with the travel service, just to make sure.'

I was starting to believe that nothing would ever be certain in Bucharest. Everything was fluid, especially faithful promises and fixed arrangements. I didn't think it was Vasile's fault. He seemed genuinely upset to have to tell me 'not today', over and over.

We sat at the same table as usual, the sun falling on my face. Sometimes he'd turn to the window and point out things of interest: pretty girls, foreign cars. He was a little younger than me, maybe twenty, but wearing an overly large suit with worn elbows. He had tacked the sleeve hems up so that, if it had buttons, they were hidden. He frequently pulled the sleeves down, as if the suit was too small, and I wondered if he'd picked up the habit from watching someone else.

The waiter stumbled across and Vasile gave our orders. I smoothed down the white table linen, rearranged the cutlery and looked out of the window, but it was the same view as ever at the lunch service. The buses and trams, with the bottom half red and top half cream, were crammed with bodies spilling from the doors and, occasionally, clinging to the sides. So many people. Could they all be on shift work, or did they go home for lunch? Vasile became edgy when I asked questions, so I tried not to ask too many.

Vasile sighed. When I looked at him he'd closed his eyes.

He murmured, 'Hotel Continental.' This was another habit of his, to sit back, forgetting I was there, say something to himself, and shake his head. 'It's the greatest hotel in the world, don't you think?'

'Have you been here before?' I asked.

He opened his eyes, looking confused. 'I saw you here yesterday and the day before.'

'I mean before I came.'

'Ah, no.' He leaned towards me. 'This is my first job as a guide.'

'Your English is very good,' I said.

He lowered his gaze and smiled more widely than usual. 'I study very hard. I hope to be the best guide.' He pulled at his suit sleeve again, then joined his hands together on the table.

'Do you live at home?'

His smile faded. 'Of course I live in a home.'

'At home with your parents, I mean.'

'Ah.' His face clouded and he turned to fix on a distant point outside. He tilted his head as if he'd remembered something. 'If Mircea Drăgan is not available, would you be open to interviewing another director instead?'

I knew he'd been leading up to something like this.

'No, it has to be Drăgan. That's why I'm here.'

Vasile persisted. 'Elisabeta Bostan isn't directing this week. She is the director of fifteen films, some very popular musicals.' He raised his eyebrows.

I shrugged. 'It has to be Drăgan. I don't get to choose who I interview, I'm afraid.'

'Do the British not enjoy musicals?'

'Some do. But Mircea Drăgan has been entered into three Moscow International Film Festivals and won awards at each, and was on the jury in another. He has more of a profile abroad.' Supposedly. Not that I'd heard of him until shortly before I was sent on this trip.

'I understand.'

The waiter arrived back with our beers, and Vasile gratefully began talking to him. I was happy with his timing too. I had never heard of Bostan, and wouldn't know what to ask her. I had only seen Drăgan's last film, so all my questions were based on that. It wasn't great. An ocean liner on fire, it didn't compare well to *The Poseidon Adventure*, out the year before, but my boss had fixed on Drăgan to compete with *Sight and Sound*. 'They can have Tarkovsky, but we'll get Drăgan. He'll be so much bigger.'

I had my doubts. Even I had heard of *Solaris*.

Vasile and the waiter were chatting fast, very excited about something. Most of Vasile's beer had gone as he drank from his glass and handed the waiter the bottle to drink from.

'Six one!' he shouted at me. 'We beat Denmark, six one!'

I clinked my glass to his. I gathered it was a qualifications match for the UEFA Championship, and Vasile could now visualise the Romanians on the winners' podium, kissing their medals.

Sport. I'd already heard way too much about Ilie Năstase, a tennis player I had heard of, and a load of gymnasts I hadn't. It was going to be a long afternoon.

'Do you see? If we can beat the capitalists at soccer and tennis, we prove ourselves.' He burped. 'I don't mean any offence.'

'That's all right. I'm not sure that I'm a capitalist.' I hoped he would take me back soon. I wouldn't be able to keep my eyes open for much longer, and I seemed to keep slipping from the bench. We had left the restaurant at dusk, some time ago, but I couldn't quite remember how we'd got to this park.

'Oh. I must note that. That's interesting.' He wriggled to right himself and nodded.

'Note it?' I asked.

He whispered loudly, 'I make notes. I am always learning more about your people.'

I nodded. 'Me too.'

He squinted to look at me. 'I haven't told you anything.'

'Don't worry, I'm not taking notes. I meant – no, I've forgotten what I meant. Romania won the football, though, I remember that. I'll let everyone know when I get back to London.'

'Ted, your voice doesn't sound like you are from London. Where did you live before?'

I couldn't be bothered to explain where Harwich was. It was too complicated. 'Nowhere. Just London. I'd never been out of the country until I came here and I'm booked to go to the festival in Moscow. I'd prefer Cannes, to be honest, but it's exciting to be abroad.'

'And how did you get your job?'

'I'm not sure, really. I just applied.' Mr Benstrup had hinted that his wife had liked my application letter, but I wasn't going to admit that.

Vasile mumbled a word to himself, then yawned and looked around. 'Where are we?'

'I have no idea.' There were trees around the bench we sat on, and I could hear some water. I couldn't hear any cars. Now I was thinking, it was pleasantly cool. The days had been warm, from my position at the window, waiting, waiting, waiting. But as for where we were, it could have been anywhere in the world. 'I hope we're somewhere in Bucharest.'

Vasile laughed, and then stopped suddenly. 'Ted, I need to ask you something.'

'Please don't ask me how we get back to the hotel.'

'No. Will you give me your trousers?'

'What?' I lit a cigarette and his face was illuminated. He looked serious as he helped himself to my packet and flicked his Zippo lighter open and closed.

'When you leave, can I have your trousers?'

I looked at my trousers. 'I'm wearing them.'

'But you have another pair.'

'I need two pairs. They have to be washed, now and again.'

'Bine, bine.' He looked sad, his head to one side. 'So you are a capitalist after all. That was a joke. But I have a serious question to ask.'

'OK.'

He lit his cigarette and edged closer to me. 'Will you take a trip for me and write an article about it?'

'A trip?'

'A historical trip to Transylvania. It explores the history behind all the Dracula rubbish. It would be very good for you to write about. I would be very grateful.'

I tried to edge away, but I was on the end of the bench. 'I'm a film reviewer. I don't write about travel.'

'Yes, but you are a journalist first. A great journalist. You can spread your ideas.'

'I really don't have time for travelling. I need to get back to London.'

'Right.'

His voice was flat. He stood up and held his hand out. I stumbled to my feet.

'Time to go back.'

We walked along paths, under trees, and along dark roads until the hotel was there in front of me. He saw me across the road and to the main doors.

'See you tomorrow, Ted,' he said.

I grabbed onto the door handle and somehow negotiated my way through. I slid along banisters and walls, and found the intimidating floor attendant sitting at her desk.

'Room 313, please.' I think I said that. I could have said anything, in the knowledge that she knew who I was.

'You have your key.'

I checked my jacket, then each trouser pocket in a slow but thorough way. 'No, I left it with you.'

'It's in your left trouser pocket.'

It was. I looked at her as if she had placed it there while I blinked. Sixtyish, stern, with every hair pulled back into a bun, and magical. I'd never have expected it of her.

'Thank you,' I said.

'Good night,' she said, and went back to looking at the empty staircase.

I let myself into my room, flung myself at the bed, and stared at the ceiling with its bare bulb. There were things I wasn't happy about in this room. Things moved, ever so slightly, when I wasn't looking. There were strange noises in the skirting board, and that stain on the bathroom floor, but it was a relief to be alone.

I sat up and the room steadied. Letter. I could use this time to write the letter I had meant to write this afternoon. I needed to explain, and that was always easier on paper. I wouldn't have to look anyone in the eye.

I tore a page from my notebook and sat by the window which I had opened fully to still the queasiness in my stomach. The night was cool and quiet, the streetlights all out. I heard a clatter in the distance. In London that would be a person, drunk or being beaten, but here it would be something pleasant. Like a fox. No one roamed the streets. It was nice in that way, at least.

I started to write, one eye closed for precision.

ROMANIAN MINISTRY OF THE INTERIOR

Compilation of REPORTS on
REGINALD EDWARD WALKER

9-15 May 1975

Day 1

The subject arrived at Otopeni airport at
13.45 on 9th May and was collected by STARLING
who escorted him to the Hotel Continental,
Bucharest. He is booked into room 313.

At 17:00 STARLING accompanied the subject
to the restaurant, allowing LEAF to examine
the subject's possessions, among which
were: two pairs of white underpants (Marks
and Spencer), one pair of black socks (no
label, worn, 2mm hole in one) and one pair of
burgundy cotton trousers (C&A), a grey shirt
(C&A), and a tweed jacket (chest size 40, too
large for the subject). The relative quality
of the jacket prompted further attention.

On examination, this jacket was found to
have a label (Towncraft, Penneys) indicating it
was a style made more than ten years earlier
in the USA - two buttons to the front, one on
each sleeve, narrow lapels, chest pocket, two
flap pockets and two back vents. Fabric is wool
(mostly blue with a thin gold-brown stripe)
with rayon lining (grey). Considering his age
and the fact this is larger than his shirts,
it is possible either the subject was given it

by an older relative, or purchased it second-
hand. He may, however, have ties to the USA
which are unknown.

A copy was taken of the information in his
British Passport, as follows:

- Cover: Reginald Edward Walker – uses
  'Ted', a potentially misleading name
- p.2 Occupation – Journalist; Place of
  birth – Harwich; Date of birth – 3rd
  July 1953; Residence – 159C Griffin Road;
  Height – 5'9"; Distinguishing marks –
  none; Spouse and Children – left blank
- p.3 black and white photo, good likeness
  which shows that his hair can be tidier
  with effort

Continuing with the suitcase contents, which
had not been fully unpacked:

- materials for bathing and shaving
- two house keys (copies made)
- an exercise notebook
- one black Bic pen
- one red pencil with black lead
- a copy of *Journalism – Made Simple* by
  David Wainwright
- a copy of *Darkness at Noon* by Arthur Koestler. Contained within this book (p.46)
  was a business card reading 'Mr Attridge,
  Travel Service Whitehall 3636' – possibly
  used as a bookmark, but this could

indicate something of significance on p.46 which has not yet been ascertained. On calling this number, LEAF was unconvinced that this was an authentic business owing to a perceptible buzz on the line.

The ashtray held three butts, identified as 'Kent' brand. There were no matches, and he has been observed using a lighter, identified by STARLING as a 'Ronson Varaflame'.

The appearance of the subject is relatively clean yet his clothes have not been ironed since they were last laundered. He is currently wearing brown corded trousers, a cream shirt, presumably further underpants and socks, and a pair of brown brogues. He appears to be physically able, and prefers his right hand to his left.

He presents as having a genuine interest in Romania generally, and the film industry in particular. The book on journalism and cited 'occupation' as journalist are potential pressure points, as his true role is 'film reviewer'. The subject seems to know little about film reviewing so it has been decided to keep the subject away from the Buftea film studios until more is known about his intentions. While we have been told that the subject is happy to act as a courier on behalf of his employer, we need to be certain that we do not expose our practices unnecessarily. LEAF is particularly concerned that the business card could indicate that he is acting for another party. Before we make our planned advances, STARLING has been instructed to view the subject as potentially hostile, and close observation continues.

Service T has put phone and light intercepts in place and these are being monitored.

No phone calls scheduled for this night.

Day 2
STARLING called on the subject early and remained with him all day. The subject did not talk much and appears to enjoy listening. STARLING reports he was able to convey a lot of positive information about the Romanian form of social progress. On a walk around the area, the subject saw people picking lime blossoms for tea and suggested that they were picking leaves to eat because they were hungry. STARLING corrected this straight away.

The subject had some conversation starters which were designed to draw information from STARLING on the Romanian film industry, film directors and recent prizes awarded within the industry. The subject offered no opinions of his own.

The subject did not display concern about the delay of his trip to Buftea, so he may be collecting other information. He looked towards the woman on duty in the travel office whenever he passed. Owing to this interest, it is suggested that someone look into MIHAELA ZAMFIR's background for any links to Britain or other Western countries. Alternatively, it might be possible to introduce the subject to a connection to progress this type of interest.

For information, STARLING was observed eating all three meals with the subject, as has been observed with other subjects.

Bin contents – *Holidays in Romania*

Noise activity - nothing coherent. Occasional humming.

Phone calls - the subject reacted negatively to phone calls from the bar asking if he would like company. After 3:00 no calls were answered — presumably the subject found a way to muffle the sound.

Day 3
The research into MIHAELA ZAMFIR continues. In the meantime she was told to cancel the subject's flight, partly to keep him in Bucharest and partly to see if she passed on this information.

At the subject's request, STARLING called on the subject at lunchtime instead of breakfast time, and remained with him all day. In the evening the football result where we crushed Denmark gave STARLING a reason to push more alcohol on the subject than before to see what information could be collected. The subject gave no contradictory information, and claimed to have no links to the USA or people from there. He confirmed that his jacket was indeed a second-hand purchase in London, and there is no reason to disbelieve this. He also stuck to his claim that he was from 'London' and not 'Harwich', as this is now where he lives.

LEAF would like to record STARLING's unprofessional focus on the subject's clothes, as overheard near the Biserica Kretzulescu. By asking for trousers he makes the state look incapable of clothing its citizens and this must not happen again. It is also noted that he wears a jacket which is too large and is ordered to find a more suitable article of clothing from the office. It was made clear to him that any repetition of unprofessional appearance or behaviour will result in action. When confronted, STARLING assumed that the subject must have reported or otherwise complained about him. As this may lead him to think twice about asking for a subject's possessions, we will not inform him otherwise.

An early concern, that of the business card, is no longer thought to be problematic as the subject has not undertaken any actions nor asked any questions which would benefit a third party. It has been decided that it is safe to take him to conduct his interview, after which we will proceed with the main aim of his visit.

Further to this, OAK has requested that the subject be used to acquire the cooperation of MARKU BOLDEA who resists providing information on his place of employment. STARLING to act on this.

Bin contents - *Holidays in Romania*

Noise activity - during his drunken state, the subject was heard to tear out paper and mumble to himself. The scratch of a pen was sometimes audible.

No phone calls scheduled for this night.

CHAPTER 2

There was a heavy banging on the door, and then talking outside. I heard keys, and pulled my pillow over my head. I could hear mumbling, and someone tugged the pillow away. I managed to open one eye.

'The car is ready,' said Vasile. 'I have been ringing your room. You have ten minutes.'

I nodded.

'Ten minutes,' he repeated, and the door closed behind him.

I forced myself to sit up. The gloomy brown room was a mess, even in the near dark with the curtains pulled. Crumpled papers reminded me that at some point I had written unfinished letters, and a blanket over the phone suggested that it had rung at some point but I didn't remember waking.

I pressed my hands into my eye sockets. Something terrible and urgent had happened, and I couldn't remember what it was.

Oh, yes.

The car was ready.

Vasile was waiting for me in the lobby as I inched myself down the wide stairs, tweed jacket in my hand. The stair treads seemed particularly red and shallow today, and I relied on the handrail to get me there safely. I spotted Mihaela at the travel desk in her booth and waved feebly. She blushed and looked away, and I felt embarrassed for both of us. I checked that I had remembered to put my notebook and pen in my pocket. The look on Vasile's face told me that I wasn't fooling anyone about being fit for a day's work.

'How much exactly did I drink last night?' I mumbled.

He shrugged. 'Not much.' He looked the same as ever. Actually, no, he was different. He wasn't smiling.

The sun bounced off the concrete block opposite the hotel entrance, and I held a hand to my eyes. Vasile took my elbow, leading me to the car parked around the corner. He got in the nearest door, so I went around to the other side. It didn't take me long to realise that a spring had gone rogue within the seat, pushing up against the thin material. At a word from Vasile, the driver pulled away, and I concentrated on trying to open my eyes. We emerged onto the wide main road, thankfully straight and true, passing grey blocks of concrete flats, and more rounded, older buildings. I'd seen so little of Bucharest, stuck inside the hotel with my view of the crossroads and grey buildings with shaded windows. Yet, while I enjoyed glimpses of little parks filled with trees, I could feel there had been a worrying shift in my relationship with Vasile. After all those days of endless talking and smiling encouragement, he was stiff and silent.

I sneaked glances at him, but his face was turned towards the window. No discussion of why Romania shouldn't be linked only with Dracula in films, no mention of the evils of Hungarian land grabs, no lists of sports men and women. Nothing.

I wished I could remember more of the previous night. I had glimpses of how it ended, and it seemed to be pleasant enough. Funny, even, but I must have insulted him somehow.

I must have been rude about Romania, or Bucharest, or – oh, God, I hoped I hadn't told him what I thought of Drăgan's films. Or when I said he couldn't have my trousers, was that it? Could I spare my trousers? They were nothing fancy, getting a little worn in the knees, in fact. But I couldn't afford another pair at the moment. Not with everything. But the silence was becoming awkward now.

I looked across again, and down at his wrist. Buttons. Buttons on his suit jacket, and surely that was a new tie. Maybe he'd been so embarrassed that he'd borrowed a suit from someone else, a brother maybe, or a friend. He turned to look at me. I smiled, but he just turned away.

I must have done something really bad. I shuddered.

I took out the notebook and pen, and tried to focus on why I was here. It wasn't to make Romanian friends, it was to impress Mr Benstrup and keep my job. I was sure I'd made a list of questions for Drăgan, but in the rush to leave, hadn't been able to find them. Had I even locked my door?

I was doodling, and Vasile was watching. I turned the page over and smoothed it out. Questions. For a director of derivative films. I remembered that his film was based on a true event. I could ask him about that, about transforming fact into fiction, the demands of the watery set.

The water. Full of sea monsters, according to my father. When I was a child he had read from *The History of Greenland* every night, picking out the sections on sea-serpents and kraken, which he never claimed to have witnessed, and the disappearance and reappearance of islands, which he said he *had* seen. For years, I didn't understand why a family of fishermen would pass down this book, but when I went out with him in the cold dawn, he told me to keep a look out. 'It will make our fortune, if you catch one of them monsters.' Our fortune. No more fishing, no more being soaked and frozen.

I concentrated so hard that my hand was sliced open by the snapped section of metal railing my father never replaced, and I nearly lost the feeling in that hand.

The doctor who stitched it up told me off for being careless.

'You've heard the stories, haven't you? Men who've been sailing for years get caught out and swept overboard. You must be aware of what's going on around you at all times.'

'I am. It was an accident. I am very observant.'

He frowned. 'That may be so, but are you observing the right things? I know your dad, he's a talker. Make sure you know what is important at that moment and give it your full attention.'

It was a big scar, but it didn't get me out of fishing.

My eyes had closed again and the pen fallen from my hand. I kept them closed until the car slowed and rumbled over unmade ground. We stopped by a medieval gateway and Vasile got out. The heat hit me straight away, and I realised how thirsty I was. I clambered from the car, remembering my pen, and followed him.

An older man was waiting for us. Vasile shook his hand, and they had walked on before I was even out of the car. This new man kept looking back at me, but the openness of the studio site meant that the dust swirled freely, making me cough as I jogged towards them.

Vasile shouted back to me. 'He wants you to know that Orson Welles visited here eight years ago.'

The man nodded and smiled. I nodded and smiled back, trying to keep the dust out of my mouth. We walked through a film set. Mexico, it seemed. One-storey buildings with rough walls and archways next to two-storey buildings with long, curved wooden struts holding up the tiled roofs. A tall, thin tower seemed to have nothing to do with this place, and the men in soft hats and long tunics who stood around looked like North African travellers who had lost their camels.

Still we walked, through dusty city streets and dustier rural villages, my mouth becoming drier.

'Over twenty films a year!' shouted Vasile. 'Many international awards!'

Smile and nod.

'Last year, Mircea Veroiu filmed *Duhul Aurului*, this year Mircea Daneliuc is filming *Cursa*.'

Were all male directors called Mircea? I didn't care anymore. My feet started to drag. I was going to die in Morocco or wherever this film set was supposed to be.

The other man ran up to me and put my arm around his shoulder. He shouted back and forth with Vasile then led me towards another set with a building with windows and steps. He helped me inside and sat me down. It was some kind of office. Still hot, but at least I was sitting.

'Water, please,' I said. 'Water.'

Vasile talked to the man, and they both disappeared through a door. I noticed a woman at a desk, staring at me. She jumped, and began typing. The man came back and handed me a glass of water. As I drank it I saw that he wasn't sympathetic anymore. He shook his head at me.

'Thank you,' I said.

He tutted and walked across to the typist, making the international sign for drinking. She shook her head and said, 'Capitalist.' Also, clearly, an international communication.

Vasile opened the door and beckoned to me. 'Mr Drăgan is ready to see you.' I stood up and placed the glass on a table, before following him along a dark corridor. He knocked on an already open door, and introduced me to the thin man standing behind a desk. He didn't look like the dark haired forty-two-year-old I had been expecting, but closer to sixty. What hair was left around the sides was grey, and his smile was nervous as he flicked his eyes between me and Vasile.

'Mircea Drăgan?' I asked.

He smiled and shrugged, and then indicated that I should sit. He lit a cigarette and offered me one, but I declined. Vasile took one, then sat behind me. Drăgan spoke to Vasile.

'Nu,' said Vasile.

'What did he say?' I asked.

'He asked if you had a tape recorder.'

I addressed Drăgan. 'No, I did have one, but it was taken away from me at customs.' I turned to Vasile.

'Nu,' he repeated.

The angry typist brought in three coffees and I burned my tongue in my desperation for more fluids. It was strangely tasteless, but after that I felt much better.

I poised my pen over the paper and began. 'What was it about the real incident that suggested a film script to you?'

We were off. Vasile said something to Drăgan, he said something back and I wrote down what Vasile told me he said. It didn't sound like any of the interviews with directors that I'd read, and I was thinking all along about how to rework and reword it before I handed it in to Mr Benstrup. But that was the benefit of not having a recording, I suppose, both for me and Vasile. He could say anything he liked.

We were finished within an hour, and Vasile led me back to the car. This time the journey to the car took only four minutes, but I was so looking forward to being able to sleep on the way back that I didn't bother to ask Vasile why he'd taken me on such a long detour when we arrived. To be a translator was to have all the power.

I got in, back on the broken spring, while Vasile talked to the driver and then turned to me.

'Would you say that I was professional, Ted?'

'Yes.'

'Would you say it, please?'

I glanced at the driver who was watching me in the rear-view mirror. 'I think you are very professional, Vasile.'

He nodded, looked pointedly at the driver, and sat back, smiling.

I had no idea what that was about. I carefully folded my notebook and put it in my pocket with the pen, and let my head fall back, heavy against the headrest. I'd make my flight tomorrow, type up the article, impress Mr Benstrup and pay off my debt. Nici o problema.

CHAPTER 3

There was a calming, murmuring sound and a cool breeze, and I didn't want to wake up fully, but I was thirsty again. I tried to turn over but bashed my head against something hard. I opened one eye. I had been left in the car with all the windows rolled down, like a dog.

I rubbed both eyes, dragged my hands down the stubble on my face, and forced myself to look through the windscreen into the light outside. Vasile, the driver and two other men in police uniform were sitting on the grass by a lake. I hadn't been taken back to the hotel.

My hands started to shake. In a film, this was the kind of place, isolated but beautiful, where you would kill someone. They were looking away from me and for a moment I was convinced that I had to run. I looked behind me to see a large white church with pillars on the right, and a taller but similar building on the left. Apart from that it was just grass and trees.

I wouldn't know which way to run, even if my legs felt capable of obeying me. I turned back to the windscreen. Vasile nodded towards me and walked over.

'Hello, sleepyhead,' he said. 'We have food and drink. Come and join us.'

He smiled. It looked genuine, like the person he'd been

before today, my friendly guide to Romania. He opened the door for me, so I straightened my stiff limbs and followed him to the others. He looked behind him, waving me on. In that moment I became convinced that there were two Vasiles, maybe twins.

This Vasile gestured for me to sit next to one of the men in police uniform, who nodded to me as I sat down, not too close. Vasile passed me a tin mug which I took a tentative sip from, but it was water, not vodka. I drank it all, and another mugful, then ate the bread and sausage as it was passed to me. It was a Romanian picnic.

I hadn't expected this. I was so relieved that I couldn't stop smiling. Vasile was back to normal and I wasn't going to die of dehydration, and the place was lovely. I looked out at the cool water, and rebuked myself for thinking of it as a murder site. It was just what I needed, food and fresh air after the hot winds of Buftea. I saw a couple of fishermen on the far side of the lake, their rods just visible in front of the thick tree line. A flock of starlings swooped and then scattered around the trees. If I'd been alone, I would have lain down and watched the ripples of the water reveal the fish, but instead I stretched out my legs, leaning on one hand while the other fed me a constant supply of food and strong cigarettes from the older policeman.

I didn't see much water in London, and I realised how much I had missed it. In Harwich we had both the sea and the estuary, salty or fresh water, within walking distance. In Plumstead there was only the brown Thames. I did sometimes walk down to the river, but it was industrial, nothing like this clean lake with the trees growing right up to the shore. I wondered how far away from the city this place was, but I wasn't concerned right now. Not yet.

It was pleasant to be a part of the group but not have to listen or respond to anyone. The uniformed man next to me was older, maybe late fifties, and his younger colleague was about the same age as me, early twenties. I hadn't heard the younger one speak yet. Like me, he seemed apart from the group. Vasile, obviously, did most of the talking. The driver did most of the laughing, and occasionally flicked his eyes towards me which made me think I was the subject of Vasile's jokes. I didn't care. My interview was complete, whoever it was with, and now I could rearrange my flight home and get back to London and normal life. I thought of Julia, a girl I'd met a couple of times. Maybe she would like to have a picnic on the common. A bottle of white wine from the Co-op and some sausage rolls from the bakery down the road. I could stretch to that.

I noticed that the men had stopped talking, then heard a second car pulling up at the church. Two more men got out, another older policeman and a man in baggy shirt and trousers, as if he'd bought them and then shrunk. I looked around. Everyone was watching them approach, apart from the younger policeman sitting with us. He was watching me. I sat up straight.

Vasile stood up and welcomed the baggy man with a pat on the shoulder. After saluting the group, the policeman walked back to the car.

Vasile turned to me. 'This is Marku.'

I nodded to Marku, unsure of why I needed to know his name, and no-one else's. 'Hello.'

Vasile then talked to the younger officer, and gestured for Marku to sit between me and himself. Marku slowly lowered himself to his knees.

'Ted,' Vasile said, 'Marku needs your help.'

'What?'

He repeated himself, pointing, 'Marku needs,' then pointing at me, 'your help.'

I looked at Marku, his eyes directed towards the ground, his hands clasped together as he knelt. He could have been praying.

'I understood the words. I don't understand how I can help him.'

Vasile opened his hands. 'I haven't explained yet.' He said something which sounded brusque to the young policeman who nodded and shrugged. 'I am going to translate as Marku explains his situation. Yes?'

'Yes.'

Vasile nodded again, and the older policeman and the driver stood up and walked off together, smoking. The younger one, who I now realised was the more important, lit another cigarette. He gestured for Marku to start and said something to Vasile. When he spoke his voice was low and hesitant, quite unlike Vasile's, and it made me shudder. No one his age got to be in charge without a good reason.

Marku talked and Vasile echoed him.

'My sister is called Ana. She was eleven when she became very ill. Not even the great doctors we have in Bucharest could find out what was wrong with her, although they never stopped trying. One day the hospital sent us a doctor from Berlin, who was an expert in skin disorders, and she asked my parents to allow her to take Ana to a special sanatorium in Germany where they could cure her. Elisabeth-Sanatorium, Sanatorium E. My mother wanted to go too, but they said they would send for her later. The translator was called Ingrid.'

Marku was repeating something else, a name, and Vasile shook his head.

'Nadia Osipova,' Marku said to me.

Vasile shouted at him, Marku remonstrated with the silent policeman, who stood and gestured for Vasile to follow him. Marku and I watched as they argued quietly, the policeman eventually pushing Vasile hard in the chest. They sat down with us again.

Vasile said, very quickly, 'He thinks the doctor might have been called Nadia Osipova, but I wouldn't put too much in that name.'

Vasile paused and lit another cigarette as Marku began to sob. Eventually, Marku took a deep breath and carried on.

'We never heard anything else. We wrote to the sanatorium and never heard back. We couldn't get visas to visit her. She must think we don't care.'

I was bewildered. This poor man had started crying again, and for some reason he had been led to believe I could help him. I was feeling uncomfortable, and just wanted to get back to the hotel and take a bath.

'I really don't see—'

'He's not finished,' snapped Vasile.

Did they expect me to go to West Germany and find her? Or East Germany? I lit a cigarette and waited for Marku to continue. Finally, after wiping his eyes on his frayed cuffs, he did.

'My uncle works in films at the Buftea studios and he takes films to festivals sometimes. Two years ago he was in Moscow and he saw the translator for the doctor who took Ana.'

'What?' I said. 'Hold on. Your uncle recognised the translator of the doctor who took your sister, how many years ago?'

Vasile didn't translate that.

'Can you ask him how old Ana is now?' I asked.

He turned to Marku and they spoke for a while. Marku took a small, crumpled photo from his trouser pocket and showed it to Vasile. They seemed to argue over it.

Finally, Vasile said, 'Twenty-three years old.' He held out the photograph. 'This is Ana when she was eleven.'

A black and white photo of a skinny eleven-year-old girl with dark hair and dark eyes, taken twelve years ago.

'I won't recognise her from that,' I said.

Vasile nodded as if I'd said something clever, and returned the photo to Marku, still nodding. Marku half-smiled as he put the photo away and pulled out another from his other pocket. This had been cut from a newspaper. Vasile handed this to me next, and pointed at the woman, half obscured by a smiling man.

'This is the woman, Ingrid.'

Again, black and white, but this time her features were distinct enough to give me an idea of how she looked. Marku was talking again, tugging at his hair, a strip of ribbon wrapped around his fingers.

'Red hair,' said Vasile.

'Do you mean ginger?' I asked.

'No, red hair.'

He passed me Marku's ribbon. It was that deep reddish brown that I'd noticed many women here chose to dye their hair. I looked up. Marku was staring at me. I nodded, holding the ribbon to my hair. He smiled and held both hands to his heart.

'Ana,' he said.

'Ana.' I handed back the ribbon.

The policeman, silent all this time, now spoke a few words to Marku and he nodded. They stood up, brushing down their trousers, and the policeman whistled for the officer in the car to start it up, ready to take Marku back. Marku walked slowly away, turning once to raise his hand to me.

Vasile clapped his hands together, the driver returned and the young policeman wandered off along the river bank to meet up with the older man who was waiting by a fallen tree.

'Dinner time,' said Vasile. 'You must be hungry again.'

I stared at him, and then got up and followed him to the car. We got back into the same seats as before, and the driver pulled away.

'I don't understand what I'm supposed to do,' I said.

'Don't worry about it. If you see the woman in Moscow you can ask about Ana, if you like.'

'If I like? But how do you know I'm going to Moscow?'

'You told me. We'll talk about it at dinner. Don't worry.'

I worried, but quietly. I watched the starlings pick at the roof of the church as we drove past.

CHAPTER 4

I managed to get away from Vasile long enough to wash off most of the dirt in a tepid bath, although the gritty soap wasn't any help, and then dried myself on the rough, grey towels. The brown stain that I had noticed on the first day was still there, under the sink. I hoped it was rust, but wasn't going to smell it.

I soaped my face to have a shave, but my hands trembled when I held the razor to my chin and I thought, best not. The water screamed through the pipes and then stopped completely. I rubbed the soap off on a stiff towel and looked at the bags under my eyes in the mirror.

Coming back into the bedroom, I struggled to remember what day it was. It seemed to be at least two days since I'd been woken in here this morning. The cleaners had been in, pulled the dusty black curtains open and tugged the bobbled candlewick tight again, which bore yet another copy of *Holidays in Romania*. Sometimes they left it on the bed, sometimes on the single chair by the window. They had put the phone back on the nightstand, and tidied bits of paper torn from my notebook, my journalism book and the novel I hadn't read much of into a pile on the dressing table. I sifted through the loose papers. I had half a memory of the letters I'd started, but they were gibberish and I had no desire to finish them. Drinking made me think about the debt I owed which refused to shrink. I crumpled them in one hand and threw them into the bin.

I phoned down to reception to see if the travel office was still open, but was told it had closed unexpectedly. I had been expecting confirmation of the time of my new flight, but I would have to assume it was the same as before.

My travel alarm said ten past eight, and I was starving now. I decided to make notes detailing what had happened earlier with that poor man, after I'd eaten.

I pulled my dusty trousers back on and my last clean shirt, and went down to meet Vasile.

He was leaning against the wall, a cigarette in his hand, same as ever. Which Vasile would I get tonight?

He smiled insincerely. That one. I was glad.

'Shall we?' he said.

I nodded.

Back in our usual place in the hotel restaurant, the last twenty-four hours seemed dreamlike, punctuated with drink, sleep and hangover.

We ordered our food, and Vasile lit another cigarette, before leaning across to me.

'Thank you for meeting with Marku earlier. It means a lot to him.'

'Did I agree to do something?'

Vasile looked at me strangely. 'Of course. If you see that translator you will ask her for information about Ana. If you don't,' he shrugged, 'you don't.'

'Why me? Aren't there other Romanians who go to film festivals, like his uncle?'

Vasile held his finger up to silence me as the waiter brought our warm red wine, and waited until he had left us.

'We can't ask them.'

'Why?'

'It's too difficult. They have work to do. You are free to come and go as you like.'

He half smiled, but he looked like the other Vasile and I didn't care what he thought of me any more. I took a large gulp of wine.

'I also have work to do in Moscow. This woman speaks German and Romanian. No-one has said she talks English. It's a ridiculous thing to ask.'

He sat back and crossed his arms. 'What would it cost you to help out a brother who misses his sister?'

'What would it cost me? It's nothing to do with me. I can't believe that your government shouldn't be the one to track down one of its people that it's been so careless with.'

Vasile looked genuinely hurt. 'How can you say that?'

'How can you ask me to work for you? And for free? What am I supposed to do if I find out something? Just walk into the nearest Romanian Embassy and ask for you? Put a message in *The Times*?'

He opened his mouth to respond just as the waiter brought over the unspecified meat pie we'd both ordered. The waiter turned to leave but Vasile stopped him and said something. The waiter nodded and glanced at me before leaving. I waited for Vasile to say something in response to me, but he started eating, so I did too. He never spoke while he was eating, as if he was scared someone would take his plate away. I raced him, finishing the pie so quickly that I could feel the pressure of heartburn building in my chest. I lit a cigarette although Vasile was still eating, and felt glad that I was leaving. I didn't have to anticipate his moods or please him any more. He'd been assigned to me, but there must be other translators who weren't so overbearing.

He finished, wiped his mouth, and lit his own cigarette.

'It's all up to you. You have been asked for a favour by a good, kind and lonely man. You can say no. You can live with that, I'm sure, with your important job. Marku is a road cleaner. It's all he has left, no parents, no sister. Just the big sky to look at and a broom to sweep. And plenty of time to wonder.' He looked away. 'I know that's nothing to you.'

The heartburn had turned to nausea. What harm would it do me? I was never going to meet that woman, or be able to talk to her. I probably wouldn't even recognise her if she was standing next to me. And Marku, didn't he deserve someone to ask for him? I sighed, and put my hand to the pressure in my chest.

'So, in theory,' I said, 'how would I pass on any information?'

Vasile suppressed a smile, and I regretted giving in. He looked towards the doorway and nodded. 'You could send a postcard to me here, at the hotel. Or, put a notice in *The Times*, if that sounds more exciting. You can always use this kind of thing as material, can't you? If you were ever going to write your own article, maybe.'

Article? I remembered that he had also known about my Russian trip. He'd been researching me. 'Have you –'

'Ah.' Vasile stood up and held his hands out. 'Ted, this is Nico.'

I turned around and saw a stunning woman, with long dark hair and the only fitted dress I'd seen since I arrived. So fitted. She held her hand out, and I pushed my chair backward to stand up before shaking it.

Vasile was all smiles now. 'Nico, this is Ted, an important journalist from Britain.'

I flushed, 'Not important, no,' but her eyes had widened in such a way that I wanted to take it back. She still held my hand.

Vasile said, 'Sit down, Nico. I'll get you a glass so you can share our wine. Nici o problema.' He beckoned for the waiter.

She sat, slowly letting my fingers slip from her grasp, and I watched her arrange the dress just above her knees. So fitted.

'Aren't you going to sit?' asked Vasile.

There was something in the way he said it, or the way he looked at me that snapped me out of it. I thought back to that man I had met at the airport who had told me a couple of horror stories, friends of friends, made delirious by beautiful women. I knew that there was nothing about me that would attract a woman like Nico. There was still dust on the seat of my trousers, and stubble which went way past rugged and manly.

I smiled, and found myself half-bowing. 'It is lovely to meet you, Nico, but I'm afraid that I have to go to bed. I am flying home tomorrow.'

'Are you?' asked Vasile. 'Isn't that more reason to spend your last night in Romania in fine company?'

I laughed. His English had improved significantly over my stay, or he'd stopped faking that learner's hesitancy.

'I'm afraid so,' I said.

Nico looked upset, and I tried to believe that it was really because I was leaving.

'Good night,' I said, and managed not to run from the room.

At the desk I arranged for my bill to be made up for the morning, an early call to tell me what time my plane left, and escaped to my room.

I packed my clothes and sat on the bed, holding the novel I had brought with me, but not read since Heathrow. *Darkness at Noon*. On reflection, this may have not been the best book to bring, feeding my growing paranoia. I'd only chosen it because Koestler was from Budapest and I'd confused it with Bucharest. And yet, it suited this trip more than

I'd anticipated. I wrote down the names that I had heard: Marku, Ana, Ingrid, Nadia Osipova, Elisabeth-Sanatorium, Sanatorium E.

I flicked through the novel, and a business card fell out. Mr Attridge. That was the man I'd spoken to at Heathrow, although I didn't remember him giving me this card. And yet, here it was, marking my place.

It would be good to get home. I was strung out with nerves and wine, and in need of a pint. I got ready for bed and lit a final cigarette. I thought for a bit and, when I put it out, I carefully manoeuvred the nightstand in front of the door. I felt pleased with that, straight out of Koestler, and made a note of it in my notebook, alongside the idea of the Vasile doppelgängers. Then I packed everything else, and settled into bed. My alarm clock said half past ten exactly, a good, early night.

I slept soundly, apart from one time when I woke, imagining someone was gently knocking for me.

CHAPTER 5

I woke rested and relieved that I was on my way home, until I looked at the alarm clock. It was half past ten exactly.

I picked it up and put it closer to my face. It didn't change. It hadn't gone off. I noticed the second hand wasn't moving either. My watch said quarter to ten. My heart began to pick up pace.

I phoned down to the travel desk.

'Mihaela, it's Mr Walker.'

'Good morning, Mr Walker.'

'What time is my flight, please?'

She cleared her throat. 'It wasn't possible to get you on the flight this morning. You are booked in for the next one, in two days' time.'

'But I have to get home.' I hoped I didn't sound as tearful as I felt.

'I'm very sorry, Mr Walker.'

She did sound sorry. She had been nice every time I'd seen her. I couldn't think of what else to say, and put the phone down.

I sat on the edge of the bed in my pyjama bottoms and put my face in my hands. It was only two more days, but I'd had enough of Bucharest. It was just a place of waiting and brown paint. I really needed a shave now. Then I would decide what to do.

Clean and packed, I carried my suitcase downstairs to Mihaela's tiny booth by the lobby to signal my determination to leave today.

She smiled sadly, and glanced at my case. 'No flight today, Mr Walker.'

'Has it left?'

'Yes.' She checked her watch. 'An hour ago.'

'But you knew I wanted to leave today. I asked you to book it.'

Her eyes filled with tears. I sighed, and took the seat on the opposite side of her desk. It creaked loudly, and I raised my eyebrows. It broke the tension. She made a tentative smile.

She leaned towards me to whisper. 'Mr Walker, I am very sorry. It was not possible to book you on that flight.' Her eyes flicked behind me as she talked. There was no door to pull closed.

'How else can I get back to England?' I said.

'There's the train,' she said, 'but it takes a very long time. Nearly a whole day will get you to Austria.'

I put the case by my feet. We looked at each other.

'I don't suppose you can tell me who told you not to book it?'

Her cheeks flushed, she shook her head.

'Will I definitely make the plane on Friday?'

She shrugged. 'I will give you the details,' she said, and wrote them down on a headed slip of paper. She slid that across, and then sighed before taking a copy of *Holidays in Romania* from a drawer. 'Maybe you will find something good to do in here, while you wait.'

'I've had a few copies of this brochure,' I said. 'Please don't give me another one.'

Mihaela wasn't making eye contact any more. She looked quite tearful. I was starting to think that she wasn't really cut out for this. Neither was I. My dad would've had a handkerchief ready for this kind of thing. I just squirmed.

'Have you read the article on Dracula?' she asked.

I had read the article, twice. The Romanians were fighting back against the film and book destruction of their heritage with a tour, *Dracula: Legend and Truth*.

'We can arrange a special two-day version of the trip for you.'

'Ah.' This was the trip that Vasile had wanted me to take. The trip he wanted me to write an article about. Vasile had stopped me getting on the plane. I leaned back in my chair, and it creaked again.

'Do you have any other things I could do instead?'

'Yes.' Mihaela's face brightened, as she began to pick out leaflets from the rack next to her. Churches, museums, art galleries. I could keep myself occupied.

'Thank you, Mihaela.'

She beamed at me. 'You're welcome, Mr Walker.'

'Could you ask someone to get a new battery for my alarm clock?'

'Of course.'

I took my case back to my room but didn't unpack it.

At the crossroads beside the hotel I assessed my four options and wondered how I would describe this city. It reminded me both of the Paris and the East Germany I'd seen in films, an accidental clashing of new and old, but the people weren't like film extras. If I was the camera, they kept looking at me, slyly, before hurrying away. It was unsettling. I wasn't used to being looked at.

Nico remained the only person I had seen to have properly

fitted clothes. Everyone else had trousers that were too wide or too short, or baggy dresses that seemed designed just to cover rather than clothe. The streets were dusty but clear of rubbish, and everyone looked tired and just this side of hungry. Wainwright's book on journalism, which I was still using to teach myself, had a series of questions to ask of any place you visited. Are the shops empty, transport links broken, the utilities not functioning, are there too many police evident? It didn't ask, do people look tired and hungry? There was something missing from Bucharest, but I was hoping I wouldn't be here long enough to work out what it was.

Mihaela had told me that it was only short walk to the National Museum of Art of Romania, so I crossed the road to head north on Calea Victoriei, people scattering in front of me. I was glad to get inside, away from watchful eyes, but there were no other people in the endless rooms of religious art, so the grim guards in each room had nothing to watch but me.

My shoes squeaked loudly on the cold marble floors so I sat down in front of enormous golden iconostasis, wondering how this possibly fitted into a Communist state now, the dozens of beautifully painted icons on an ornate golden background, with further large icons and an intricate door underneath. I supposed it was like Stonehenge, an ancient relic of a past people, admired but not understood. Not by me, anyway.

It took only a few minutes for someone to join me on the wooden bench. I waited for Vasile to speak.

'No trips for you, then,' he said.

'No. No trips.'

He raised his head to the ceiling and then looked around.

'You don't like the gold?' I said.

He looked at the wall of gold in front of us. 'The gateway in heaven's wall. My mother believed in that kind of thing. It's not important to me.'

'Isn't this the Romanian heritage you want people to know about?'

'Our leaders are the heritage we need to promote.' He took a breath. 'I could make the trip even shorter, just for you, because I respect you. We need to put something up against this stupid Dracula idea. We don't want people to see us as a superstitious and ignorant people. We are brave and loyal and fierce.'

I tried not to smile. He changed tack, speaking low and confidentially.

'I have an uncle who would be very grateful for a positive article on the historical roots of your stupid Dracula novel.'

Everyone had an uncle here. No-one had aunts. 'Listen, Vasile, I saw a program about these Dracula tours on the BBC last year. People in Britain like vampire stories. If that is what gets them over to spend their money, what is the harm?' I didn't say that people in Britain also liked to view most other countries as full of peasants.

'But our *Legend and Truth* tour is better than the films,' he grumbled.

I said, 'I like Bela Lugosi.'

'No!' he cried, before realising. 'Ah, you are tricking me. We talked about that Hungarian beast.' He folded his hands. 'Romania is a modern society where the socialist project raises everyone. We don't need your money.' His eyes slid to the icons. 'We want you to understand our history. That is all.'

'I know what we should do. I'll interview you about the history, and then I'll write a review as if I have been on your tour. I can't promise it will be published, but we can try.'

'Ah,' Vasile said, looking at the floor. 'Maybe, maybe.' He decided. 'Yes, that will be a good thing to do. Do you have a pen?'

'Not here, not now. Let me explore the city today, and I'll see you tomorrow.'

He nodded. 'Tomorrow.' He shook my hand. 'Tomorrow.'

I watched him walk away before leaving myself. Alone, but for who knew how long this time, I decided not to try to find any other recommended places, but just to follow my nose and see where I ended up. I soon realised that this wouldn't be a good plan. I passed new grey blocks, and old grey blocks. No churches or museums or anything. There was a group of people ahead eyeing me suspiciously, and I took a sudden left so I didn't have to walk past them.

I walked through a small park and sat by a concrete-walled lake, before becoming self-conscious when an old man stood and stared at me. I moved on. This direction was more promising. An English-looking church was followed by a strange white box of a church, with two high towers, like dovecotes. Panels had been painted in muted colours, and the far end was angled like half an octagon. I was tempted to step inside, but somehow I didn't dare.

I decided to get back to the main road but, in my changes of direction, found myself in front of the British Embassy. I felt quite tearful as my eyes ran over the brass plate. It was homesickness. I wondered if I should go in and tell them that I had been kept here against my wishes, but imagined them viewing my booked flight on Friday with a stern eye. If I was delayed again, I would go inside and tell them.

I saw a Kent cigarette packet discarded on the ground, and picked it up. This little bit of Britain shouldn't have rubbish outside it. I held it tightly as I found my way back.

CHAPTER 6

The wind had picked up during the night and I had woken often. I kept hearing birds squawking and pecking although I could see it was still dark through the gap I'd left in the curtain. I turned over and over again, but the noises continued and it seemed that every time I had nearly drifted off my eyes pinged open.

In the morning I regretted remembering to set my alarm, now working again, but dragged myself downstairs for breakfast. Mihaela was in her booth, and Vasile was at the doorway to the dining room, waiting. Of course.

'Did you sleep well, Ted?' he said. It was good Vasile, but I wasn't in the mood to be polite.

'How did you get into my room the other morning?'

'You didn't lock your door.'

'I always lock my door. I lock it in London and I lock it here. I don't forget that kind of thing.'

'You were very drunk, my friend. Don't worry about it.' He slapped my shoulder. 'You look like you need a good breakfast.'

I grunted. We took our seats. Vasile turned his chair to face the window and leaned back, his hands behind his head.

'Nico was asking if you were free tonight,' Vasile said, looking at me from the corner of his eye. 'She's a very good girl. Well,' he snorted, 'good might not be the right word.'

I blinked. 'I have a girlfriend, thank you.'

The waiter brought our coffees and we ordered meat and cheese. The same as every other morning, there being no actual choice. Vasile turned his chair back to the table.

'You have a girlfriend.' He shrugged. 'You don't like Nico?'

'She looks very friendly.'

Vasile leaned in. 'Is something wrong?'

I rubbed my face. 'I slept really badly, much worse than the other nights. There were weird noises and I woke up too many times to count.'

'It might be a guilty conscience.'

He looked serious, but there was a twitch in his mouth that looked like the start of a smile.

'When will you be ready for the discussion about tourism? I have lots of material for you. It will be the best article you've ever written.'

I couldn't be bothered with this. 'You know the magazine I write for, *International Film Monthly*? Can you guess what we write about?'

'I know you usually write about films, yes. I must say, Ted, I'd never heard of your magazine. I know *Sight and Sound*.'

'Oh yes?' Like I hadn't heard that before.

'And *Film Review*, of course. That went up to ten pence on the cover, I saw.'

I drank my coffee.

'*Screen International*. That's a good name.'

I put my cup down on the saucer a little too hard.

He concluded, his arms spread wide, 'But now, Ted, I will search out *International Film Monthly* just to see your name.'

That didn't cheer me up. The reviews I'd written so far, small summary pieces, didn't have my name under them. I had a horrible feeling that Mr Benstrup was aware that employing me was a terrible mistake and he'd sent me to Romania to give me time to realise it myself. Who cared about the Romanian film industry?

I realised that Vasile was talking to me. 'Sorry?'

'I was asking whether you had ever worked in film. Maybe behind the scenes, acting, or even scriptwriting?'

'Screenwriting. I haven't, no.'

Vasile looked surprised. 'No desire to write for film?'

'Not really.'

'But maybe other kinds of writing?'

This was getting too close for comfort. I began to wonder if he'd been in my room at other times and seen my book on journalism. I had been drunk the other night, but I definitely remembered turning the key. Even if the grumpy woman had a spare, and I was sure she did, my key would have stopped another getting into the keyhole. If he had been in my room, he might have read my notebook on ideas for articles. I shifted in my seat, signalled to the waiter for more coffee, and changed the subject.

'I want some time to get cleaned up after breakfast. Shall we chat for an hour before lunch?'

'We can start then, and carry on over lunch. Good idea.'

I sat up straight and clenched my hands. One more day. One more, and I could leave.

I managed to escape Vasile after learning more than I would ever need to know about the evils of Hungary, and the wonders of Vlad Țepeș, who I was pretty certain was well known for impaling people. Vasile hadn't mentioned that.

Outside, finally alone, I let the hot wind blow me along Calea Victoriei in the opposite direction to the day before. I visited the National Museum of Romanian History, or a tiny part of it before I was told they were closing, and felt annoyed with myself that I hadn't used my first few days to visit more of it. I'd just stayed in, as I was told, and waited for Vasile to arrange the trip to Buftea, or listened to Vasile ramble on and on, when there were places like this to see. What a waste of my time here.

I didn't return to the hotel straight away, but wandered down towards the river which ran through Bucharest. When I got there, there was only river on the right of me. The left side had been covered over by road, hidden within a tunnel. I went right up to the water, crossing the tram lines, and leaned on the balcony, watching the water disappear into the hole. I listened to the cream and red trams passing behind me and the odd car rumbling along. There was black graffiti on the concrete bank, but I couldn't guess what it said. Further along there was a red star with a black line through it.

On the far side of the river there was a woman sweeping the street, and a man passing her with a kind of urn strapped to his back. It had a long spout, and he offered the cup to her, but she shook her head. I felt that I shouldn't be watching. It seemed to be a private moment, even on the street. This part of Bucharest didn't feel like a capital city at all, but a village. After living in London I had got used to adverts, noise and lights everywhere. Here they didn't even have streetlights at night.

I felt the inevitable shadow of someone standing next to me.

'Not again,' I said, but it wasn't him. It was Mihaela, blushing, and looking down. 'Sorry, Mihaela. I thought it was Vasile.'

She looked up at me, smiling awkwardly. She had make-up on now, blue eyeshadow and bright pink lipstick, so she looked even younger than usual. Was she even eighteen? She reached out and put a hand on top of mine. She was blinking so much to keep back the tears that it began to make my eyes water too. My heart sank. Someone had told her to do this.

'Mihaela,' I said, 'you're very lovely, but I think you should know that I have met a girl in London. I would very much like to have a walk with you, though.'

That got a genuine smile. I held my arm out and she slid her hand through the gap. We walked left, along the invisible river and she began to point out interesting buildings, ignoring a poster of Ceauşescu looking paternal.

We crossed the road onto a little patch of green, scaring off a handful of dusty sparrows, and she pointed out where the river re-emerged.

'It used to flood all the time, so they put it underground,' she said.

How symbolic.

'It's a very beautiful city,' I said.

Mihaela glanced around, and shivered. 'It was.' She held her hand out to me and I hesitated before taking it. Her fingers were so small, her palm rough.

'Ted, please could I ask you a favour?'

'Like what?'

'I have a sister in England, and I haven't seen her since our mother died. Could you take my mother's ring back to England for her?'

I hesitated. I wanted to help her, but at the back of my mind was the thought that this was something I shouldn't do. And yet, if I didn't, my flight could be postponed again.

'Of course. We should go back,' I said. 'It's cold without a jacket.'

She looked at my jacket, my covered arms, and said, 'You won't give me your jacket because you love your girlfriend. Yes?'

'I can lend you my jacket,' I said, but she put her other hand on mine.

46

'Tell Vasile that is why. I don't want to get into trouble.'

Then she let go of my hand and we walked back in the direction of the hotel. All the while I thought about what I'd said. I didn't know Julia well at all, and using her as an excuse felt cheap.

Had Vasile wanted to use Mihaela to get my jacket? I remember thinking that maybe he was stealing a pair of my trousers while I was out, but it wasn't a pair of trousers that I discovered were missing, but the notes I'd made from the meeting with Marku. I could have thrown them away by accident, but I didn't think I had.

CHAPTER 7

On the way to the airport, Vasile was more excitable than usual, his leg jiggling up and down. He rolled down the car window and let the dust blow in.

'Fresh air. It's the best.' He rolled it up again, and tried to push his hair down. 'Will you send me a copy of the article when it is published?'

'On Drăgan?'

'Yes, maybe, yes, OK. But the one on tourism too.'

'If it's published, you mean. I don't know where you live, though. Where would I send it?'

'To the hotel. They know me there now.'

'Probably.' I was trying to think whether I'd taken everything from the bathroom. It felt as if something was missing. It wasn't my trousers, or the jacket I was wearing.

The driver pulled up at the airport entrance, and Vasile fetched my suitcase from the boot.

'I can take it from here,' I said.

'No! You are a guest in my country. I will carry your suitcase. Nici o problema, my good friend.'

I followed him into the building, and he went straight to the plastic seats of a small bar.

'One last drink for the journey.'

'Just coffee for me,' I said. I checked my watch. Enough

time for a last effort at conversation. I would be happy when I could walk around unhindered by the thoughts that spilled from his head. He put my suitcase next to a table.

'Sit down, I will get it.'

I took a flimsy seat and sat down gingerly. It didn't collapse. I checked where Vasile was, and then leaned forward to pull my suitcase towards me, and clamped it between my legs. Now I had my case, my passport and my tickets, he couldn't stop me catching my flight, and I could relax. I noticed how tight my shoulders were, and I rotated them before stretching my shoulders back.

'We have very good treatments here,' said Vasile, putting two coffees on the table. 'You should have said if you were suffering from muscle pains. Was the bed not good?'

'It was fine. I'm just anxious that my employer will be cross that I took longer than was agreed.' The bill had been bigger than I was expecting, even taking into account the extra days. I'd handed over the American Express card that Mr Benstrup had entrusted me with. What else could I do?

'Ah, when you show him the second article he will be pleased with your hard work.' Vasile sipped his coffee, and pointed to mine. 'Drink up.'

That made me anxious. He was definitely after something. I held the cup to my lips and pretended to sip.

'That book in your pocket.'

I looked down. I'd put *Darkness at Noon* there for the aeroplane journey. I hadn't finished it, and wasn't sure that I wanted to now. It would always remind me of Vasile, talking and watching.

'If you have finished with it, could I have it? It is useful for me to read books in English and expand my vocabulary.'

I handed it over to him, and he held it to his chest like a prize. He was so pleased that I felt a bit bad then for resenting his many requests. He looked down at his feet, and then stood, pushing his chair back.

'Your suitcase! Someone has stolen it!'

'I have it, Vasile.'

I knocked on it, leaving it where it was. He sat down, and looked under the table. Don't ask, I thought, please don't ask. He leaned across to me, his voice low.

'Do you have any spare trousers?'

'I don't.'

'You are wearing trousers. You have other trousers.'

'I do.'

Vasile scowled and stood, his chair skidding away from him. 'I will go now.' Still clasping the book, as if he'd stolen it, he walked out of the airport.

'Enjoy the book!' I shouted after him, and then added, 'I like Bela Lugosi!'

That made no sense, but it felt good to say it and I saw him shudder. I sighed, picked up my suitcase and went towards the image of a plane which I hoped meant Departures.

On the other side, in the waiting area, I was still annoyed about his final request, especially after I'd given him the book. I opened my case, took out the notes I'd made of his Dracula extravaganza and put them in the nearest bin. I smiled for a bit. I'd finally got one over on him. Then doubt began to creep in. Why had I done it here? I should have waited until I was at Heathrow, among people who had enough trousers. The seats around me were filling up, but I couldn't hear any English being spoken.

I put my suitcase on my lap and tried to remain calm. I'd be home soon. I could go and see if Julia was around. Maybe Mr Benstrup would be so impressed by the interview that he would write me a great reference when I finally found a traineeship in journalism to apply for. I told myself this, even though I knew it wasn't going to be possible for a long time. I'd have to go to night school and take some courses first, and when would I be able to afford that? I knew why none of my applications to newspapers had led to an interview. They wanted their trainees to have O levels, or at least one. I applied to Mr Benstrup's advert in the local shop because I was desperate, and he was equally desperate with the deadline for visas coming up, but when the film I was most looking forward to seeing was *Jaws* and not another interminable tribute to *The Seventh Seal*, I knew that I was in the wrong job.

Now I looked back to the bin, realising I'd just thrown away material which I could use to write a proper article on. Not the bits about the tour, but the attitude of Romanians to something that British people had actually heard of. Then again, I had more material than that which Vasile had fed me. I decided, while it was fresh, to write down anything I could remember that might make a good travel piece, not for Vasile, but something that might have a market.

I sat down in a café area, took my notebook from the suitcase and stared out of the window. The sun was bright outside, and it made the interior of the airport look grubby.

I wrote down the names of the museums and the hotel, and then all the names that I had heard or used: Vasile, Mihaela, Marku, Ana, Ingrid, Mircea, Nadia Osipova, Elisabeth-Sanatorium, Sanatorium E. I wrote a description of the church by the lake, the lake itself, the streets I had walked around, the feeling of watchfulness. I'd come with no understanding of what to expect, Romania didn't make it into the papers often, but if I wrote an interesting piece on visiting the city maybe a broadsheet would pick it up. Unlikely, without a news story to go with it, but now I vaguely remembered something about President Ford arranging a visit to Bucharest in the coming months. It might be enough.

I listed what I had been served for my meals and I described the hotel room. I didn't mention the stain in the bathroom, but it was in my mind. Would the article be positive or negative? I didn't feel it could be neutral. I'd check the papers when I got home and see where they pointed. I wrote down what I remembered about 'Drăgan's' appearance, so I could check this against photos of the real film director.

I also wrote down Marku's story about his sister, and wondered what could be behind that. Could I follow this up? Was there a story I could write? Vasile hadn't seemed to care whether I was going to follow that up or not, and that made me want to more. I couldn't see how I would bump into a Romanian-speaking German woman, or German-speaking Romanian, at a huge festival in the centre of an enormous city. Still, it was a story, and stories were what I had to focus on.

I bought a coffee with sterling and opened my Wainwright. I'd neglected my journalism training recently and he probably had hints on what I should be focusing on before it started to fade into memory. I tried, but I couldn't focus on the words. I had to soak up this last bit of Bucharest, this place of stern faces and polished shoes, while I was here. Would Moscow feel similar? I was determined to do a better job in the USSR. By day a film reviewer and by night an investigative reporter, if I could find something to report. Unlike Romania, the USSR was always newsworthy.

I looked at my watch and saw it was nearly time to board. I finished my coffee and lit a cigarette, my last in Romania. Thank God. I checked one last time that my passport and ticket were still in the left pocket before I went to the boarding gate.

It still felt odd to have a passport. For years I'd watched all those ships leaving Harwich and never been able to get on one. I'd asked Mum if I could get a year passport, just to go across to Holland and see it, wouldn't even get off the boat, but she said we didn't have any spare cash for jaunts like that. And we never had, not until she made Dad sell his fishing boat. Didn't keep him off the water, though, and that's where I would still be if he'd had his way. I preferred aeroplanes.

I'd been unprepared for this trip, but it wasn't as alien as I had been expecting and this made me wonder what I had missed. I would be more observant next time. I put the pen in my right jacket pocket, and felt something odd. I pulled out a small, hard box. A ring box. I looked around. No-one was watching me. I opened it. There was a thin gold ring, maybe a wedding ring, sitting in a cream silk slot.

Had Mihaela put this in my pocket when she said goodbye? Who was I supposed to give it to? I tried to lift the silk, see if there was a note, it was empty apart from the ring.

I closed the box and put it back in my pocket. I definitely had to ask more questions.

ROMANIAN MINISTRY OF THE INTERIOR

Compilation of REPORTS on
REGINALD EDWARD WALKER

9–15 May 1975

Day 4
STARLING called on the subject early and
remained with him all day. The subject looked
very unwell in the morning, so it can be
certain that he was inebriated the previous
night. This makes what he said more credible.
The subject was driven to the Bucharest Film
Studio, Buftea, at 9:00. After a short walk
around the film sets, STARLING introduced him
to ASH taking the role of "Mircea Drăgan".
The subject showed no signs of suspicion, and
conducted the interview as well as he was able
in his state. STARLING adapted the words of
ASH to make more sense.

The subject fell asleep in the car after
this, so STARLING did not have to explain
why they were driven to Meeting Place 3. OAK
brought BOLDEA to the meeting where STARLING
was to translate.

Background: MARKU BOLDEA works in a factory
at which our best informer was murdered.
We have been trying to get him to agree to
assist us in the normal ways (patriotism,
money, other advantages) but the only thing

which we have found to sway him is finding information about what happened to his sister (ANA BOLDEA) some years earlier (see addendum, below). It was decided that using an outsider figure would impress BOLDEA as to our efforts to discover the truth, and find his sister. Added benefits were that the subject would understand only what STARLING told him. It was not necessary at any point for the subject to go along with the plan, as long as BOLDEA was unaware of this. This depended on STARLING being able to accurately read the expressions of both parties.

What was not expected was that the subject would agree to help BOLDEA. He has proved to be entirely malleable and eager to assist. We are sure that we can make something of this revelation. STARLING will provide a full personality evaluation. In order to facilitate this, the battery was removed from the subject's travel clock alarm so the subject would 'miss' his flight.

On arrival back at the hotel, STARLING introduced the subject to NICO, with a view to gauging the subject's interest in her. NICO was rejected. It could have been assumed that the subject was just overtired, but noise surveillance revealed the sound of the subject moving furniture against the door. He did not respond to knocks on his door. It has still been noted that he continues to look at MIHAELA ZAMFIR, and we could focus here next.

While he was out of the room with STARLING

and NICO, a piece of paper was found with restricted information. The paper was removed, and LEAF summoned STARLING for an explanation of this information. STARLING explained that OAK had insisted that the subject be given this name, as BOLDEA had been assured that everything he said would be translated for the foreigner who had promised to help him. LEAF remains unhappy about one name in particular but it is hoped that the subject will not pay too much attention to it.

Following up on the observations from the previous night, LEAF was able to recover a number of partial letters from the bin. These are reproduced here:

1. Julia Julia Jul (all crossed out)
2. Mum I'm sorry I know I promised. It will take me a bit longer [illegible] forgive me [illegible] pay you back
3. Julia [illegible]

Addendum
Father ——, of the Biserica Buna Vestire Belu, reported that one of his parishioners, ANA BOLDEA, was presenting with a condition which threatened to undermine social cohesion. She, or another, had created injuries in her wrists, ankles and abdomen which (it was said) mimicked the wounds of Christ. He called it fabricated 'stigmata', and said that his church was empty because everyone was queuing

outside the BOLDEA residence to worship at the bedside of the child (11 years old at this time).

Father — warned that this was escalating into a situation which could threaten the state. People were describing her as a sign that they should rise up against the President of the Republic, that he was the embodiment of the anti-Christ, and she could lead Romania back to spiritual purity. The girl became a focal point for treacherous sentiment.

ANA BOLDEA was removed from the family home for medical tests, and her mother was allowed to accompany her. The mother was not allowed physical access in case she was responsible for the injuries. There was no improvement and pilgrims started to gather outside the hospital. This meant word spread even more widely.

It was decided to remove her to a place that her family would not be aware of, and return her when she had been cured. To encourage this, a German-speaking contact (NADIA) and translator (INGRID), told the family that ANA was being taken to a sana-torium in the German Democratic Republic where they had specialists in blood disor-ders. There would be no danger of requests for visits as few people could travel to the German Democratic Republic. Thus, the interest would die down and the girl would be forgotten as a symbol of resistance.

NADIA and INGRID removed the girl with the parents' agreement, and she was driven to a different sanatorium to that named, Sanatoriu 4, Minsk. However, when they stopped for a meal break, the girl disappeared and has not been traced.

Day 5
The subject was heard to get up and pack in time for his flight, before phoning MIHAELA ZAMFIR who then had to inform him that his flight home today was 'cancelled'. The subject showed some discomfort, as did ZAMFIR. It may be that the investigations into her background and that of her family should cease in order to keep her more emotionally stable. She asked if someone else could take over her dealings with the subject, but we intend to build on the interest he has in her.

The original purpose for the subject's visit was to see whether he would be happy to carry items to and from London. STARLING was originally going to be used to ask him to do this, but it has been decided that ZAMFIR would be a better person to ask as the relationship between the subject and STARLING appears strained. After the subject's response to BOLDEA's story, LEAF came up with another family-orientated suggestion for the request. If the subject agrees to this, it can be assumed that he would be amenable in other places while carrying out his official 'work', as hoped.

The subject left the hotel alone and was followed to the National Museum of Art (CALEA VICTORIEI). STARLING was able to catch up with him here, and discussed an idea for a second article to be written on the Romanian tourist industry. The subject was unwilling to go into much detail, and they arranged to meet later.

The subject visited a number of rooms (see Appendix) and then left the Museum. Took STR. C.A. ROSETTI (cont. after crossing B. DUL N. BĂLCESCU), left onto STR. ALEX SAHIA, left STR. PICTOR VERONA, through PARCUL GRĂDINA ICOANEI, EREMIA GRIGOESCU, left STR. DIONISIE LUPU, right J.MICHELET, left B. DUL N. BĂLCESCU, right STR. 30 DECEMBRIE and CALEA VICTORIEI back to hotel.

Points of interest:

It looked as if the subject was going to take STR. ICONANEI before taking STR. ALEX SHAIA. There was a queue for food ahead, which may have been the reason, but it was one of many sudden changes in direction which could indicate inept attempts to shake any tail.

Outside the British embassy the subject picked up a cigarette packet, mostly likely a dead letter box. LEAF will be alert to finding what may have been in this box.

The battery taken from the subject's travel alarm clock was replaced

Bin contents – *Holidays in Romania*

Noise activity – nothing worth noting

No phone calls scheduled for this night

Day 6

With the subject showing most interest in ZAMFIR, an arrangement was made to provide her with make-up and clothes appropriate for her new role. This is all she has asked for at the moment. LEAF instructed her to make contact with the subject when he next left the hotel and instructed her in how to introduce the idea of the package.

STARLING also made an agreement with the subject that he would write an article on the Romanian travel industry, partly to refute the Western obsession with associating our country and heroes with monsters.

The subject left the hotel after talking to STARLING, and took CALEA VICTORIEI to the National Museum of Romanian History. It is positive that he is conducting independent research unconnected with the film article he came with the intention of writing. LEAF believes that we should consider delaying more visitors' flights to see how they fill their time.

When the subject left the Museum, he continued south on CALEA VICTORIEI to the DÂMBOVITA river. OAK observed ZAMFIR approach the subject who looked happy to see her there. She made physical contact, but has reported that the subject claims to have an emotional attachment in London which prevents him from acting on any interest. (See letters, Day 4.)

While the subject was out, LEAF was

able to check the notes he had made during his conversation with STARLING, and they look positive. The subject has put leaflets provided by STARLING within this notebook, and intends to write it up when he returns to Britain. There was a discussion about delaying his return further to encourage him to write it more quickly, but LEAF disagreed with this.

The subject had a final meal with STARLING and he reports that they ended on good terms. STARLING insisted on escorting the subject to the airport to see him onto the plane.

Bin contents – *Holidays in Romania*

Noise activity – mumbled to himself. The name "Vasile" was audible multiple times

No phone calls scheduled for this night

Day 7

STARLING called on the subject early to breakfast together, and escorted the subject to Otopeni airport for his flight at 9:30. STARLING says that, unprompted, the subject gave him the novel he was carrying – a copy of *Darkness at Noon* by Arthur Koestler. Contained within this book (p.46) was the business card referring to Mr Attridge. STARLING handed the book over to LEAF and it was later established that its positioning could indicate the word 'pince-nez' ('pinch nose', or could refer to a type of corrective 'eye glasses'). It has been noted that STARLING has displayed a habit of acquiring items from visitors to our country. He has been heard to explain this as providing evidence that the people of the West are wasteful and do not value their possessions as they have too many of them. However, LEAF believes it to be a mere craven desire to acquire Western goods for his own use. Previous items acquired (razor blades, 'Zippo' lighter, pens, a pair of socks) have not been correctly logged and cannot be found in the archive.

On leaving STARLING the subject displayed some odd behaviour, shouting, 'Enjoy the book! I like Bela Lugosi!' STARLING has no explanation for this outburst, and there was no evidence of the subject having consumed any alcohol. Given this behaviour and the acquisition of the book, it must be considered that the placing of the business card was a signal of some kind to STARLING, and the card itself could be a way for STARLING to contact persons unknown in the British Secret Services. Enhanced surveillance of STARLING is to be strongly recommended.

On passing through the airport, the subject was observed to place some papers in a bin. These were later retrieved and proved to be the notes he had made on the article suggested by STARLING. It must be considered that STARLING is pursuing his own ends in a way which alienates foreigners.

MINISTRY OF THE INTERIOR

The subject has potential drawbacks. The meandering journey on Day 5 and unresolved purpose of the cigarette packet leave some points unanswered. Equally the unfinished letters retrieved from the bin could have been left there on purpose to confuse our picture of him, yet they tally with other reports of his behaviour. He rejected NICO, but also claims to be in the early stages of an emotional attachment. The biggest concern is that he put the notes (from his discussion with STARLING) in the bin, having agreed to a course of action that either he did not mean to stick to, or meant to at the time and reneged on. The uncertainty over the behaviour of STARLING (below) makes this difficult to ascertain. (It has further been noted that STARLING has an uncle who heavily invested in a hotel in the area he is promoting. The service cannot and should not be used for this kind of personal or familial advantage.) We wait to hear whether the subject successfully delivers the package.

Conversely, the subject has many positive attributes from our perspective. He is agreeable company, he is not overtly political and does not try to promote the Western form of

society. Neither does he mention the differences between his social experiences and material goods and our own. He did not offer any
provocations, and he did not submit to any.
He appeared to be open to different points
of view, and is accommodating to the point of
being malleable. Most importantly, he took the
proposal of finding out information for the
unknown Romanian as an important assignment.
This could be from a sense of honour, a willingness to please, or a deception (although
this is thought unlikely).

This introduces one of the pressure points
we have identified. This sense of honour or
willingness to please could stem from a low
self-esteem which would be easy to manipu-
late. His interest in how much things cost
could indicate that he has little income,
or has recently had little. The letters
offer another approach: there is something
he feels he needs to apologise for to a
parent concerning a promise, a repayment and
forgiveness. If this were to be linked with
honour and money, it might suggest that he
owes them a debt that he cannot currently pay
(he defers the payment rather than rejects
it). Therefore, our assumption is that all
three pressure points are linked by the
third.

The potential complications related to our
source in the London office have been assessed

to be slight. The subject would not know her by the name of 'Nadia Osipova'. Nevertheless, she has been alerted to the issue.

It is unlikely that the subject will return to Bucharest specifically or Romania more generally so it has been agreed that this file will be passed by STARLING to Colonel — through the usual channels, in the hope that it strengthens the bond between our two organisations and produces reciprocal information.

Additionally, LEAF was very impressed with ZAMFIR, and she has agreed to undergo further training.

LONDON

CHAPTER 8

On the plane the man who sat next to me, stinking of cheap Romanian cigarettes, looked at me in a way which was unsettling until I realised that he just wanted to try one of my Kent cigarettes. He didn't speak English, so we exchanged signs. The meal was standard and dry, the wine was sharp, and I woke up as we landed.

All very uneventful, and yet I felt like kissing the tarmac at Heathrow, like a sportsman who has come home with the trophy. After I'd dumped the notes, I'd nearly convinced myself that Vasile was going to storm back in to prevent me getting aboard my plane. Those policemen from the lake would appear and drag me off somewhere dark and cold.

But, no. I had my suitcase, with trousers, and I was through customs with only the standard amount of guilty eye evasion, and on my way to the train. I had an unnatural affection for my fellow British men, and thought, maybe this is why people go abroad. The grumpy businessmen had a new charm as I joined them on the way to the train, and I looked around with a sense of affection before I spotted a familiar face. I struggled to remember his name. Mr Attridge, of course. The business card. Which I'd now lost, it being inside the book I'd given to Vasile.

He removed his hat to wave it at me, and made his way through the people waiting on the platform.

'Mr Walker, how was your trip? First time abroad, wasn't it?'

'It was interesting, thank you.' I felt my hand creeping to cover the pocket with the ring box. He noticed the movement but didn't say anything.

'Did you achieve everything you wanted?' he asked.

'Eventually, yes.' I hadn't thought about how I was going to explain what happened. 'Thank you for your warnings about the friendly ladies.'

'Oh.' He waved his hat again. 'We businessmen have to look out for each other.' He looked at his watch. 'I have to go and meet someone who is landing. I'll see you soon, I expect.' A final wave of the hat, and he strode back towards the terminal. His dark suit was entirely smooth, as if pressed moments ago. I would have to ask for tips, as my trousers looked as if I had slept in them. I thought of Vasile. At least I had two pairs.

When he'd disappeared, I exhaled. I didn't know what I was going to do about this ring. I'd take the box apart properly when I got home, and see what was there. I wondered how much it was worth, just for a moment. Just if I couldn't find out who to get it to.

I sat down on the train, watching people get on and off as we headed towards London. They were heading for home with food and spare trousers, and I was glad I didn't have to go back to Romania. Being in a country like that made everything feel not quite as stable as it used to. Governments could change, wars could break out, and everything you were ever confident about could disappear. At least here, should someone speak to me, I'd know it was just because they were interested in what I had to say. I was of no more value than anyone else. And I could understand what they were saying behind my back.

On the underground I noticed a woman sitting opposite who I was sure had got on the train after me at Heathrow. She had black hair, brushed high and thick, and vibrant red lipstick. She was reading a book titled in another language, *Sonnenfinsternis*. The author was Arthur Koestler. The novel that I had given Vasile, *Darkness at Noon*, was by him too. The woman glanced at me and I looked away. At the next stop the seat on my left became free and she swapped seats to sit next to me. The tube started to move again and I kept my gaze fixed on the dark blur outside the window, not her reflection.

She leaned towards me, her perfume pungent.

'Do you have something for me?' She had a strong accent, but I didn't know what it was.

'I'm sorry?'

She tapped her finger. I fumbled in my pocket and pulled out the ring box. She took it and kissed my cheek. I looked around to see if anyone had seen, and then focused back into the darkness. She got off at the next stop and I watched her walk away, her book in one hand. Was that the right thing to do? How on earth did she know who I was?

Still shaken, I paused at Charing Cross for a sandwich and a mug of tea from a stall outside. I had to decide whether to face Mrs Cunningham first, or try to get my pay for the week from Mr Benstrup. Or I could see if Julia was around. Home, work, and then Julia.

I'd noticed people looking at me oddly, and as I got on the train I noticed in my reflection a smear of red on my cheek. Lipstick. I tried to rub it off all the way to Plumstead, but it just seemed to spread itself over my face.

Seeing the long stretch of Victorian terraces all the way up Griffin Road made me feel safe. I let myself into my boarding house halfway up the steep hill, closed the door and listened for Mrs Cunningham's footsteps. Every Friday, at each sound of the front door, she would race to her private entrance which kept the downstairs separate to the rooms she let out upstairs. She poked her head around the door and frowned.

'You gonna have my money by six?'

'Oh, yes.' I checked my watch. It was half past four already.

'In and out, I don't know. You'll wear the door out.' Her frizzy curls bounced as she moved her head in demonstration. 'Where ya been? Haven't seen you in days.'

'I went to Bucharest. I did tell you.'

'I don't think you did tell me, and that Barry didn't know either. Next time leave a note, or I'll end up letting your room to someone else.'

'But I paid my rent.'

'Yeah, well.' She closed the door.

She wasn't kidding. She kept the advert up in the Co-op on the off-chance, or in the hope, that me or Barry would do a midnight flit. Ever since I'd moved in, I'd only seen her face poking around the door and, in my nightmares, she'd become a disembodied head. From my room, at the front, I could hear the radio on all day. Other than that, I had no idea how she spent her time. There was no sign of a Mr Cunningham and I thought he'd had a lucky escape, even if that meant he'd died.

I looked upstairs and my heart sank. I'd got used to not having to lock any doors when I used the bathroom attached to my hotel room in Romania. Here, Barry would be straight into my room, going through my things. Every single time I'd forgotten to lock my door, I'd found him in there, 'looking for me.' He never had a reason why he wanted to see me, though.

I took my suitcase to my room, and unpacked it on the bed. I took the hotel receipt and the credit card, changed my shirt, and scrubbed my face before I left the house again.

I walked back down Griffin Road and, at the bottom of the hill, turned right at the station, past the Radical Club, and ran up the two flights to the offices of *International Film Monthly*. Suzanne had already left her desk, but Mr Benstrup was still in, his cough giving him away.

'Ted!'

He said it as if he'd heard I died, and was more surprised than pleased to see me. I often had the impression that with his wide and varied repertoire he was waiting to be spotted by an agent. An agent who specialised in the more mature man. Definitely a character actor.

'Come for your wages, have you, even though I expected you back days ago?'

I took the papers from my pocket and spread them out. 'I'm very sorry, Mr Benstrup. The interview was delayed, and the hotel cancelled my flight twice without asking. I did get the interview though, and it's all ready to type up.'

He looked at the receipt. 'Don't you think this is a lot?'

'It's in leu, so I wasn't sure. It did seem more than I was expecting, but I thought I might have worked out the conversion rate wrong. And it was extended from three days to seven, which might explain it. I didn't have any choice. They kept cancelling my reservations.'

'Hmm.' Mr Benstrup had unfolded the hotel invoice. 'Ted, there's rather a lot of alcohol on here. And food. You have been entertaining, I take it?'

'Is there?'

He turned the invoice around and I saw that it contained not only what I'd had, but everything that Vasile had consumed too.

'My guide wouldn't leave me alone. He ate with me every night,' I stuttered, 'but I had no idea that I was paying for it.'

'You weren't paying it, though, were you?'

I hadn't even told him about the tape recorder yet.

'You've been here six weeks, Ted. We don't know each other well, but I expected more of you. You know what I'm aiming for. An internationally renowned film magazine. It's in the title. But, if I can't trust you to manage my money...'

He was going to cancel Moscow. That was fine with me. In fact, if I'd known this was a possible outcome I'd have invited more people to the table. I needed the job until I found something else, but it was going to be impossible to look around properly if I kept going away.

'Ted, I'm going to have to think about this over the weekend.' He looked about as devastated as I felt. 'See you on Monday. By the way, Suzanne is very angry that you didn't let us know where you were. You might want to apologise to her.'

I was dismissed. At the bottom of the stairs I slumped against the wall. No big date for me and Julia. I'd dip into my savings, again, to pay Mrs Cunningham her rent. Next week things would get sorted out.

I walked up to The Old Mill on the common, just in case Julia was there, with 60p in my pocket. Enough for a pint and a packet of cigarettes before I had to face Mrs Cunningham and work out what I was going to eat this week.

I was 2p short for a pack, inflation, so I bought five singles from behind the bar. I stretched out my pint for over an hour, but there was no sign of Julia and I went home.

CHAPTER 9

It took days for Suzanne to forgive me for not contacting the office. I wasn't sure why she'd taken it so personally. I didn't think she even liked me.

In the weeks following my return I'd sorted my savings into piles but they kept dwindling. From the £140 I'd borrowed in February I'd only saved up £80 to give back. What with rent before I got a job, and food and too much drinking in those first weeks of freedom, and some lost along the way, clothes which became an essential, Mr Benstrup docking me wages, and £5 for the passport which I'd bought before anything else, I wasn't doing well in saving up to pay the money back to Mum. The thinness in the sole of my right brogue had finally worn through, but it would have to wait.

I pushed most of the money back into the biscuit tin, saving a pound for the weekend, and put it back in the bottom drawer.

A chest of drawers, curtains, a lamp, a bed and a chair with no desk, all for £8 a week. I could have got somewhere cheaper, I realised afterwards, but by then I was keeping my head down and avoiding 'that Barry' across the landing. It was as badly decorated as my Bucharest hotel room, but at least that room had space to breathe and the wallpaper wasn't peeling off. I wasn't even sure what the chair was for, as I wasn't allowed visitors. Just a change of scene, maybe, so I could look out onto Griffin Road in comfort, which I didn't do.

I had typed up the interview at work and Mr Benstrup had grunted for a while, and then decided to let me go to Moscow anyway. I knew he'd rather go himself, and I'd rather he went, but Suzanne had told me that his wife had cancelled all trips abroad for the foreseeable future. I'd seen the back of her once as she went into Mr Benstrup's office, remembering only her fur stole and high heels and the lingering scent of her perfume, and wondered what on earth she wanted him at home for. In any case, the visa had to be applied for weeks in advance. It was me or no one. She was the reason I had a job.

I jingled the change in my hand. A pound. I could get a sandwich and a pint and a full packet of cigarettes. That would do. But, before I got to The Old Mill, I saw Julia walking across the common. Her overlong jumper was stretched over her hands, knotted hair pulled to one side. I'd asked her once how she got it so rigid. She said, 'soap'. From then on, I'd worried about her getting caught in the rain.

I ran to catch up with her.

'Hi,' I said, falling into step.

She looked at me, confused.

'I've been away.'

'Yeah? Where have you been?'

'Romania.'

She nodded.

'For work. I'm a journalist.'

She looked mildly surprised.

'I thought I told you before.'

'Yes. That's good.' She was walking fast, as if she was trying to get somewhere.

'Where are you off to?'

'There's a meeting. Isn't that where you're going too?'

'No. I was just heading to the pub. What kind of meeting?'

'The London Squatter Campaign. Wanna come?'

I laughed nervously. 'I can't right now.'

'Suit yourself.'

'I was thinking, wondering, if you wanted to go out one time.'

She frowned, as if she was trying to remember something.

'I'm Ted. We talked a couple of times, last time about the Plumstead Make Merry. In June?'

She shook her head.

'You said 2p was too much for a programme. Indian dancing and piano smashing?' This was awful. 'It doesn't matter. I wondered if you'd like to see a film, or something?'

'Don't you think films just divert the masses from real life, from solving real problems?'

Her eyes were a little unfocused, but she was looking at me and I felt, maybe, it would be worth going along to these meetings just so I could sit next to her. She wasn't leaving yet, though. If I could just keep talking, I could keep looking at her, and the way her smudged eye make-up made her eyes look huge.

'I'm going off to Moscow soon. I just had to get my visa sorted out. It's 20p now to get a set of photos, you know, in a booth.'

'Oh, you'll be writing about Moscow?' Now she was interested. She even pushed some hair away from her eyes.

'Yes. It's a fascinating place. I'll be there for a couple of weeks. If you wanted to meet up before we could talk about it.'

'We're off to the Hackney marshes tomorrow.'

'Your squatter group?'

'And some others. I'll see you when you get back, maybe.'

She didn't remember me, which was bad, but I'd had a conversation with someone that I didn't work with, which was good. And she might remember me next time. I went for a celebratory pint.

It was later, in bed, that the implications hit me. Julia would want to know what I had written about. She might even ask where she could read it. If I told her I'd covered films, those diversions of the masses from their miseries, she wouldn't want to see me again. I wasn't entirely sure that she did want to see me, other than to hear about Moscow. Did she want to know about housing? I should have asked.

That Barry started to bang around in his room at that point, and I gave up on trying to sleep and sat on the edge of my bed. Twenty-two, and all I had achieved was a dirty room with a noisy neighbour, a rude landlady, a job I didn't think I would ever be good at, and a debt that I thought I'd have paid off by now. I should have.

I pushed myself off the bed and looked out of the window. The hill was almost empty, just a stray dog sniffing its way around a gatepost before walking away. I thought of Julia, and wondered where she was now.

I took my tin from the drawer and counted the money again. The memory of Mum replayed itself, explaining how it was the only way she could get Dad off the boats, the only way she could stop him.

'He can't take another winter at sea, Ted. You saw the state of him. That pneumonia nearly did for him, and I can't let that happen again.'

I added the money up to the same total. Maybe I should give up on London, take back what was left to Harwich, and work my debt off on the boats. Yet I wanted to return with more than I left with, the hero. And with the girl? Would it be too much to ask?

London wasn't what I thought it would be, that was certain. I thought I might have a friend or two by now, someone to go to the pub with, but it wasn't that kind of place. The soldiers had their pubs, the dockers, the power station and motorcycle factory workers had theirs. Any new face was a threat. It felt smaller than Harwich a lot of the time. I had ended up spending my weekends as cheaply as I could and in the same way as I had done back at home. All Saturday in the library reading newspapers, and a pint or two at a pub in which no one would speak to me. It wasn't what I had hoped for.

I had tried. I had asked Suzanne at the office if she wanted an after-work drink, but she gave me a strange look and reminded me she had a boyfriend. I spoke to people in shops, I sat on the riverfront looking approachable. I was not approached. So I watched the boats on the Thames, the rubbish gather in corners, kids with no shoes in the street and cats fighting in alleys.

I thought of home, how Mum had the candles sitting on the sideboard and batteries ready for the radio in case this time the power cut was not as temporary as most. People were hungry for more than they were given. In Harwich I had seen people getting poorer, but it was worse here. Hooligans and skinheads occupied set corners of Woolwich and Plumstead, spitting at any passing Sikhs or Nigerians, squaring up to the squaddies from the barracks, while the police watched with their batons at the ready, and underneath it all the threat of all out strikes, of society crumbling, of utter moral degradation — if you chose to read that kind of newspaper. You could read another kind which asked, why worry about terrorism and cults when there are supersonic aeroplanes, and, yes, there's the oil prices, and famine, and dying cities and the desertification of the countryside, but what we really need to think about is reducing taxes, because one day you might be rich enough to worry about that too, and here's who won the Pools.

And there were worse papers than the ones in the newsagents. The National Front sent out their members with their paper to schools and train stations and football matches and sold them to people who wanted to believe that it's all the fault of those people over there, not like us, the different ones. Whenever I saw them standing outside Plumstead station, I walked a bit faster.

And yet, there were spaces of hope, even in London. Notes pinned up in the library and in corner shops spoke of derelict warehouses taken over for artistic spaces, rock bands needing members, people like Julia making empty houses into homes for squatters. There were queues outside the job centre, but also giant lava lamps in the windows of chemists for the kids to stare at, open-mouthed, a swagger in the stride of teenagers, and a feeling that things could be better, more equal, more fair. I would find my place here, eventually.

Then there were films. With all of this going on, I could see the appeal of sitting in the dark for a couple of hours, living someone else's life. And as much as I wanted to be a part of that other world, spotting the lies, the way facts were twisted and people were misrepresented, I understood why we needed films. I would never tell her, but Julia was wrong. They weren't always a distraction. Sometimes they were a magnifying glass, and the more I read and watched, the better I understood what was happening. That had always been my role, not quite a part of the action, but good at watching it all unfold. And I was good at that. I'd been told. Bucharest had taught me that I needed to be better.

It was all about observation, both films and society, applying the rules to your own country as well as others abroad. Using the same questions that Wainwright prompted me to apply to Bucharest, I now looked at London: are the shops empty, transport links broken, the utilities not functioning, are there too many police evident? Do people look tired and hungry? Yes.

CHAPTER 10

I'd only walked in the door when Suzanne, arms folded, had me pinned in a corner.

'Did you go through my filing cabinet last night?' She was anxious, but trying to make it look as if she was angry. She clearly didn't know that she was one of the last people I'd mess with.

'What?'

'Did you?'

'Of course not. No. Why do you think that?'

She looked over her shoulder at Mr Benstrup's closed door, and leaned back against the wall. 'Someone has been through the files, and my desk.'

'How do you know?'

She opened her desk drawer and closed it again. 'I can't say exactly. You know when something just feels off?'

'It wasn't me.' I couldn't keep denying it. I sounded more guilty each time.

The noise of Mr Benstrup's door opening made us both jump. He looked from her to me, but didn't ask what we were doing.

'Got that review of *By the Law*?'

'I'm just going to type that up now,' I said.

Mr Benstrup nodded, and disappeared behind his door.

I sat at my desk, pulled my notebook from my pocket and sighed. Mr Benstrup's big idea was to fill in some of the extensive gaps of my knowledge of Russian cinema before my visit to Moscow. Sometimes I went to press screenings in the morning along with shift workers, hospitals and British Rail being well represented, but those were more for new British or American films. Mr Benstrup wanted to strengthen my knowledge of film techniques, history and sources. I wondered if he was reading Wainwright too. In between Bucharest and Moscow, twice a week I took the bus to Charlton and knocked at the basement flat of a man called Lev. I assumed Mr Benstrup decided what I should watch, sent a bit of paper to Lev, and Lev put the film on and handed me the bit of paper so I knew what I had watched.

Lev, bent over and shuffling, would let me in and, in his already darkened room, opened a silver tin and put another film on his projector for me to watch in his slightly smelly armchair. Clearly, I couldn't understand any of the words on the screen or words spoken, but Lev didn't help me out with this. I wasn't sure if he spoke English at all, as he didn't say anything. The only soundtrack I could follow was Lev's snuffling and the quick chatter of the projector. Some films I felt stretched the idea of film as a visual medium, and I checked for reviews in the library to see if I'd got the right idea. What Mr Benstrup most liked was when I drew links between the Russian films and Hollywood, as long as the influence was of Russia on Hollywood.

By the Law, the silent film that Lev had shown me this morning, was easy to write about, but I had to make it work as a longer piece with the other reviews. I began typing, then realised that the office was too quiet. Suzanne was still looking at the filing cabinet.

'What was missing?' I whispered.

'Nothing.' She pressed her fingers against her throat. 'I must be mistaken.'

Mr Benstrup called me into the office after lunch. He'd made a couple of corrections, but that wasn't what he wanted me for.

'After Bucharest,' he frowned, 'we have come up with a clear set of rules for Moscow.'

I nodded.

'Suzanne has been in contact with the London Inturist office to work out how much money you will need for the hotel and full board, and has paid this to them in advance. She could order travellers cheques for any extra you want to take, but was told that you can use sterling in the only shops you'll be going in.'

'Sterling.' I nodded.

'So bed and board,' he paused, 'for one person. Beer or wine in moderation, no spirits.'

The vodka had been Vasile's idea, after the football results.

'You will need to show me that Bucharest was a one off, and you're there to work.'

I nodded. I wondered, not for the first time, how he funded this magazine. At a bigger organisation I wouldn't have to worry about expenses. I could ask around for other jobs in Moscow, but they would all be film related too.

'Do you have any questions, Ted?'

'No, Mr Benstrup. Bed and board. It's all very clear.'

'Good lad.' He coughed twice and cleared his throat. 'Suzanne has your itinerary ready, and your wages for the next two weeks so you can pay your rent. And I got a surprise for you, too.'

He reached into his drawer and pulled out a book, *Smith's Moscow*.

'Published last year, so it should be bang up to date.'

'Thank you, Mr Benstrup. That's really thoughtful.'

He sighed. 'I bought it for myself, but Mrs Benstrup won't let me dilly dally abroad anymore. Have a good time, Ted. Not too good.'

Back in the main office, Suzanne was carefully closing the cabinet drawer and locking it.

'You saw me lock it, yes?'

I nodded.

'Good.'

'Shall I check it's locked?'

'No need for that,' she said, but she glanced back at it twice as she picked up her bag and left the office. It was as if she expected it to move when she looked away.

I caught up with her outside. 'Listen, Suzanne, is something going on?'

She blinked but didn't answer.

'I know you don't want to go for a drink with me —'

'Let's go for a drink,' she said.

I followed her to the Rose and Crown. It was hot for the first time this summer, and even hotter in the dark interior. I pulled my shirt away from my armpits and put 'a lighter jacket' on my shopping list for the future.

'I'll go to the bar. What do you want?' she asked.

'Pint, please.' I sat down on the worn corner seat and wondered what this was about. She brought the drinks over, the pint for me and something clear with a lemon for her.

'I prefer pints,' she said, 'but I don't want my boyfriend to smell that I've been drinking.'

'That doesn't sound . . . like a good situation.'

'That,' she pointed at me, 'isn't your business. What I wanted to talk to you about was things moving around in the office.'

'The filing cabinet?'

'That, but I've noticed a couple of other things, too. I always pile the toilet rolls exactly on top of each other. I always put the plant so that the flower faces into the office. I always make a right angle with the stapler and the ruler in my desk drawer.'

'I had no idea.'

'Obviously. And I know it's not you, but I need to ask. Have you touched any of those things?'

'No.'

She took a gulp of her drink. 'There's something else, too. I think someone followed me home yesterday.'

'Did you get a look at them?'

'No. Just glimpses, dark clothes, that kind of thing. It's just there were glimpses of dark clothes all the way back.'

I didn't know what to say.

'And, yes, I'm sure.'

'I don't doubt it. But you don't think that was me as well?'

'No, completely different build to you.'

'Taller?'

'No, shorter.'

I was pleased about that.

'Do you think Mr Benstrup is involved in something strange?'

She wrinkled her nose. 'I don't know, but I doubt it. He is worried about money, but anything dodgy would give him palpitations. You're the one that would know. You get sent places. You got any ideas?'

'No.'

She looked as if she had something to say, but she must

have changed her mind as she finished her drink and stood up.

'I'm sorry I can't help you with any of it.' I tapped my glass. 'Can we do this again though?'

She downed her drink. 'Probably not. See you when you get back. Don't miss your flight again.'

CHAPTER 11

There was something strange in the air that night. The men who gathered around the bar seemed snappy with each other, as if something was brewing. I nursed my pint, as I always did nowadays, and stayed out of it. It felt like a fight was going to break out, that kind of tension, and then there was a ripple of interest as someone came through the door.

The hair brushed up high was familiar, and I realised it was the woman from the train. Then, as she stood at the bar in her high heels with her back to me, I knew exactly who she was. I could smell her perfume from where I sat. I watched her, waiting for her to sit down so I could slip out, but she sat down at my table. She slid a glass towards me.

'Ted, I wanted to thank you for that favour you did.'

'That's all right, Mrs Benstrup.'

'It was very important to me, my mother's ring. I'm sure you understand how difficult it is to send packages in some countries.'

I nodded. Mihaela had said this ring was for her sister, but the more I looked at Mrs Benstrup the less I believed they were related. It wasn't just that she was older. She lifted her glass and waited for me to lift mine.

'Vodka. To good relations between countries,' she said, and

clinked glasses. I sipped while she drank the whole measure. 'Have a good time in Moscow. I would be very grateful if you felt able to bring something else back for me. If it's no trouble.'

I felt the pressure of her hand on mine, and wondered how she rolled her 'r' like that.

'No trouble, Mrs Benstrup.'

'Nadenka, Ted. No need to be formal.'

She kissed my cheek and I stiffened, worrying she would leave another mark, but this time there was no stickiness. The rim of her glass was scarlet instead. As she left I noticed the men at the bar watching her, and then looking at me. I finished the vodka with a shudder and left.

I looked forward to getting home, out of the humidity and heat. A nice cup of tea. Then I remembered that my milk had gone off. In cold weather I could keep it on the windowsill, but that wasn't an option now. I was lucky if it lasted a day under a wet cloth, something my mum did in the summer. I half thought about cutting down Brewery Road to buy some, but remembered I was going to Moscow. And I laughed. Just a short sound, but enough to attract the attention of a group of skinheads across the road, standing in the glitter of broken glass.

I faced forward and picked up my pace.

'Oi, poofter!'

Faster. As fast as running without running.

'Long-haired pansy!'

Was my hair too long? I wanted to feel how far it came over my collar, but I had to pretend they weren't there and get home. Then they'd know where I lived. Griffin Road had never felt so steep or so long. My calves were burning.

Halfway up the hill and I couldn't hear anything. Had they crept up behind me? Were they waiting for me to turn and look? I strained my ears, but there was no sound other than my panicked footsteps until I opened the front door and closed it behind me.

In my room I peered through a gap I made in the net curtains and I could see them, back down by the Brewery Road junction, five of them. They weren't interested in me.

I sat on my bed and waited to get my breath back. It was too stuffy, the sun still shining directly into the room. I undressed, panting, then had to give in, so carefully, revealing nothing, pushed up my sash window. I could breathe, the breeze was good as I was high up the hill, but I could still hear them, laughing and goading. I hoped it was directed at each other. Hopefully they were just going to do some graffiti and go home. They were probably responsible for the new NF symbols down by the station.

I concentrated on packing. I'd bought some new clothes and, while I resented spending the money, I was pleased to be arriving in Moscow a little smarter than I had arrived in Bucharest. The journalism book and my notebook went in my case, and in my jacket pocket I put my guide to Moscow that I intended to read on the aeroplane. I laid out what I was going to wear on my desk chair. There was something I had forgotten. The squawking from the skinheads was stopping me thinking.

My rent. I needed to pay two more weeks to cover my rent. And a note to make sure I had a room to return to. With a sigh, I took my money from the advance pay. £79 remaining after I'd taken £5 for cigarettes and extras, and £5 for emergencies. Just over half what I owed.

I didn't have anything in for dinner, but I didn't want to spend any money or risk seeing those skinheads again. I made myself a jam sandwich with the last heel of bread, black tea with powdered milk, and listened to the radio until I was tired enough to sleep and to forget all about my conversation with Mrs Benstrup.

At Heathrow I bumped into Mr Attridge. Again.

He waved his hand high above his head. 'Mr Walker.'

This was starting to become odd, but I couldn't pretend I hadn't seen him.

He strode over and shook my hand. 'Off on your travels, again?'

'Yes. Moscow.'

'And what is that for?' He tilted his head, as if interested, but I had the feeling he already knew. He was too alert. I was tempted to lie, to see what his reaction would be.

'There is an international film festival. I'm going to cover it for my film magazine.'

He widened his eyes. 'How wonderful.' He checked his watch. 'Do you have a little time before boarding?'

I nodded. He gestured for me to follow him. As I did, I looked at his suit, briefcase and impossibly shiny shoes. Whatever his job was, it seemed like a good one, and an easy one. Maybe I could hang around airports chatting to travellers.

My hands felt empty, so I stuck them in my pockets. I'd checked my bag into Aeroflot and battled the sense that I'd forgotten something.

Mr Attridge had arrived at a small counter. 'Would you like anything to eat?'

I was hungry, but I would have felt uncomfortable eating in front of Mr Attridge.

'Just tea, thank you.'

'I'll bring it over.'

He gestured to a Formica table away from the counter, and I sat down. I smoothed down my new cords. Whenever I put them on I thought of Vasile and felt a little guilty, but now I had the horrible suspicion that Mr Attridge knew what I had brought back from Bucharest and was singling me out. Maybe I could explain it was work-related, if he asked.

Mr Attridge put the two cups of tea on the table, placed his briefcase on the floor and unbuttoned his suit jacket. I straightened my own tweed jacket and checked that my ticket, passport and visa were still in my pocket. I'd dressed for Moscow rather than London, and was starting to get warm in my jacket and wool turtleneck, but Mr Attridge was watching me, so I left them both on. I took my copy of *Smith's Moscow* out of my pocket, and put it on the table.

'Mr Walker, I had hoped to have had a chat earlier, but you didn't come in as requested.'

'As requested?'

'We sent you a letter?'

That Barry. I knew he was taking my letters. And who was 'we'?

'I didn't get a letter.'

'Ah.' Mr Attridge took a sip of tea, grimaced, and pushed the cup away. 'That's a shame as you could have met the other Britons attending the film festival. We like to have a quick chat with anyone travelling to,' he lowered his voice, 'the Soviet Union. There are a few dangers we like people to be aware of.'

'Didn't we have this chat about Romania?'

'Yes, we did. But the USSR is much more sophisticated, so it bears repeating.'

I took a sip of my tea. It truly was disgusting. A smile flickered over Mr Attridge's lips. I sat back and folded my arms.

'Go on, then.'

'Mr Walker, I assure you, this is in your interests, not ours. In Britain, we have laws telling us all what we cannot do. The thing you need to understand about Russia is that they have laws telling you what you can do. If you are told you can exchange your money in an Inturist bureau, you do not change it on the street at a much improved rate of exchange. Obviously, don't agree to take anything across borders. If an offer looks too good to be true, it will probably land you in the Lubyanka prison, and maybe Lefortovo after that.'

I was unsure why he thought those names should be familiar to me. Taking things across borders was the only bit that meant anything to me, unfortunately.

'As in Bucharest, if you are approached by a woman for sexual favours, put your ego to one side and assume she is being instructed to pretend to find you attractive.' He looked back to his tea. 'The same goes for a man, of course.'

I smiled uncomfortably. It didn't sound terrible. Nico had looked very attractive, in fact, and I managed to say no.

'I'm being very serious, Mr Walker.'

I adjusted the neck of my jumper. 'This all sounds very unlikely. I don't know anything interesting.'

'Everyone says that, Mr Walker. All information is of interest to someone at some point. A quick fumble may be of no consequence now, but in the future you may find yourself in a job which would not benefit from photographic evidence of your preferences.' He sighed. I suspected he had given this speech multiple times. 'Any Soviet citizen who approaches you will want something from you. No Russian who isn't working for the KGB would come anywhere near you. Use your best discretion. If you can. And, of course, should anything come to your attention which you think we should know . . .'

'Who is "we", exactly?'

'Ah, you know.'

He picked up his briefcase, stood and buttoned his suit jacket, before looking me and down once more.

'You do know that it was 67 degrees Fahrenheit in Moscow yesterday?'

'But Moscow is cold.'

Mr Attridge shook his head. 'You're not very prepared at all, are you?'

I hadn't found out about the temperature. That didn't mean I wasn't prepared. I thought back to my new C&A easy-care polyester trousers, tapped *Smith's Moscow* and raised my eyebrows. He sighed and left me to the cold cup of tea.

I took out some of the money I'd allowed myself and headed towards the duty free. I wouldn't have to buy any cigarettes in Moscow. Hopefully I wouldn't have to buy anything at all and my emergency money would return with me.

Attridge to MOSCOW CONSULATE
(direct to C.H. if possible)

9th July 1975

A British visitor, Reginald Edward WALKER (known as Ted), is on his way to Moscow to attend the biennial Moscow Film Festival. His tickets, arranged through Inturist by Suzanne PROUT, INTERNATIONAL FILM MONTHLY, indicate that he will be in the Inturist hotel 9th-23rd July (arriving one day before the festival and leaving on the final day).

I have met with WALKER on two occasions, neither being particularly productive. He first came to my attention when he was sent to Bucharest by the film magazine he has just started working for (INTERNATIONAL FILM MONTHLY, Plumstead High Street). We have an ongoing interest in this magazine.

The manager, Stanley BENSTRUP, started the magazine in spring 1972 with a small inheritance from his mother. He attended film festivals in Berlin, Locarno, Edinburgh, and the Tashkent arm of the Russian Film Festival (running in even years, the Moscow festival running in odd years). In Tashkent he met a young woman who was given papers to come to Britain with BENSTRUP after a sudden marriage in Tashkent (October 1972). This raised flags, as you can imagine, papers like this being difficult to acquire for those in the USSR.

BENSTRUP has not travelled to any festivals since his marriage, and this may be because Mrs Benstrup wants to remain Mrs Benstrup, and not revert to her previous name. It is a complication of the marriage taking place in the USSR that her name on the marriage certificate appears to be an obvious fake: Nadenka DEVUSHKA (Nadenka being a derivation, and devushka meaning 'girl'). Enquiries are continuing, but it is unlikely that we will be able to ascertain her legal name. (See cross-check report.)

Due to the urging of DEVUSHKA, BENSTRUP has been looking for a film reviewer who is willing to travel to foreign festivals and be paid very little for it. His aim with this publication has been, since his marriage, more closely focused on the cinema behind the 'iron curtain', and it is suspected that DEVUSHKA is the reason for this. As a matter of interest, it is expected that BENSTRUP will run out of money for his magazine by October, so this problem should not reoccur.

(Incidentally, I pulled up WALKER's passport application and found that the photograph was certified by BENSTRUP who could not have known him long enough. Suggest this is added to BENSTRUP's file.)

Previously, WALKER worked at 'Dovercourt Bay Holiday Camp and Lido' in the summer months (June – September), and assisted his father on a small fishing boat during the rest of the year. In early February 1975 he moved to London without having any work arranged. It is unclear how he arranged this financially. He applied for the post of 'Chief Reviewer' with some rather massaged 'experience', and was accepted in March. He lodges in a small terraced house close to the magazine's office (159C Griffin Road, one room and shared use of bathroom facilities).

I met him in May at Heathrow Airport as he left for Bucharest and considered him to be very naïve, sexually inexperienced, and unaware of the political and personal dangers he faced in a Communist country. I then met him on his return very briefly, just to show my face. He seemed surprised by this, showing signs of anxiety. I did not pursue my doubts as I knew that I would be in touch with him again as we had been alerted to his visa application to the USSR. I sent him the usual letter, asking him to attend the general briefing, but he did not arrive. When I met him earlier today he claimed not to have received this letter. I tried to warn him again, but he was rather blasé about the risks, and suspicious of me personally. He tried me get me to admit who I worked for, and his attitude was, on the whole, insolent and arrogant.

This would not necessarily be cause for alarm. Plenty of stupid British businessmen survive a few days in Moscow, as we know. However, this particular business was already a concern. What is a further concern is that we received a murmur from Bucharest in the last couple of weeks that the Securitate found him to be 'agreeable' and 'malleable', and that he agreed to undertake a task for them. He has the arrogance of youth, but seems quite unprepared for the sophistication of attack for which we know and admire the USSR. As you know, any idiot can become a useful one. We are unsure what this task might involve.

I would recommend a similar level of surveillance to before, although with any luck he will not become a problem if he can be encouraged to do his job. I am also alerting another experienced festival attendee to make friends with him and keep him on the straight and narrow, which should reduce the time you need to spend on him.

There will be a continuing 'light touch' investigation into WALKER and the DEVUSHKA file is attached.

CROSSCHECK REPORT: DEVUSHKA

Despite the earthquake there in that year, the Film Festival in Tashkent opened in October 1968, running in alternate years to the Moscow Film Festival. Both festivals, as well as others in Eastern Europe, are designed around the promotion of communist films and political ideas. The 1970 Tashkent festival had to be cancelled due to an outbreak of cholera, making the 1972 festival the second one held, and the first attended by BENSTRUP.

Stanley BENSTRUP came to our attention in October 1972 when, after attending the International Film Festival in Tashkent (USSR), he came back with a wife. Nadenka DEVUSHKA (per the marriage certificate) had managed to get a marriage licence and an exit visa with suspicious ease. This suggests that she has political advantages, clearly, but why these should be linked to BENSTRUP was very unclear. An investigation has not resulted in many facts, but we have established some key points.

DEVUSHKA is almost certainly a KGB officer, not least because her passport with her married name was available to her within two days. BENSTRUP is a magazine editor. The interest of the KGB in such an insignificant character started to become more evident as the focus of his film magazine shifted to international film festivals held behind the "Iron Curtain". His first 'Chief Reviewer', Joseph NORTH (employed January 1973), travelled to:

1. FEST Belgrade, Yugoslavia – February 1973
2. Berlin International Film Festival 'Berlinale', West Germany – 22 June – 3 July 1973

3. Moscow International Film Festival, USSR – July 1973
4. Pula Film Festival, Yugoslavia – August 1973
5. FEST Belgrade, Yugoslavia – February 1974
6. Berlin International Film Festival 'Berlinale', West Germany – 21 June – 2 July 1974
7. Karlovy Vary International Film Festival, Czechoslovakia – July 1974
8. Pula Film Festival, Yugoslavia – August 1974
9. Kiev International Film Festival 'Molodist', USSR – October 1974

(The specific dates for the Berlin festival are covered in the extensive notes for these festivals.)

NORTH first looked like a problem in Berlin where it is easier for us to carry out surveillance. The decision was taken to watch and wait, rather than intervene. The ease with which we found letters and packages in his luggage convinced us that NORTH was not trained for subterfuge, nor entirely aware of the illegality of his actions. We anticipated that his 'favours' were carried out either for BENSTRUP or DEVUSHKA, and we swiftly discounted BENSTRUP.

NORTH went missing in Kiev during the 'Molodist' festival. We are unaware of either the date or precise location that he was last seen. It was not until November 2nd that the office secretary, Suzanne PROUT, contacted the local Plumstead police in some distress, and it took some time to be referred up the chain to us. We have people asking around on the ground, but our sources in Kiev are limited in number and scope. The authorities provided documentation that NORTH had boarded an aeroplane back to London, but he did not walk off that plane.

On the positive side this did give us a reason to interview BENSTRUP and PROUT in the magazine office, allowing us to get a good sense of what they both believe was happening. In the course of these discussions, PROUT agreed to answer occasional questions regarding the business. She has told us that she had been ordered by BENSTRUP not to tell WALKER about NORTH.

The addition of interviews with directors to WALKER'S travel made for an unfortunate extension to our remit. While we can cover festivals with fixed dates and multiple attendees, it is much more difficult to watch individuals.

There are clear threats to WALKER who is blithely unaware of the existence of NORTH and his disappearance. However, there seems to be a further threat to BENSTRUP. At 52, he is not of a particularly advanced age, and yet he seems to have acquired a series of chest related medical issues. Until we gain access to his house we cannot be sure what is being done to him, but PROUT has reported on his increasing ill health, most notably a serious and persistent cough. She is aware of his having five visits to the doctor in June during work hours, but the condition is worsening. Meanwhile, she has heard DEVUSHKA tell BENSTRUP to 'stop complaining like a baby'. Should anything happen to BENSTRUP, DEVUSHKA would be the sole beneficiary. She acquired right of abode on marriage to a British subject, and therefore freedom from immigration control (Immigration Act, 1971).

It must be assumed that someone in Moscow may try to pass a letter or package to WALKER, and anything to avoid this scenario would be welcome. It has been decided that it would be better to keep him ignorant of events.

MOSCOW

CHAPTER 12

Although I'd made a good start on *Smith's Moscow*, I started to feel less confident about what he described as I queued up at Sheremetyevo Airport, passport and card visa in my increasingly sweaty hand. There were stern faces and uniforms everywhere, dark green with flashes of red and gold on the shoulder and cap. That's when it hit me that I was in the Russia of the films, not the version sold by Smith with a pleasant wave through customs. I could have seen the Donald Pleasance from *Telefon*, or the Angela Lansbury from *The Manchurian Candidate*, and I wouldn't have been surprised. Although, they were both English, I realised now. I wondered what the Russians thought about that.

I was called forward, showing my papers, like offerings, to a scowling guard. My suitcase was rummaged through (new pants, luckily), and I found myself in the arrivals hall where a driver was waiting for me with a sign: 'Waker'. Could have been worse.

Getting into the car, I noticed it was a little chilly and I wished I hadn't struggled to remove my turtleneck in my plane seat. Mr Attridge wasn't as reliable as he thought. I'd mention it when I got back to Heathrow, as I seemed destined to always bump into him.

Still outside the car, my driver lit a strong-smelling cigarette and looked up at the heavy grey sky. He opened the passenger door, took some windscreen wipers from the foot well and fixed them onto the car. He didn't say a word to me, just got in, started it up and drove away from the airport.

It was a longish drive, but the car was big and I didn't have to think about where I was going. It was relaxing after the rigour of customs. I knew I would be assigned a hotel, but I'd forgotten to ask Suzanne if she knew which one. I felt it was probably written down somewhere, but I didn't have a choice so I didn't worry about it.

Although I had read through *Smith's* description of the journey in by road, it was different seeing it. The trees and fields, with the occasional small wooden houses in the drizzle beyond turned into pale concrete shapes studded with dark windows. The buildings were enormous, over twenty storeys, the roads wide and quick, and it made the smaller dark outlines of people look tiny. I didn't think that London's roads would ever be so clear, or the cars so quiet. I didn't hear anyone beep their horn, but there was a lot of lane-changing and acceleration. As we neared the centre of Moscow, the buildings shrank a little, to five or six storeys, and it felt less intimidating.

The car pulled up at a doorway. The driver took my case from the boot, and stood beside my door. I got out. The rain was pouring down now and had found a route down the back of my neck. The driver handed me the case, pointed to the door, and said, 'Hotel.'

'Thank you.'

I walked past the doorman, through a cloud of cigarette smoke, and up to the desk where there was a slight young woman, smiling at a man she was talking to. I waited for them to finish. She looked at me and carried on talking.

'Hello,' I said.

She looked at me again. 'Wait.' She carried on talking, as the man reached out and pulled at a tendril of her curled, brown hair.

The rain dripped from my own hair, and I tried to brush it back with my fingers. She kept talking.

I put my case down and looked around. It was poorly lit although, as far as I could tell, all the lights were on. There was an Inturist booth, written in English letters. At least I could read that. They were the people who would organise everything I needed. An older man came in with a suitcase to keep me company at the desk. The bald patch on top of his head looked wet, and I was surprised he didn't have a hat. Most men here did. He took his jacket off and gave it a gentle shake. I glanced back at the receptionist who was still ignoring me, and looked towards the entrance but I couldn't tell if the rain had stopped. There was a couple of red chairs near the doors which had men lounging in them, hats still pulled low over their eyes, and papers in front, smoking but not drinking. The smoke was thick and heady.

I was thirsty now. It had taken a while to get through customs, and I'd turned down the last offer of a drink on the aeroplane, being unsure about aeroplane toilets. I turned back to the girl and raised my voice.

'I need to book in, please.'

She turned to me slowly, and glared. The man slunk off and I wished I could too.

She knocked the desk with her knuckles. 'Papers.'

I slid my passport across, and she snatched it from my fingertips. She took it over to a box of papers, flicked through them and then returned, triumphant, and threw the passport back to me.

'Wrong hotel.'

'What do you mean?'

She stretched out each syllable. 'Wr-ong ho-tel.'

'But my driver brought me here.'

'You were booked here.'

'But not now?'

'No.'

'Where should I go?'

She crossed her arms and shrugged. 'I don't know. You could ask Inturist at the Service Bureau.' A flash of a real smile, and she turned away to ignore the other man waiting.

I was starting to panic now. One thing I had learned from the guide book was that I couldn't book where I wanted to stay. I was allocated somewhere and that was it. If I'd been unallocated I would have to leave. Maybe I'd made the girl cancel my booking by being rude and interrupting her.

I picked up my case and walked towards the Inturist office. There was one woman free in there, four others were busy. I waited until she called me over. I couldn't anger too many people. I depended on them knowing what I didn't and being nice enough to tell me.

She beckoned to me. 'Yes?'

'I was booked at this hotel, but now I'm not.' I handed her my passport.

'Mr Walker?'

'Yes.'

'You have been transferred to the hotel next door. The Natsional.' She pointed to the smoke-filled entrance. 'Please turn right, and you'll find it.'

'Thank you.' I'd read about the Natsional. 'What hotel is this one?'

'The Inturist. Natsional next door.' She pointed to the entrance again.

'Thank you.'

I moved towards the doors, to find the man who had been

waiting next to me at reception. He held his hand out. I tensed myself, waiting for something I wouldn't understand.

'Did they sort you out?' he asked.

English. I shook his hand.

'Yes, thanks. I've been moved next door.'

'The Natsional? Lucky you, I like that one.'

'Are you being moved?'

'No, I just hung around in case you needed any help. Those Inturist people are great usually, but sometimes two people are better than one. I'm Alan Sullivan.'

'Ted Walker.'

He tipped an invisible hat, 'See you around,' and headed towards the stairs.

Alan Sullivan. It was good to know there was an Englishman in the hotel next door, but I wished we were in the same hotel. As I walked to the entrance a uniformed woman came in, leading a group of twenty people, all talking English. Her blue uniform and red collar were familiar. A Thomson package tour, of all things. Everyone English was staying in the Inturist, it seemed. But not me.

I stepped back outside and paused under the awning. The rain was even heavier, but the sun illuminated the shining wet building opposite, light bouncing from the upper windows. No one seemed to have an umbrella as they walked quickly, heads down, their dark coats and hats. If anyone caught my eye they quickly looked away. The streets had traffic, but there wasn't the urgency you'd see in London, and the cars were much cleaner than in Bucharest. I watched pedestrians negotiate a dripping downpipe and it all felt oddly familiar, maybe from films.

I turned to the right, my eyes on the large red building ahead, like The Natural History Museum in style except it was red brick instead of cream stone. There was no point waiting for the rain to stop. I launched myself into it, keeping my head down, and bumped into a man walking quickly in the other direction.

'I'm sorry,' I said, but he didn't turn around. I checked my pockets, but everything was still there. Just rude, but not a pickpocket.

I continued round to the small canopy which I assumed was the entrance of my new hotel, nodded to the doorman, and went in.

CHAPTER 13

I stood in the lobby of the Natsional, in front of four enormous near-naked statues, hesitating on the dark red rug. There was no reception desk. I turned back to the doorman and he pointed me forward and to the left.

The long reception was lit by huge yet dim chandeliers, the heavy velvet curtains and the wooden panelling seeming to have absorbed the light. Through the window and the rain, though, I could see a second red building with a tower next to what I now thought of as the Natural History Museum. This wasn't the right hotel. I knew it from the doorman, the leather armchairs and the view. I was just going to find out where to go next, and hope the rain didn't get worse. My passport, held underneath my jacket, seemed dry.

I didn't want to drip all over the reception desk in this nice place. I stood next to a small table by the window, put the case down with a sigh and removed my sodden jacket with fingertips and placed it on the arm of the chair. The tweed had soaked up every raindrop. The check-in desk had five clocks on the wall, illuminated against the dark wood. I could see the two people behind the wooden desk looking at me, but I tried to seem purposeful and looked towards the door. I caught the eye of a man, settled in one of the armchairs. He quickly looked away. I wondered if all hotels had men sitting in chairs by the doors. This reminded me of my book on Moscow, and I pulled it from the jacket pocket. It was warped, and I knew it would fatly blossom in that way thoroughly wet books do. I put it on the table and sighed.

I was starting to shiver and wanted nothing more than a bath and hot drink. I hoped my hotel, wherever it turned out to be, wasn't far. I needed to get to a room, any room. When I picked up my jacket I noticed with horror that there was a dark stain on the pale yellow upholstery.

I picked up my suitcase and book, draped my jacket over one arm and walked quickly towards the desk. I could hear a slight squelching in my shoe, my wet sock starting to bunch up.

The woman behind the desk looked at me and tried to smile, as if she'd been ordered to.

'Passport.'

I placed it on the desk and tried to explain. 'I was taken to Inturist, next door, and they said to come here. If you could tell me where to go now I would be grateful.'

She looked at me, my passport, and then at something on her desk. She spoke to the man next to her in Russian, and he fetched an envelope. She was busy writing something, and he went back to his post on the far side of the desk. She kept writing. I started to look around. Had she forgotten I was here? I waited. She kept on chatting to the man who flicked his eyes at me.

A Russian man came up to the desk, spoke to the man and left. An American couple came up, asked for their passports and were told, 'One more day.'

'We were told today,' the woman said.

The receptionist held up one finger. 'One more day.'

The man tutted, and they grumbled to each other as they walked away. I looked to see if the man would make eye contact with his colleague, maybe raise an eyebrow, but there was nothing.

I put my case down and wondered what was taking so long. The woman had dark hair with a red hint to it. Her white blouse was open at the neck, and a thin gold chain was visible just underneath.

I started as I noticed she was looking at me.

'One moment.'

I nodded and turned back to the window. The clouds had broken, and a burst of sunlight made the wide road outside shine silver like a summer river. The more I looked at the red tower, and the white one behind it, I was sure that it was the Kremlin. My guidebook would tell me, but I didn't want to look as if I needed help. I should know if it was the Kremlin.

'Registration form.'

I filled it in.

The woman put the envelope in front of me and her paper on top. It was a map.

'Is this to my hotel?'

'No. This is your hotel. This is a map to get you to the Festival opening tomorrow morning at ten o'clock.'

This was my hotel.

'You will go to the Rossiya Hotel for the festival,' she pointed with her pen, 'past the Kremlin, past the cathedral and left, here.' She patted the envelope, 'Your list of films and cinemas.' She picked up a slip of paper. 'Room 302. Each floor has an attendant. You'll see the desk. Please leave the key with the floor attendant when you go out. She will take your breakfast order the evening before. If you need anything, like laundry, she will arrange this. Keep your Customs Declaration safe.'

If this was my hotel, I didn't care how tiny my room was.
But I needed to be sure.

'My trip was paid for in advance.'

She didn't disagree.

'And I have meal vouchers. Can I use them here?'

'Of course. Give this paper to your floor attendant, and
she will give you the key. You will need to show this paper,'
she waved it, 'whenever you come in and out of the hotel. Do
not lose it.'

'Thank you.'

'Nichevo.' She rang a bell, and a boy arrived to escort me
upstairs.

I followed him up quiet carpeted stairs, past huge pieces of
dark furniture and dim lighting. On the third floor we turned,
and he handed me over to the floor attendant. Silently, she
took my paper, studied it, and then opened my door before
handing me the key and the paper, closing the door behind
her.

There had been a wonderful mistake. It was a large room
filled with antiques. A door opened onto a bathroom: cast
iron roll top bath with taps large enough for giants, a ceramic
toilet with dark wood seat, an enormous basin. I turned the
bath taps on, and went back to see if I'd imagined the four-
poster bed, but it was still there. I stripped off my wet clothes
and got in the bath.

When I'd had a wash and laid my clothes on the side of the
bath to dry, I opened the envelope and looked at the list of
films I had to see. Only a couple of directors meant something to me. I looked in drawers and cupboards, and had a
fiddle with the small television in the corner, but I couldn't
get it to work. There was a radio on the sideboard, but all I
could find was classical music.

I took my meal vouchers out and choose a 'dinner' one. Or should it be 'tea'? It was five o'clock. What time did 'lunch' finish? Then I remembered about booking my breakfast, and searched for a menu. I found some brochures for Inturist and started to fantasise about coming back to travel the Trans-Siberian railway — *Paris to Tokyo in twelve days*. The other covered a lot of rules regarding what you could photograph, but I didn't have a camera. Eventually I found a menu. It didn't look like breakfast, but that's what it said. I decided on tea, white bread, butter and jam, and wrote it on a bit of paper to give to the attendant.

I dressed and wondered what to do about my shoe. The cardboard I had carefully laid over the hole was soaked and mushy. I took the photograph information card, and tore a corner to lay inside.

By now I was starving, so I took my meal vouchers and locked the door to my room. I gave the key and the breakfast request paper to the woman attendant in the hall on my floor, and asked her where I could eat. She shook her head. I showed her my vouchers. She pointed to the stairs.

I went downstairs. There was a restaurant on the first floor, but I doubted my voucher would work in there. It looked very expensive, and I was conscious of Mr Benstrup's disapproval. I went back to the lobby and back to the woman who had served me before.

'Could you tell me where I can eat with my vouchers, please?'

She sneered at them. 'Hard currency is better.'

'But I have these.'

She sighed, and pointed out restaurant, café and bar in different directions.

The café would do for now. She'd said the vouchers were fine before, so I couldn't see why she was sneering about them now. People were changeable, I thought, and then I wondered whether it was the same woman. I was pleased I hadn't tried to explain about my shoe.

I hesitated at the bottom of the stairs. Dozens of people were suddenly on the move around the hotel: four Asian women with long black hair in tunic tops and loose trousers, the American couple I'd seen earlier, three North African men, and me. On my own.

I was tired and I needed some food, but it was reassuring to know there were British people next door.

CHAPTER 14

I sat in the bar with my glass of red wine, working things out. One pound was one and a half roubles. This drink was 38 kopeks, 25p. It was what everyone else seemed to be drinking, but was not quite what I wanted. I was looking, as subtly as I could, at the snacks people were eating and wondering which to choose.

The people here were a mix of Westerners, British and American, and from everywhere else. There were snippets and sounds from so many languages I didn't recognise, let alone understand. I didn't think I could hear much Russian. I lit a cigarette and just listened out for English voices. Maybe some of these people were connected to the festival and they would mention it and I'd find out what I should do. Did I try to go to all of the films, or some?

I looked back at the menu again (in English, French, German and Russian) and noticed my feet were tapping. I was in Russia, in Moscow, and free to do what I wanted, unlike in Bucharest, and it was unnerving. I looked around towards the window, in case Vasile was staring in, and smiled to myself. Then I turned back again. I had recognised someone. That man from the other hotel, Alan Sullivan. He was sitting with a striking black woman who looked much younger than him, a bottle of red wine between them. She caught me looking. I quickly turned back to my drink and lit another cigarette.

'Ted!'

I turned to see Alan waving.

'Come over and join us.'

I hesitated and then thought, I did need someone to explain things to me. I carried my wine to their table.

Alan held his hand towards the woman. 'Ted, this is Ursula Koskinen.'

Not a wife, then. Lover?

'Ursula, this is Ted Walker.'

We shook hands. Her fingertips were cold but her grip was strong. I wanted to stare at the way her hair was pulled back in twists, the way the gold earrings lay against her neck, but there was something in her gaze that stopped me from looking too hard.

'How's your new hotel?' asked Alan.

'It's very nice. Much nicer than I expected, a huge room with a massive bath. I can actually lie down in it.'

'Do you have a view of the Kremlin?'

I thought. 'I haven't looked out of the window yet. I don't know.'

'The first thing I did was look out of the window.' Alan clearly did most of the talking. 'Next thing was to test the air conditioning and check where the pool is. You two don't have either of those things, because you have history. Ursula is in this hotel as well.'

'Did you come over together?'

'No, we travelled separately. We always decide where we'll meet the night before it starts because we never know which hotel we'll be in. It was a good job we did chose to meet up in this one. At least we get to avoid the Thomson tour lot in the Inturist. You don't come all the way to Moscow to listen to people from Maidstone.' He topped up both of their glasses.

Ursula said, 'You're not from Maidstone, are you, Ted?' Her voice was low and smooth, with a slight American accent.

'No. Not that far away though. Where are you from? Are you American?'

'No, I'm not American.' She sounded bored, as if she'd said that too many times. I could feel my cheeks blushing.

'You do sound American,' Alan tutted. 'I don't know why you get so cross about it. You must learn to sound more like us if you don't want people to think that.'

Ursula punched him gently on the arm.

Alan continued to smooth things over. 'Well, I thought you might be American too, and I'm good with accents. I knew Ted wasn't from Maidstone. Suffolk, is it?'

'Essex. North Essex, though, not far from Suffolk.'

'Not that good with accents, then,' said Ursula.

Alan put one hand to his ear, like a shell. 'I'm getting old. My hearing is going.'

What was their relationship?

'I live in London now,' I said. 'Is that where you live, Ursula?'

'No.' She sipped her wine.

'Just tell the poor boy. She's Finnish,' said Alan. 'She's just being difficult because they gave her a hard time at the border. They always do, so we always spend our first night like this.'

He flicked the wine bottle and patted her hand. Ursula sat back and folded her arms. She was wearing a wedding ring.

'I know you didn't deserve it, but Ted here seems like he's on his first trip to Moscow.' He looked at me and I nodded. 'Be nice.'

'I'll be nice after a good sleep,' she said, and yawned. 'Those trains give you bruises on the inside. All my organs feel like they've settled in the wrong place. And the guards.' She made a disgusted face.

'Well, an early night and you can forget all that nonsense,' said Alan. 'We have the opening speeches in the morning.'

'Are you here for a conference?' I asked.

'The 9th Moscow International Film Festival,' said Ursula, and yawned again.

My stomach leapt. 'Me too.' I wouldn't have to be alone. This was a nice surprise.

Alan nodded. 'That's good. We can walk over together.' He patted Ursula's hand again. 'Do you want to get up to bed? We can meet in the lobby at half past nine and wander over.'

'They always start late,' said Ursula, still petulant.

'I know, but we get to watch Ted here experience the delight of St Basil's and then the horror of the Rossiya.' He turned to me. 'Only the outside is bad, like Inturist next door. The inside is good. Not falling down, like this old place.' He stood and shook my hand. 'See you in the morning, Ted.'

He downed his wine, Ursula left hers, and they walked off, arm in arm.

The other good news was that I had decided I wanted soup. I ordered it at the bar, with another glass of wine. Borsch Moscow style, the bar man corrected me, not 'soup'. Although it was a soup. It was good and rich, and the dark bread that came with it was filling, although I nervously left the cream on the side. When I finished, I noticed that there were more Russian voices than before, although I wasn't entirely sure I was able to pick out Russian from Polish, or Finnish, for that matter. But the room was warm and smoke filled, the wine was good and I felt quite at home.

I closed my eyes to listen to the noises around me, and smell the food. Having forgotten to bring my notebook downstairs,

I would have to write all this down when I got back to my room. One thing I had found in the newspapers in the library was regular interest in Moscow. Opinion pieces, travel pieces, everyone wanted to understand what it was like to be in this secretive city. So secretive that Thomson ran tours here, and it seemed the whole world visited but still, articles describing weekend breaks to Moscow were published. I had hopes that a couple of good articles could erase my lack of qualifications, and I was happy to play up the idea of secrets to get into the National Union of Journalists.

One more glass of wine, and I decided to wander outside and look at the illuminated stars above the Kremlin. The Kremlin wall was the other side of a wide road and some gardens, further than I'd thought, and on the path running up a slope alongside it I could see an army of cleaners, with trucks washing the paving down after all that rain.

Couples strolled along the road, foreigners talked loudly and I felt utterly safe. It may not be true that there was no crime in the USSR, as the Soviets claimed, but I felt a lot safer here than I did in London. It was early to do this, and I was in a hotel, but first impressions are important so I ran through my list. Are the shops empty, transport links broken, the utilities not functioning, are there too many police evident? Do people look tired and hungry? No.

I stood on the street, smoking a cigarette, and thanked Mr Benstrup for never following up my references.

CHAPTER 15

I woke to a knock on the door. I froze. I had half-expected the constant phone calls which I'd experienced in Bucharest, and had covered the phone in case of this, but I hadn't heard anything. Now there was a knock and, although it was morning, I was scared.

I crept from the bed, and opened the door a little. A maid in black uniform with white lace trim was holding a tray. My breakfast.

I opened the door properly and put my hands out to take it from her.

'Nyet.' She manoeuvred past me, and placed it on the round dining table.

'Thank you.'

'Nichevo.' She had a swagger that I had to admire.

I rubbed my eyes and sat down. I looked in vain for milk to put in the tea, but there was only a lemon. I drank half of it anyway. The bread and jam were good.

I dressed and went downstairs to wait for Alan and Ursula. I was early on purpose so I could see if Alan was coming from the hotel next door or Ursula's room. It would be a clue. The leather chairs already held the inert bodies of men with newspapers and hats. I wondered if they had been there all night.

Alan came in looking tired, and lifted his hand in recognition.

'You look dreadful,' I said.

His face looked baggy. 'I was woken up a lot. Did you get any phone calls last night?'

'No.' I felt a bit left out. 'I did in Bucharest, but not here. Not yet, anyway.'

'Lucky you.' He smiled. 'I've got my technique honed now. You have to muffle the phone with towels, anything you have, but last night I forgot to prepare everything. You can't leave it off the hook or they complain. It's psychological warfare.'

'It's hard to believe, isn't it? Everyone seems so nice, except for the receptionist at your hotel.'

He patted me on the back. 'It's nothing to worry about, as long as you don't say yes to anything. They're just trying to see what they can get away with. Ah, here she is.' He kissed Ursula on the cheek, and we headed out of the door into brilliant sunshine.

She was wearing an olive-green blouse and black trousers. He was wearing an ironed blue shirt and dark blue trousers. I was wearing a crumpled grey shirt and dark brown cords which, I now saw, had a drop of dried soup on the thigh. I would have to up my game.

I hadn't stood up next to Ursula, and now I realised she was taller than me. I checked her shoes, and was relieved to see that she wore high heels. Even so, I drifted to walk with Alan between us. He was taller too, but not by much.

We crossed the road, and Alan pointed behind us.

'Who's luckier? The one in the ugly hotel which looks out at the beautiful one, or you two?'

The Inturist hotel was a grey office block from anywhere, while the Natsional was curved, cream and decorative.

'That's my room there,' said Ursula, pointing. 'First floor.'

She had a better view than me. I'd checked when I went to bed, and saw the square courtyard at the heart of the hotel.

Alan led us up the cobbled incline, past the queue for Lenin's tomb that he pointed out and the women sweeping, their heads covered in black scarves. The brushes were bundles of twigs, their shoulders bent, but their voices boomed if they saw someone drop a cigarette butt. The soldiers watched them approvingly.

'That's the big shopping arcade there,' said Alan. 'Every year I think that I'll go and get a handmade pair of shoes. If you fancy it, they're on the top floor, but give them a couple of days to make them. Ursula went to a fashion show there once, didn't you?'

'Do you come to every film festival?' I asked.

'We have done for—' Alan looked for Ursula to finish his sentence.

'This is my fifth,' she said, 'so it's your sixth.'

Alan nodded. 'I'm sure you're right. Goodness.'

Finally, a clue. 'So this is where you met?'

'Yes. And they're every other year, so that's ten years we've known each other.'

'No, eight years.' She counted them on her fingers. '1967, 1969, 1971, 1973, 1975.'

'Yes, you're right. I first came here ten years ago. Did you ever go to Tashkent?' he asked her.

Colleagues. Film festival colleagues. I watched the easy way they interacted. This festival ran from the 10th to the 23rd July. That was two weeks. They'd known each other for eight weeks in total.

I stopped at a raised round area constructed from white stone. There were steps up to it, and a closed metal fence around it, but nothing there.

'What is this?' I asked, but they had gone.

'Are you coming?' called Alan. They'd moved ahead so I ran to catch up. We walked around St Basil's which was starting to look a bit silly up close, and then Alan pointed at a large, ugly office block. 'The Rossiya.'

'Blimey.'

'Twenty-one floors, four thousand rooms. We stayed here in '73 when they moved the festival to this hotel. If you need a nightclub or a post office, they've got it. They even have a barber, and a police station.'

'You're kidding?'

'No,' said Ursula, 'look out for the black door next to the barber. That goes to the cells.'

It was a weird kind of teasing. She didn't smile at all.

'But a brilliant movie theatre,' said Alan. 'Two, actually. And a concert hall. That's why lots of festivals and conferences are focused here.' He checked his watch. 'We'd better hurry. They like us to be on time, even if they aren't.'

I followed them, arm in arm again, around to the main entrance where there was a crowd of people, all dressed up. I looked down at my clothes again. As we got closer to the doors I could see a group of children, each with a red handkerchief around their neck, holding out pieces of paper for people to sign. A few women were handing out red and white carnations, and a series of banners in different languages hung over the entrance. I found the one for me: 'Greetings to the participants of the IX International Film Festival in Moscow'.

We made it past the shiny newspaper kiosk and clear phone booths, and through the glass doors of the hotel into another crowd in a bright, double height lobby. There was the grand Russia of the Natsional, and then this modern Russia of veneer, plate glass and mezzanines. As I gazed around I noticed with horror that the women who were directing the crowd to the auditorium were wearing grey and brown, the same as me.

'Is it what you expected?' asked Ursula. She stood out with her height, but also in the comfortable way she eased her way through the crowd. I was continually jostled, smelling food and soaps and cigarettes and cigars and aftershaves and washing powders from around the world.

'A bit busier than I was expecting,' I said.

'The whole world is here,' said Alan.

'Are there other British people?' I asked.

Alan lowered his voice. 'There is another British man, Terence, but you really don't want to get stuck with him. Or maybe you do, but not until you have a drink in your hand. He's unbelievably dull.'

'All right.'

We followed the swell of languages and colours and I began to feel excited. Everyone was smiling and eager. I gazed up at the light fittings above the reception desk and wondered if they were deliberately modelled on Sputnik, before noticing the grim faces of men looking down on us from the mezzanine.

We were welcomed as we entered the cinema, and Alan guided me to the right, up onto the overhanging balcony section. Ursula was already arranging herself and shooing away people from our two seats. We sat down, and the murmur of languages grew louder.

Two weeks of films in a couple of very different posh hotels. I could see why Alan and Ursula kept returning. I could be one of them. I could draw the contemporary references from the fictional worlds I saw. I could come to understand serious, complicated films. I might even come to like them.

CHAPTER 16

I was separated from Alan and Ursula in the crush after the introduction, and went alone to my first film of the festival. It was from North Vietnam, not an area of film I knew anything about, but that's why I was here.

I had got lost in the corridors, arrived late and, instead of heading to the balcony, had been pushed into one of the lower seats by an usher. The four women in the seats along from me were, I was sure, the group of women from my hotel that I had seen the day before. I looked around. Everyone in this section of the cinema was Asian, and I hoped I hadn't taken someone's place.

There was a woman translating at the front of the cinema into Russian, the soundtrack was quieter than normal and my headset had a woman translating into English. With the door opening and closing, and three versions of the film running, it was surprising that anyone could follow it. But I did. It was amazing what you could get used to.

When I started to well up I half-wished I had been more distracted by the swinging doors. I managed not to cry until I realised everyone else around me was sobbing. I supposed they were North Vietnamese. The lady nearest me passed me a handkerchief, and that was it.

*

I met up with Alan and Ursula in the café. Their table was full, but the two people sharing left soon after I'd spotted them. The waitress remonstrated with me, pointing at people waiting by the bar, but Alan pulled my arm so I sat down hard in the green tub chair, and then there was little she could about it. She smoothed down her white apron so her white blouse with red embroidery puffed above her waist, tutted and left. I was hungry, and hoped she would come back. I held the menu up to signal this.

'How was your film?' asked Alan.

I blew air from the side of my mouth, wondering how to put it.

'Hard going?'

'Yes.' I lit a cigarette, keeping the menu loosely upright, and changed the subject. 'The translations were intense. Are they recorded?'

'No, they're live. They have a whole load of women in the back, watching the films and translating sometimes as they watch, and sometimes from a script. Sometimes they haven't seen the film.'

Ursula added, 'Sometimes they don't even know the language they're translating from and they have to make it up. They do a pretty good job. They are great at reading the content from the images. But they can usually cover every language.'

'It's like the United Nations,' I said.

'It is the United Nations,' said Ursula, 'in a way.'

I thought back. 'There was a lot being said at once, though. You have the film, the translation, and then there's the woman shouting the Russian translation from the front.'

'It can be overwhelming, but it generally works, somehow,' said Alan. 'The Illusion cinema uses earphones from the war, but I think the ones here are newer. What about the film itself?'

'It was the Vietnam war from the perspective of a small girl. I think it had actual war footage. It was a bit – it was amazing.' Thinking about it again, I wasn't sure that I was still hungry. I looked at their plates. 'What did you eat?'

'Blini,' said Ursula. 'Pancakes. They're good.' She leaned towards me. 'Do you like herring?'

I blinked, and looked at Alan. He was smiling.

'Ursula wants to go to a Beriozka to get some herring. She's having withdrawal symptoms, but I said no one would want to sit next to her and we all have to see Kurosawa later.'

She pouted. 'I'll just eat it on my own tonight. I don't have to share.' She looked around, and tried to attract a waitress over with her hand. One saw her, and turned away. 'I'm going to the bathroom.'

Alan watched her walk away, biting his lip, so I watched too. Ursula cornered two waitresses who looked at her, and then carried on talking. Their eyes suggested they were talking about her. Ursula spoke to them, and they spoke back. The one that had tried to stop me sitting was loudest, but Ursula silenced her with a lot of finger pointing and then left the café. The waitress who had been over before sent the other over, still blushing, and Alan ordered me blini and kefir.

'What was that about, with Ursula?'

Alan bowed his head towards me. 'She gets a lot of abuse here. The Russians swear blind they're not racist, but they are. Very. They were standing over here before, right behind her. Ursula can speak Russian, so she likes to listen to what they're saying and then tell them she'll report them for being inadequately Communist and shaming the state in front of foreigners.' He sighed. 'It works during the festival because no one is quite sure who is who, and who has power. But it gets to Ursula, being on guard all the time.'

'Do you speak Russian?'

'Yes, no, thank you – that's it. Not even all the basics. Every year I leave convinced that I will apply myself to learning it for the next two years, but it hasn't happened yet.'

The waitress arrived back, slammed the plate with the blini down with some force, and the glass of kefir with slightly less, but enough for it to slop over the dark orange tablecloth.

'I think she doesn't like being told off.'

'Oh, they never do. Some service staff think that it doesn't show them to be equal if they have to serve people. Even though that is what they have agreed to do as a job. There's this phrase you get, something like, "I'm a human too". And then you see them with someone in a uniform, and they behave exactly like a servant.' His eyes went back to the door. 'She's been a while.'

This was the point at which I should ask what was between them, but then Ursula came back in, glaring at the waitress in her path. She sat down.

'How's the blini?'

'Oh.' I'd eaten half without noticing. 'Really good. And this drink is strange, but I like it too.'

'It's called kefir, but sometimes translated as yogurt.' Ursula looked at her watch. 'We have a little time before the film. I think I'll go for a walk by the river.'

'I'll come too,' said Alan. 'If that's OK?'

'Of course.'

Definitely more than colleagues. The waitress sat three new people down on my table, but didn't bother to clear the dishes. With the small tulip-shaped lamp in the middle, there was nowhere to put anything else. I nodded to them, but had no idea what language they were speaking. They looked

Indian, or Sri Lankan, maybe. I couldn't guess. The world was a big place. I finished quickly, and left.

Now that the lobby was emptier I could appreciate the space. The floor was a series of grey and black marble slabs, polished nightly, Alan had told me, by a team of women with rags tied to their feet. The women behind the reception desk wore white blouses with black pinafores, and the phones next to them were a startling yellow. They still had chandeliers in this modern palace, but contemporary and simplified, constructed from golden tubes.

I could also now see the men guarding the doors in their black uniforms, as well as the men in no uniforms who were smart and stood too still. I remembered the cells and the police station and, for some reason, thought that the least suspicious thing to do would be to look at the items for sale in the glass cabinets, and the Russian language newspapers that I could not read.

I wanted to go to the river, but I didn't want Alan and Ursula to think I was following them or that they had to look after me. I picked up a couple of Inturist leaflets and found a red armchair to sit in, next to the window. I lit another cigarette, and read about what I could do in Sochi and Novgorod.

A group of five women walked past the plate glass window, one man in front of them and one behind. I watched and wondered if this was part of the gang of translators, getting ready for the big film, Kurosawa. And then I remembered the task that Vasile, or Marku, had set me. The woman in the photo, Ingrid, had been photographed here. Did that mean she spoke Russian? She had spoken Romanian to Marku's family, but she must have spoken German too, or they thought she did. Maybe she just translated between Romanian and German, or Romanian and Russian. I watched the last of the women walk past the window, and then turned to watch them walk through the lobby towards the cinema. All ages, all heights, sizes, hair colours. I didn't recognise Ingrid, although I wasn't sure that I could. A couple of women noticed me staring, and I turned away. I wasn't going to be challenging those security guards to get close to any of them, but I was interested to see if Ingrid was real.

I went back to my leaflets and had a last cigarette before Alan and Ursula came over to fetch me. We all went in together.

Marku had said his uncle had been here with a film company. I wondered if anyone was keeping an eye out for me, too. I turned to Alan.

'Was Mircea Drăgan at one of the festivals? Is he here?'

'No, he's not here this year. He won a diploma at the last festival. Do you remember what the film was, Ursula?'

'*Explozia*,' she said. 'Explosion. But in English I think it was called *The Poseidon Explosion*.'

'Yes, I saw that,' I said. 'What did he look like? Drăgan?'

Alan thought. 'Quite thick set, dark hair. Why?'

'I was supposed to interview him, but the man I saw was thin and balding.'

'How odd,' said Alan. 'Didn't you ask why he didn't look like Drăgan?'

'I thought it might have been an old picture that I saw, when he was younger.'

'You really need to do more research, Ted,' said Ursula. 'You can't let people take advantage of you.'

The lights went down and we settled back in our seats, headphones on.

CHAPTER 17

It felt as if it should have been dark when we came out, but the sun wasn't near setting. Alan sighed every couple of minutes.

'I mean, he's just perfect, isn't he?'

I exchanged a glance with Ursula.

'We've seen the winner. We might as well go home.'

Alan seemed drunk on Kurosawa adoration, wandering a bit behind us on the cobbles of Red Square.

'Do you want to have a bath before we eat?' asked Ursula.

I looked at Alan, then realised she was talking to me.

'Yes, all right. Shall I meet you in the café?'

'We usually spend our second night in the Metropol, our way of celebrating the festival opening. Come to my room about eight, and we'll have something to eat before we go.'

'Before we go out to dinner?'

'Yes. It can take an hour to get a single course in the Metropol. It's never a good idea to go there when you're hungry.'

She told me her room number, 103, and I went ahead while she waited for Alan to catch up.

I had a bath, then I checked in *Smith's Moscow* what that round platform was that I had seen in Red Square: 'Lobnoye Mesto', he said. 'Place of the Skull'. I flicked forward. Hundreds of deaths by hanging, whipping, scalding, molten lead straight down the throat. But that last one was just for traitors.

I changed my clothes to less closely resemble the festival hotel staff, and knocked on Ursula's door on the first floor a little early. I noticed her long turquoise dress, a gold tint on her eyelids, and I felt underdressed, again. Her bare feet pressed into the thick Chinese rug in the centre of the floor.

She had a suite. A dressing room, a drawing room with an ornate waist to ceiling mirror, a bathroom with an even larger bath than mine, even an iron balcony with French doors. She didn't show me the bedroom, but I'd seen enough.

'How did you get this room?' I asked.

'I slept with the right person.' She smiled, slyly. 'Really, it's just the luck of the draw. Hungry?'

She led me back to the drawing room. There was white and black bread, cream, olives, crackers, red caviar and, I smiled, herring.

'Help yourself.'

'Why does cream come with everything?'

'It's sour cream. It goes well with savoury food. Try a bit of it all. Especially the herring.'

I loaded my plate, and Ursula poured champagne into three glasses. I hoped Alan would take his time. I didn't feel that I knew Ursula at all, but I wanted to.

'Are you married, Ursula?'

She brought my glass and whispered into my ear. 'Ask me personal questions at the restaurant.'

I shivered. She clinked her glass against mine, and saluted the mirror with it.

'Kippis!'

She sat in an armchair next to the window, and lit a Prima cigarette.

'Did you order this food from the restaurant?'

'No. I dragged Alan to the Beriozka. He likes it really. There's a brochure around here somewhere.' She flicked through a pile of magazines on the floor next to her. I saw *Sight and Sound* and other film magazines. She'd been doing her homework. I had asked Mr Benstrup about getting some subscriptions into the office, but he'd sent me to the library. She found the right magazine and held it out to me. I sat in the chair opposite her own, plate on my lap and champagne on the floor. I flicked through the brochure, and laughed at the huge lumps of meat next to tinned peas.

'Vegetables are a rarity,' said Ursula, when I pointed it out.

Everything else looked better than what I had at home. Jars of olives and béarnaise sauce, caviar and hot dogs, milk in strange little pyramid containers, thirteen types of cheese, not including processed cheese. 'Knorr soups?'

Ursula wrinkled her nose. 'I didn't like those. But, here, if it's Western, it's seen as worth having.'

The last half of the booklet covered alcohol and tobacco with large, full page adverts of Heineken, Cointreau, Beefeater and Marlboro.

'I wish I ate this well,' I said. 'They've got everything.'

Ursula shook her head. 'It can be in the brochure, but not in the shop. Like the menu, it's a promise of what is possible, only.'

'But, still, I thought the Russians were badly off.'

Ursula put her glass on the table. 'These shops aren't for Russians, Ted. They're for foreigners. They're for us.'

There was a knock. Ursula let Alan in. He was wearing a tie. I felt my open collar, and wished I'd at least brought one.

'Hello, hello,' he said, rubbing his hands together. 'This looks delicious. Except for the herring.'

'Ted is being polite and trying it. Maybe you should too.'

Alan waved his finger. 'I fell for that emotional blackmail before. Maybe we should ask Ted what he thinks of the herring.'

'It's fine. I couldn't eat a lot.'

Ursula laughed, and handed Alan a plate. 'I've hooked him.'

'Did you bring your itinerary, Ted? I can tick some of the good films for you.'

'No. I'll bring it tomorrow. I started writing some notes up about the North Vietnamese film, though.'

Alan picked up his champagne and sat down. 'You can't write about *Girl from Hanoi*, Ted.'

'But that little girl was an amazing actress. And it was a great film.'

I thought of the two little girls running across the bridge and started to well up again. I busied myself lighting a cigarette. It was too late. Ursula had noticed and came across to put her arm around me.

'I'm all right,' I said.

'I know.'

Alan topped up my champagne. 'You have to remember the politics. It shows the Americans as violent imperialists, just the kind of thing the Soviets want us to take home as a message. Any American films they show will be the seediest, grubby side of America. Anywhere that is even vaguely Communist will be idealised. I'll go through the list for you so you don't watch things you can't write about.'

'All right, but that seems self-defeating. All films have some kind of sub-text. Think of *Casablanca* and its message about the war. It doesn't make it a bad film.'

'True,' said Ursula, 'and there is a huge amount of good in these kinds of festivals. Where else would you see films from Mongolia, Cuba or Syria?'

'Or Finland,' added Alan.

'And of course they often give awards to revolutionary governments rather than films, but you could say Cannes awards them to style over substance. And there can't be anything bad about seeing what is out there and allowing other cultures to influence your own.'

Alan grunted, 'Not too much.' He added, 'The films you absolutely should never watch here are the British films. They cut them so badly. Russians don't even notice that the films they see are hacked to bits.'

'What do they cut?'

'Sex, mostly. Not that there'll be any sex in *Great Expectations*. I mean, what a choice to represent Britain. Have we got nothing going for us but a Victorian writer and a dubious history of child exploitation? Why do we keep promoting Dickens to ourselves? It's not like society has improved that much, is it? What's Finland got this year, Ursula?'

'*Home for Christmas*.'

I finished my plate full of samples. I didn't like the herring one bit, but I finished it. The caviar was fine, and I half-heartedly dipped some dark bread into the sour cream.

I wasn't sure about Alan's opinion, and I wondered what Ursula thought about it, but I didn't want to start a real argument while they enjoyed their pretend arguments so much. I liked listening to them, back and forth. Without them to guide me, I'd probably be sitting in my room, worried that the telephone would ring. Even so, was he serious that I couldn't write about it? Wasn't the point of film to see other places and other lives? I decided to write it anyway, and see what Mr Benstrup thought.

Ursula was standing by the door, a midnight blue silk shawl draped over her shoulders and Alan draped on her arm. She held out her other arm to me. 'Shall we, gentlemen?'

We walked down the wide stairs like that, in a row, and I felt so proud. I caught sight of two of the North Vietnamese women, who half-bowed their heads, and smiled. They liked me because I'd cried at their film. Alan and Ursula liked me because they were kind. I fitted in with them without even trying. For the first time ever I felt at home. Home for a couple of weeks, anyway.

CHAPTER 18

The gardens across the road were full of people making the most of the warm summer evening. I had fallen behind the others, and Ursula stopped Alan so I could catch up. People looked at us as we walked past, clearly not from here, but they were interested rather than hostile.

We crossed roads and, as they talked, I looked at the people carrying loaves of bread, their string bags full of paper packages. As we approached the Metropol, Alan pointed out the Bolshoi and saluted the statue of Marx.

'Do they mind you doing that?' I asked.

'They get a lot of people who mean it.'

Ursula said, 'The problem wasn't really Marx. He just had the idea. It was other people who implemented it.'

Alan separated himself a little to look at her face. 'I didn't know you were a Marxist.'

'I'm not.' She looked confused. 'You don't have to believe something by learning about it. It's not all fixed, and I like to understand what I am rejecting.'

Alan shook his head. 'I'm just not interested. I like my world the way it is. Do you know anything about Communism, Ted?'

'Not a thing. This is my introduction.'

'No it isn't.' Alan laughed. We'd arrived at the doors of the Metropol. 'Watch what happens now.'

The doorman nodded to us, and opened the door. We unlinked arms to pass through.

'Think that happens for the great hordes? What you have to remember is that you can only fly to Arkhangelsk, and you can only take the train to Murmansk.'

'What do you mean by that?'

'That you'll never really know what's going on here, only what they show you. It doesn't have to make sense, it's just the way it is.'

Alan headed towards the stairs on the left, and was stopped by a slim, smartly dressed man who greeted him by name. I was starting to think everyone in Moscow had a suit but me.

'Christopher, this is a surprise.' Alan introduced me, and we shook hands.

'Christopher Hughes,' he said.

Alan said, 'I'm sure you remember Ursula.'

'I do indeed.' As Christopher shook her hand he made a slight bow.

'How's your wife finding Moscow?' asked Alan.

Christopher looked thoughtful. 'Ah. Moscow didn't agree with Martha, I'm afraid. She headed back quite a while ago. Not long after I last met you.'

'Oh, that's a shame. I am sorry, Christopher.'

'Never mind. It happens.' He shook it off quickly with a professional smile. 'You're keeping up your tradition of first night at the Metropol, I take it?'

'We are. This is Ted's first visit to the Metropol, and Moscow.'

He looked at me. 'I hope you enjoy it.' He turned back to Alan. 'I would try the other restaurant tonight, Alan. Your normal venue is pretty packed. You'd be much better off on the fourth floor.'

Alan nodded. 'Would you like to join us?'

'Another time, thank you.' He shook our hands again, and waved as he left.

'What was that about?' asked Ursula.

'I'm not sure.' Alan was still watching Christopher through the doors. 'We were being warned off.'

'I don't mind going to the tea-room,' said Ursula, 'but it won't be the same for Ted.'

'We can come back another time.'

We headed for the stairs.

'What a shame about his wife,' said Alan. 'I suppose not everyone can put up with it here. I think they were only just married when I last saw him. Sweet little thing, Martha. She called him Kit and I thought it suited him. I really thought they'd last.'

'He doesn't look old enough to be married and divorced,' I said.

'He's not much older than you,' said Alan, 'mid-twenties, I'd say.'

Ursula said, 'He acts much older than that, so serious.'

Alan said, 'I suppose that when he's speaking to us he's hard at work, representing Britain. I've met him a few times, yet I know next to nothing about him. If I hadn't met his wife I wouldn't even have known she existed. He smiled a lot when he was with her. What a shame that ended.'

We'd reached the first floor when I felt my meal voucher in my pocket. 'Does this place accept vouchers?'

Ursula shook her head. 'That settles it. We have to go to our usual place.' She walked across the corridor, and looked through the restaurant door. 'Whoever it was must have gone. It's half empty.'

She sat down and beckoned to us. Alan shrugged.

'I'll blame you both, if he asks.'

We sat either side of Ursula, a spare chair between Alan and me. A waiter brought us menus, and Ursula quickly ordered some wine before he disappeared. She put her hand on my arm. 'I will order for you. There are certain things you have to try to know that you have been to Moscow.' She lowered her head, 'I promise they are all better than herring.'

I was embarrassed that I hadn't disguised my feelings better, but relieved that she knew. When the waiter returned, Ursula ordered for us all again.

'Now we relax, drink, and wait until we are nearly starved.'

Alan still looked preoccupied, scanning the other tables. I had a look too. There was a large table with about eight women, and half the others had two or three people on them. No one was paying us the slightest attention. The room was strangely bright for a restaurant. A fountain trickled in the centre of the room.

'Ursula, you said you would tell me about yourself when we got here.'

'Yes, I did. I am married, and live in Helsinki. I have two children and a dog.'

I was surprised it was so straightforward. 'Why didn't you say that before?'

'That mirror in the room. I'm convinced there's a camera behind it.' She lowered her voice. 'In fact I have covered the one in the bedroom with a blanket.'

I looked at Alan.

'Not because he'll be there.' She laughed. 'It's just the principle. Privacy is important.' She waited for Alan to say something, but he was still distracted. 'That first year we were here together, I'd had enough of the provocations, so I asked Alan to pretend to have an affair with me. Now every other year we have our fake Moscow fling, and no one bothers us. No one believes it, but everyone pretends to. Alan is married too, aren't you? Alan?'

She patted his hand, and he came back to the conversation.

'Yes. Thirty-six years married.' His eyes slid away again. 'Ursula, do you recognise any of those women? You're good at faces. Are they from the festival?'

'They are right behind me,' Ursula hissed. 'I can't turn around, it's too obvious.'

I didn't recognise anyone at the women's table, but I'd had such a quick look as the group of women at the festival had walked past that I wasn't surprised. There was a lot of talking going on, not one conversation, but many, and I caught snatches of different languages as well.

'Are they translators?' I said.

'Maybe,' said Alan. 'They're not allowed to talk to the attendees, but I suppose they are just talking to each other.' He nodded his head towards the empty bottles on the floor by their chairs. 'That's a lot of wine they've gone through. Is anyone— Oh.' He put his head down. 'I've spotted a couple of minders. Don't look.' He pointed with his finger in a way which made not looking much harder. 'I think you're right, Ted.'

Ursula sighed. 'What we do now is talk about anything and everything. We don't look around and we don't second guess. Only this table exists and the food which, with any luck, will start arriving within the hour.' She held Alan's hand. 'Yes?'

He smiled. 'Yes.'

I'd thought that Alan was in charge of this strange couple but clearly, just because Ursula found it hard to get a word in, it didn't mean he dominated things.

'Didn't you want to try a banya, Alan? Now you have someone you could go with.'

'A banya?' I said.

'A bath house.' Alan looked at me. 'Would you fancy a bit of massage and bathing?'

I nearly agreed, but Ursula was giggling. I felt I was missing some crucial information.

'I'm not sure.'

'It's not a summer thing to me,' said Ursula. 'We prefer our saunas in the winter. But if you ever wondered whether you'd enjoy getting beaten with birch branches in the nude, you should give it a go.'

'Ursula! He's not going to agree now, is he?'

'So you weren't going to warn him?'

I had no idea how much of this was true, but I suspected that I'd had a lucky escape.

Alan said, 'I got a list of the other films being shown from Inturist, if anyone's interested.'

'At normal cinemas?' I asked.

'Some of them. We see the official press showings, that's why there are so many languages translated. There's plenty of others shown, in Udarnik or the Palace of Sports. It's only 50 kopeks a ticket, so they always sell out, and the Palace is a massive venue. There was nearly a riot during *My Fair Lady* when the translator tried to translate the songs. I wish I'd been there for thirteen thousand Russians all shouting, "No translation! Don't translate the songs!" Was that '65?'

'Maybe,' said Ursula. 'And, despite their extraordinary range of swear words, they ban them from being translated in cinemas.'

Alan lowered his voice. 'I saw that the Illusion cinema is showing Tarkovsky's *The Mirror*, but only because Michelangelo Antonioni refused to stay at the festival unless they showed it. The Soviets refused to let the Cannes and Berlin festivals show it, and only foreigners are allowed to go to this showing. I will never understand how they restrict their best work. Like *Solaris*, they barely showed it. Did you see that, Ursula?'

'I didn't like it,' said Ursula. Alan made a face showing mock horror, and they were off on one of their good-natured arguments.

Ursula topped up all our glasses with the excellent red wine that she'd chosen, and we toasted each other, the festival, the Metropol and film makers everywhere. We'd ordered a second bottle before the first course arrived. As I became more relaxed, I found it harder not to look to my right, over Ursula's shoulder, at the older woman in the bright purple hat who had caught my eye.

'FISHERMAN' BACKGROUND REPORTS: FOR ADDITION TO WALKER FILE

'International Film Monthly' office, Plumstead High Street

22.58 7th July

Entry was made to the property shortly before 11pm. There are a number of local public houses nearby, and it was suggested that 'kicking out time' might provide cover, if necessary. 'Kingfisher' made a general search while 'Flycatcher' opened the lock on the filing cabinet which allows both small upper and large lower drawer to open.

Nothing of interest was found outside of the filing cabinet during the time we were on the premises, but a scaled map is included as an appendix.

Contents of desk belonging to PROUT: stamps, ruler, stapler, pad for telephone messages, rubber, 2 pencils, hairbrush, address book containing business contacts

Desk belonging to the target does not have a drawer

Contents of filing cabinet:
    Top drawer: 7 pens (4 blue, 2 black, 1 red), paperclips, box of staples

Bottom drawer:
    Old copies of International Film Monthly

    Copies of wage slips (subject earns £20 per week, employed since March 1975)

Copies of job application letters from PROUT and subject (see below)

Copies of insurance forms taken out by Mr Benstrup for the trips taken by the subject. This raises two points: subject's 'next of kin' is listed as: Joan and Reginald Walker, 16 St Austin's Lane, Harwich (to follow up); the amount for the insurance (£50,000) seems in excess of his worth to Mr Benstrup – I suggest that there should be further investigation into his motives here.

Concealed at the bottom, underneath newspaper, a birthday card in an opened envelope addressed to PROUT (92 Abbot Road, Charlton). Message reads: 'When you have had enough, this will get you home. Mum.' Card contains £25 (5 x £5 notes)

'Flycatcher' was alerted to someone being in the office belonging to BENSTRUP by severe and prolonged coughing. We left shortly afterwards.
     BENSTRUP's marital status may be about to change, which could impact on the direction of the magazine, and could explain the large insurance amount as a form of gambling as he needs an injection of cash, personally or professionally.

<u>Joan Walker – 16 St Austin's Lane, Harwich</u>

11.35 10th July

Early 60s, brown housecoat worn over a brown skirt, pink slippers. Hair is grey with a permanent wave growing out.
     I assumed the role of an employee of the market

research company, *Research Services Ltd*, discussing life insurance options. Joan answered the door and was reluctant to let me in so I offered £5 as an incentive. There was no suspicion regarding the large amount. She told me that Reginald ('Reggie') was out fishing.

After my listed questions, I managed to move her on to a photo I had identified as the target. She said that he had left home and was working in London, but offered no details of this. Neither did she name him, referring to him as 'my son'. It may be that she has not had any details of where he is living or working. When she went to the kitchen to make a pot of tea, I looked through the letter rack on the table and could identify no letters from the target. Most of the letters were Airmail from Australia.

The question about teachers having a positive or negative influence on the young produced the name 'Miss Slater'. She 'gave him ideas', she said, but would not expand on this.

I tried to introduce politics into the discussion, but she is uninterested in voting or who runs the country. I discussed the electricity shortages, but she claims that they have not impacted on her as she 'goes to bed early'. Questions on the Common Fisheries Policy produced the surprising answer that her husband was in favour of membership of the EEC, despite being a fisherman. 'Reggie wasn't in the war, but his brothers were and they were saved by the French, fetched right out of the water.' As for fishing, she wants her husband to retire and has already forced him to sell his boat after a period of ill health.

Once it got to half past twelve she was eager that I should leave before her husband returned. I observed him go inside the house at 12.44.

Agnes – Corner shop, Eastgate Street, Harwich

12.52 10th July

Late 20s, curled hair with dark roots. A shop tabard covered her clothes. Nicotine stains to fingers of her right hand.

I assumed the role of a customer, discussing the front pages of a few newspapers with Agnes as she filled the sweet jars.

I asked her if she knew how Joan was getting on, that I hadn't seen her for a while. She expressed dismay that 'Teddy' could do such a thing. I agreed. She went on to talk about how long Joan had been saving up, how much she'd had to push Reg to agree, and all while she was scared of setting foot on a plane. And weren't planes amazing, and so cheap nowadays. She then finished by saying how she hoped Teddy would turn up with that money soon. She swiftly moved onto gossip about other neighbours, and then started asking me questions.

I bought cigarettes and left.

Keith Ball – The Alma Inn

14.10 10th July

Late 50s, stained work trousers, thick green jumper with two large holes in the body, peaked cap. Boots were of good quality, old but well maintained with newer laces.

I approached as he finished his second pint and offered another. He accepted, and we sat together at the bar. He provided a lot of information, confirming Reggie's age as 57, his wife's desire to take a holiday to Australia, his illness last year and his wife's desire for him to stop fishing entirely.

Bringing up WALKER led to a long conversation about BALL's own children and their reluctance to go out on the boats. On WALKER himself, BALL hinted at problems at the Dovercourt Lido, with WALKER expecting a promotion which he didn't receive. He used derogatory language in relation to WALKER and his desire to work in an office, and returned to the subject of his own children.

At 15.00, last orders were called and BALL went home.

Miss Slater – Upper flat, 188 Marine Parade, Harwich

16.31 10th July

Late 50s, pale blue twin set, black shoes (scuffed). Sitting room has multiple bookshelves, and there are piles of opened letters, and exercise books on the table in front of the window.

I telephoned and assumed the role of a university student, writing a thesis on changing approaches in teaching. She was very happy to contribute to this and arranged a day and time. When I arrived, a copy of *Who Killed Enoch Powell?* by Arthur Wise was face down on the arm of the chair by the window. She blushed when she moved it for me to sit down.

I tried to lead her to talk about the target (children of fishermen, only children, children who had to leave school early), but in the end I had to introduce his name directly into the discussion.

She described him as being a quiet and lonely child. He was good at English, and little else, spending his time avoiding the larger boys. She remembered giving him particular praise for a piece of writing, commenting on how observant he was and having the strong sense that no one had really praised him for anything before this. She told him that, if he worked hard, he could make a living by writing. He asked what kind of work, and she said a writer, a teacher, a journalist, but then he left at the age of fifteen to work on the boats. 'Another one lost,' she said. 'But I wasn't ready to give him up.'

'We used to meet in the library for him to practise writing. Every Saturday. He thought that, if he could create a kind of portfolio, his lack of qualifications might not be such a sticking point. I think he sent some off to the bigger newspapers, but he had nothing new to add to the articles he'd read. Who wants to read about the fishing industry, or coastal holiday parks?'

She did allude to some kind of problem the target had at work, an accusation of theft which was unresolved, but led to a loss of a promised promotion. She believes that it was at this point when the target made the decision to leave. 'There was never anything here for Ted. I'm glad he left. Now or never,' she said.

CHAPTER 19

On Friday morning neither Alan nor Ursula was watching an early film, so I walked over to the Rossiya on my own. It was my first Hungarian film. Nestled in my seat, I was warm and the voice of my translator through the headset was calming. Hardly any accent at all, I remember thinking, just before I fell asleep, waking only when half the cinema audience began loudly applauding.

Ashamed, I started to scribble in my notebook the title and what I recalled of the opening minutes, only to see a piece of paper fall to the floor. I picked it up: 'Tomb of the Unknown Soldier, 12pm'. I looked around. Who had left this? Had I picked it up by accident? Then I remembered Mrs Benstrup, Nadenka, asking if I would bring something back for her. I had agreed, but now I was here I didn't want to do it. There was something about her that worried me. I decided that I would say I forgot, or didn't get the note. I crumpled it and let it fall to the floor, under my seat.

I went to the usual café, with its view of the Kremlin, and ordered an early lunch with coffee. There were other cafés within the Rossiya, but this was Alan and Ursula's preferred one, and now it was mine.

When my dumplings arrived, I smoothed my list of films

out on the table and crossed out the title from that morning. It wasn't one that Alan had ticked as a 'must see' as we waited between courses the previous night. I still didn't feel comfortable as a film reviewer. I probably never would be, but I needed to be better at faking it. Maybe the next festival I'd be sent to would be Cannes. I could get used to that. Three men took the other seats at my table, with a nod. I listened to them talk. Maybe Italian?

I had an Italian comedy marked on my list for this evening, but didn't fancy anything in between which gave me time to have a look around. Alan had ticked it, of course, and had also ticked a Japanese police procedural for tomorrow. He'd given me a one sentence synopsis of every film on the list. I still felt unprepared but was lucky to have his help.

I had ticked an Argentinian werewolf film, *Nazareno Cruz and the Wolf*, leaving him laughing in disbelief. I tried to explain that I was here to expand my knowledge of film, as well as review the best ones. We agreed to disagree.

'You just have to think,' he said, 'does this come from a Communist country? And if it does, it's going to promote a Communist world view.'

'All films are propaganda,' I said. 'We talked about this.'

'Yes. But some are our propaganda.'

Ursula said, 'Don't listen to him. Watch whatever you like. Where else will you see films like this? The London Film Festival often seems an excuse to show foreign films with nudity. And *The Texas Chainsaw Massacre*? They showed that at Cannes, and then at Locarno, and it sounds like they will show it in London. Is that really the best film has to offer?'

She wasn't faking her dismay, she was genuinely angry. We went back to the list and whether translators should translate the spirit of the film (Ursula) or the literal translation (Alan).

As well as films, there were trips planned for foreign reviewers, to Lenin's mausoleum on the first Sunday, and a river cruise on the following Saturday. Alan and Ursula were reluctant to visit Lenin again, so I was going without them. Ursula wanted to organise a tour of the Kremlin through Inturist instead, but Alan was unmoved by her request as yet. What I was waiting for was the Romanian film, *The Actor and the Savages*, on Thursday. This had got a tick from Alan, despite its Communist roots, but I was most wanting to see who the in-cinema translators would be.

I looked out of the window and wondered what I could do for a couple of hours before my next film.

The passers-by that I was coming to recognise as the everyday kind of Russian were walking across the space between the Rossiya and Red Square, in dark, wide trousers for the men, and thin shapeless dresses for the women. They weren't the kind of Russians that I'd seen in the hotels, their heads uncovered by headscarves or hats. The sun was warming me through the glass now, so I put my notes back in my pocket and prepared to leave. Mr Attridge had been right eventually. The weather was warm now.

A group of women passed in front of the window, and I raced to the lobby so I could stand facing them as they walked past. Their minder went first, the women walking behind him in pairs or threes, their faces mostly turned from mine. I reminded myself I was looking for red hair and a small mouth. I scanned their faces, but still didn't see anyone who seemed familiar, except for one woman. It wasn't Ingrid, it was the woman from the restaurant last night, still wearing that striking hat which drew my eye. As she removed it I could see she had dark brown hair in a bun. She was the only one who made eye contact with me.

I went outside thinking, if I caught the translators on their way in before the Romanian film, which would be late on Thursday afternoon, it would be my best chance of finding Ingrid. Or maybe I should follow these ones out, to see where the translators rested between films. I felt uncomfortable at the thought of that, having just been seen to watch them walk in. I had days to catch them in a more natural way than chasing them around a hotel.

I checked my watch. Half-past eleven. I had seen that the Tomb of the Unknown Soldier was near my hotel, so I didn't want to walk in that direction and accidentally keep that appointment with whoever was waiting for me there. I looked the other way. The river.

I crossed the road and went up onto the bridge. There was a square section sticking out which looked like an observation point, so I stood there, next to a low wall which ran around it, and looked across the river. What surprised me most was the number of people lying on the river bank in what looked like their underwear. There was an occasional boat, and some people walking along the riverside, including a group of those children in white shirts and red scarves. I sat on the wall, looking back at the Kremlin. There were so many towers and trees within the walls, like a tiny city. The original city of Moscow.

I felt a hand on my shoulder and jumped down. It was the man from the Metropol, Christopher Hughes.

'Guilty conscience?' He smiled. 'Are you waiting for someone?'

'Just admiring the view.'

'Yes. I forget to do that now, but it's well worth it. The embassy is just over there.' He pointed to the left, across the river. 'So it's all become too familiar. Familiarity breeds contempt, as the saying goes.' He coughed. 'The Kremlin is very impressive though. The red and green always reminds me of Christmas. I was never keen on St Basil's.' He checked his watch. 'I'd better go, I have a meeting, but it was nice to see you again.'

'Can I just ask, what is that uniform I see children wearing, white shirt and red scarf?' I gestured towards Red Square so I could watch his expression while he wasn't looking at me. I was very unsure about him. The way Alan had responded to his instructions had felt odd. I wanted to concentrate on how he spoke to me, whether his face changed.

'Oh, they're Pioneers. They've made a pledge to be good Communists.' He didn't pretend to be interested in me, or my question.

'Like Scouts.'

'Not exactly.' His eyes continued to pass over the distant view. 'There is very little crossover between British organisations and Soviet ones. When you've been here a little longer, you might be able to see this for yourself. My role is for people like you to never have to think about that side of things.' He looked back at me, and I felt I had failed his assessment. 'You wouldn't believe what people agree to do.' He smiled, but his eyes remained critical.

People like me. 'Is that right?'

He tapped his watch. 'Anyway, I do have to go. See you soon.'

I raised my hand as he walked away and realised that it hadn't felt as strange as it should have, to bump into someone I knew in such a distant place. Maybe I should have asked him where I should go now, what I should see, but then I realised that I didn't have to be anywhere or do anything. Everything was organised for me, and I suspected he would have reminded me of this, reminded me to go only where I was supposed to.

I sat on the wall again and looked around. The deep red

of the Kremlin, the childlike scribblings of St Basil, the surprising space leading up to Red Square, and the Rossiya sitting squarely on the right. Now that I thought about it, there was a matching observation point on the other side of the bridge from where I could easily watch people enter and leave the Rossiya. For a second I considered tracking the translators in and out from there, but realised I would look exactly like a spy. I could imagine what Mr Attridge would say about that.

On the one hand I just wanted to enjoy the food and the posh hotel, and continue my pretence at a career until I worked out what on earth I was going to do next, yet finding Ingrid was starting to feel like a real possibility. It was remarkable how Marku's story had got to me, but that was a personal aim. Professionally, I needed to find out more about Soviet Moscow, find the story which could move me towards reporting news.

Another group of children with red scarves, or maybe the same group, was heading towards Red Square. I thought about following them up there to get an ice cream from the stall I'd seen, but there was no rush. I looked back to the river and saw Christopher on the road that ran below mine. He must have doubled back down the steps. Had he crossed the river just to speak to me? I noticed a man stumbling towards him, his thick coat pulled tight and a hat pulled low. It was far too hot to be wearing so many clothes. Christopher checked his watch again; he seemed to be looking for a chance to cross the wide road, over to the water. The man swerved to meet up with him and Christopher turned away, although he must have seen him.

The man hesitated, pulling something from his coat pocket. It looked as if he was trying to put it in Christopher's pocket, but Christopher stepped away. The package fell to the ground. It must have been metal because I could hear it clang on the pavement. Christopher darted across the road, leaving the man standing there, his hands hanging by his sides. Two more men emerged from underneath the bridge I stood on and one of them picked up the package. The man followed them without a word being spoken. A car pulled up and all three got in.

I watched Christopher walk away and, when the car had passed, he stopped and looked around. He saw me on the bridge, watching, and turned away again.

He could have taken the package, and maybe they wouldn't have taken the man away. Christopher had let that happen, and I was sure he'd let me go just as easily.

CHAPTER 20

After my ice cream, I got back to the Rossiya in good time and went to the café for a coffee. The woman from earlier, the one in the purple hat at the Metropol, was sitting by the window. That surprised me. I didn't think that translators were allowed in here. She smiled at me and waved me to her table. Before I could react, I felt someone take my arm, and Ursula turned me towards her. Her clothes looked thrown on, and she was worried.

'Have you been with Alan?' She dragged me to an empty table.

'I haven't seen him. Why?'

'He was supposed to meet me at half past nine. I tried calling his room, but there was no answer.'

'He'll definitely be here for the Italian film. He was looking forward to it.'

Ursula bit her lip. 'That's what I'm hoping.'

I ordered coffee from a passing stone-faced waitress. 'He's probably just gone to one of the other cinemas.'

'But that's where we'd decided to go together. We were going to take a walk along the Moskva and go to the Illusion cinema to see *The Mirror*. He loves that film, and he never forgets about me. When we have a plan, nothing would stop him keeping to it. Nothing small.'

I didn't know what to say. She'd clearly thought through all the options. She looked around the café and then watched the people approaching the hotel from Red Square. I turned to look too, hoping I would see him rushing towards us, eager not to miss anything. I noticed that the woman in the purple hat had gone.

Ursula pushed her coffee away and drew herself upright. 'We know he was aiming to see this film, so let's go and watch it, see if he turns up. If not, we'll go to the Inturist and knock on his door. Either he's in, or the floor attendant has his key. It will give us an idea, anyway.'

I said, 'He probably just had his phone hidden in the wardrobe and couldn't hear it.'

'Yes, the strange calls. Do you have them?'

'Not yet.' That was weird, now that I thought of it again. I hadn't had any here.

I finished my coffee, and we went through to the cinema with a group of Italians. We took seats at the back and put our headphones on, Ursula watching whoever came in and out the doors. I'd expected them to be closed for the duration of any film, but people were in and out constantly. What with the light from the door, the shouted Russian translation, the film soundtrack and the translation through the headphones, the film had to be really good to hold your attention.

The lights went down and the film started. There was no sign of Alan.

When the film ended, he still hadn't turned up. I'd been distracted by the film, but I was sure Ursula would have noticed him. As we walked from the Rossiya she took my arm. I was the new Alan. That was fine by me.

We passed the ice cream stall on Red Square, the cobbles pressing against the card in my shoe.

'What do you think might have happened?' I asked.

'I don't want to say it aloud.'

I looked around. No one was near. Did that mean she didn't trust me?

We entered the Inturist hotel, but were stopped by the doorman.

'Papers?'

I made a show of searching my pockets. 'I must have left it in my room. We're with the Thomson tour.'

He shrugged and let us past. Ursula guided me to the lift.

'Huh. Brains open doors. What is a Thomson tour?' she whispered.

'It's a British package tour. I saw them arriving on Wednesday.'

In the lift, she pressed 8 and we waited quietly. She was breathing very fast. I had missed something, some reason for her concern. What had Alan been up to?

We stepped out of the lift, and the floor attendant watched us walk to 812. She looked almost identical to my floor attendant; late sixties, grey haired, brown smock-like top. Ursula knocked for Alan. There was no answer. I looked at the attendant, but there was no clue on her face. She just watched.

Ursula put her ear to the door. 'Alan?' She turned to the attendant and spoke to her in Russian. The woman put her upturned hands in front of her. She didn't know. Ursula said something else, and the woman became angry. She started shouting at Ursula, and Ursula was shouting back.

The door to 808 opened, and a man looked out. Ursula tried Russian, and then English.

'Have you seen the man from this room today?'

The man shook his head and closed the door.

The attendant got up from her desk, and moved us towards

the lift. She continued to argue with Ursula until we were safely back inside and on our way down.

Ursula took some deep breaths. 'I am not a relation so I can't be told anything. I tried to say that you were related, but she wasn't having it without papers. Relatives are always put in the same hotel, she said.'

Back in the lobby, the receptionist from my first day was waiting for us. She grinned.

'Wro-ong ho-tel,' she said, and escorted us out.

We stood on the pavement, watched by the doorman who had crossed his arms.

'What do we do now?' I asked.

'Let's get something to eat.'

She took my arm again, and we headed to the almost full Natsional café, joining a couple of Russian men at their table.

'I'll just have wine and blini, please.' She sank her head into her hands, and ignored the chatter and movement around her. When the waitress arrived, I ordered the same for both of us and waited for Ursula to come up with a plan. Alan, as far as I knew, had done exactly what Ursula had done. They left the hotels together, they ate together, and they watched films together. I couldn't imagine what he could have done in the time he spent alone. Well, I could, but I couldn't see him *doing* any of it. He was so aware of the pitfalls.

Our blinis arrived. When she'd finished, Ursula said, 'We can't ask anyone Russian. We don't have the right. The festival organisers won't want to get involved in anything like this. That leaves the British Embassy. Your embassy. I can't go in.'

'I have a copy of *Smith's Moscow* upstairs. It has the embassy opening times and phone number.'

'No, you need to go in person. Tomorrow.'

'But, it's Friday. It won't be open until Monday.'

'Oh God. Are you sure it's Friday?' She put her head in her hands. 'I should have gone straight away, or phoned them. Why did I wait?'

'It was reasonable to wait. They would want you to. A missing person isn't technically missing for a couple of days.' I said it without believing that it would be true of Moscow. London, maybe. 'They will take it seriously if he isn't back by tonight, but I'll bet he will be. Maybe he had a small accident and had to go to hospital.'

Ursula looked at me. 'Yes. An accident. They wouldn't tell me that, would they?'

'No. Probably not, if you're not family.'

'No.'

I was amazed that I seemed to be saying the right thing. 'So, we can just relax over the weekend and, if we don't find out anything, the embassy can chase him down on Monday.'

'I can't wait until Monday.' Ursula lifted her head fully, and sat back in her chair. The café was loud and busy. She was still thinking it through. 'We have to wait, though, don't we? Do you have the itinerary?'

I pulled it from my pocket and tried to smooth it.

'I need to stay busy,' she said. 'Tell me what you are seeing, and I'll tell you what I want to see. You don't mind us pairing up?'

'Not at all.'

We decided that on Saturday morning we would have a long breakfast in the upstairs restaurant of our hotel, and films in the afternoon and evening were booked for both Saturday and Sunday. On Sunday morning I was taking the tour of the Lenin mausoleum, so I would collect her for lunch.

'I'm sure he'll be back long before that,' she said.

She was so convinced that I began to feel uncomfortable for suggesting it. If it didn't come true, she might blame me.

'And tonight, we will go to the Beriozka and get some wine. The leftovers from yesterday are in my refrigerator, if you get hungry, but I will buy any food you like. As a thank you.'

'There's no need.' I mentally counted my change. I'd take what was left of the £5 note I was saving. 'We can go halves. I just need to go upstairs and get my money.'

'I'll meet you in the lobby.'

I ran up the stairs, not wanting her to be alone too long. I felt responsible for her, but I didn't mind.

I asked the attendant for my key, and opened my door. There was something different, unlike any other day. Something I couldn't exactly put my finger on, like the faintest of smells, yet I was sure.

Someone had been in my room.

CHAPTER 21

We hadn't even drunk a bottle of wine between us when I left Ursula to go to bed. She gave me some bread and olives to take back to my room. I bathed and got into my bed, but I was too hungry to sleep so I got up and ate first the olives, then the bread. I kept having the feeling that I'd forgotten something, but it was just the sense that something had changed. The maid had cleaned, but I hadn't noticed anything different except clean towels in the bathroom. I wondered if the person I was supposed to meet at the tomb had taken a more direct approach, but I couldn't see that anything had been left. There was something else which had changed that I couldn't see.

I didn't sleep well. In the morning I suspected I looked as unrested as Ursula. I'd learned nothing new about her the previous night. I couldn't ask anything personal and she couldn't touch on anything that made her think about Alan. That left food, and I headed to the restaurant to meet her. I hoped that she was going to make it through the day without him. She had put make-up on, which I thought was a good sign.

'Good morning, Ted.'

I awkwardly half stood for her, and she laughed.

'Let us eat well and honour our ancestors.'

'Is that what you say in Finland?'

'No.' She leaned in. 'We say, when you try to be friends with a Russian, keep a knife close.' The waitress came across. 'Tea with lemon, tea with milk, and for both of us black and white bread, butter, soft boiled eggs and ham. OK?'

'Yes,' I said. 'I didn't know I could get tea with milk.'

'You just ask for milk. It's not a good way to drink tea, but you can.' She tried to smile. 'Tell me about where you live, Ted.'

'I'm living in London. It's just a room in a house. I haven't been there long.'

'But your employer is sending you around the world. You must be clever to get that job.'

'Just lucky, I think.'

I fiddled with my cutlery. She looked out at the Kremlin. It was cloudy in the distance yet the red brick was bright, as if the sun was a spotlight.

'I'm sorry,' she said quietly. 'It was a big deal to come back here after that first year. It was so stressful, and Alan was the only person who understood. He still gets the phone calls, but I haven't felt threatened since we teamed up. I feel adrift without him.'

I tried not to take it personally, but she noticed.

'I know you care what happens to me. You just haven't experienced the bad bits yet.'

'I'm pretty sure someone searched my room last night.'

She tilted her head. 'Weren't you told that would happen?'

I rubbed my neck. 'I'm not sure I was paying as much attention as I should have.'

She drew herself upright. 'Well, hopefully Alan is recovering from a twisted ankle, and everything is fine.'

As our food arrived I realised that there were other people from the festival around the dining room. The group of North Vietnamese women that I'd been sitting with were on one table, and I recognised a few Spanish people on another.

'What's Helsinki like?' I asked.

'Oh.' She swallowed. 'Full of rich Russians stocking up on everything they can't get here.'

'Rich Communists? How does that work?'

She put her fork down. 'Are you joking?'

Mouth full, I shook my head.

'You are kidding me.' She buttered her rye bread, smiling to herself. 'The Russians still think Finland belongs to them. Apart from that, it's very nice. Good schools for the children, good jobs, good economy and welfare state. Just a bit chilly. Alan taught me that word. Chilly.'

'It's a lot warmer here than I was expecting.'

'This is nothing. Even at home it can get very hot.'

'Why did you settle in Finland?'

She answered quietly, avoiding eye contact. 'I didn't settle. I was born there.'

It was back, that tightly buttoned look of the first night when I'd asked if she was American. Why didn't I keep my mouth shut?

'Do you and Alan see each other at different festivals?'

'Just here.' Her voice was flat. She'd gone back to worrying about him.

We finished the meal in silence.

On the way out of the restaurant I asked, 'Would you like a walk before we go over to the Rossiya?'

'No. I'd like to hang around to see if Alan appears. I left a note for him yesterday. I'll leave another one, saying where we'll be until the evening. Hopefully, he'll have collected the first one. We'll see.'

'Do you want me to take it?'

'No. They don't like you much at his hotel. I'll run upstairs and write a note. Could you wait here and walk me over?'

'I'll get my notebook, and meet you back here.'

Back first, I stood in the lobby, the chairs all being taken by what seemed like the same men I'd seen on the day I arrived. A smartly dressed man came along the corridor, shoes tapping, and I guessed he was American. I tried to listen to the sound of my shoes on the marble floor, but they just squeaked. Maybe I should see if I could get some of those handmade shoes from GUM. I'd wait and see how much money I had left.

Ursula came down the wide staircase, and took my arm.

I waited for her outside the Inturist, then we walked across to Red Square. Ursula had changed into flat shoes and we were nearly the same height. I pretended that she was happy to be with me. She gripped my arm hard, and I stopped.

'It's that man, what's his name?'

A slight man with fair hair.

'Christopher Hughes,' I said. 'Of course, he'll know. Or, if he doesn't know, he can ask the right people.'

Ursula raised her hand and called to him. He looked around, saw us, but examined his watch as we walked over as if we were wasting his valuable time.

'Good morning. Off to see another film?'

Ursula nudged me. I prepared to be fobbed off.

'We are, but we are a bit worried about Alan. We haven't seen him since Thursday night.'

He looked horrified. 'Thursday night? But it's Saturday. Why on earth didn't you let me know yesterday?'

I looked at Ursula. 'We thought he'd turn up,' I said.

'Christ!'

Ursula pressed her lips together, removed her arm from mine and turned away. Why was he blaming us?

I ploughed on. 'We checked his hotel. We couldn't get in, but we're sure he's not there. We thought you could check the hospitals.'

Christopher checked his watch again. 'Of course, yes. I can't do that right now, but I'm sure you're right.' He put a hand on Ursula's shoulder. 'I can't do this until later, Mrs Koskinen, but I will later today. I will meet you for breakfast tomorrow and let you know where he is, how about that?'

Ursula nodded, sliding her arm back into mine.

'Sorry, I overreacted. It's a busy day, and I have a lot to get done.'

I said, 'I'm going to the Lenin mausoleum tomorrow morning, so we could meet before that. Or we were going to have lunch.'

'Lunch?' Christopher asked Ursula. She nodded. 'At the Natsional or the Rossiya?'

'Noon at the Natsional,' she said.

'Fine.' He checked his watch again. 'I must dash, but don't worry, we'll get to the bottom of this.'

We watched him hurry away.

Under her breath, Ursula said something I didn't understand.

'Are you all right?' I said. 'I'm sure he will sort it out.'

She looked across the square. 'When you flee from a wolf, you run into a bear.'

I looked to see who she was looking at, but I didn't recognise anyone. Did she mean Christopher?

'Don't you like him?'

'There's just something—' She made shapes with her hands, and let her fingers fly apart. 'Slippery.'

I watched him turn a corner, and he was gone.

CHAPTER 22

Ursula cheered up as the day went on. At least, she gave that impression and I suspected it might be for my sake. We talked about the films, I stole some of her comments to write in my notebook, and we talked about the people around us. She pointed out a couple of American reviewers who were sitting together in the café, and we sniggered as she told me how they hated each other, why and for how long. We didn't talk about Alan.

In the evening, after our second film, we turned left and walked along the river. She pointed out the Illusion, where she was supposed to meet Alan, then turned left again. We were taking a different route to the Metropol, past parks and squares and Metro stations. She pointed at a large building and whispered.

'The Lubyanka.'

Across, past the traffic and the roundabout with a statue, it was an imposing block. Grey at the bottom, cream above that, full of windows for them to see out and no one to see in, and full of the KGB. I shuddered. I couldn't stop thinking about Alan.

'They keep the lights on all night,' she said. 'They like to keep people wondering.'

'How easy is it—? You would know that you were doing something illegal, wouldn't you? You wouldn't *accidentally* do something bad?'

'You'd know,' said Ursula. 'You really should have had a talk before you came.'

'I did. Kind of. Don't change money on the street, assume that anyone interested in you is faking it. That kind of thing?'

She frowned at me. 'Yes. They're the common ones. The first year I came to Moscow I was in the Beriozka when a security guard tried to arrest me for shoplifting. It was Alan who came to my rescue. He'd seen a woman slip something into my pocket. He pointed her out and made such a fuss that they had to let me go. Otherwise I'd have ended up there.' She pointed towards the Lubyanka.

At the same moment we realised we were standing across from the KGB, pointing at them. We started walking again, Ursula pulling me in the right direction.

'You're thinking that Alan might be in there?' she asked.

'No, of course not.'

She shrugged. 'It happens, but he was very aware. He's not new to Moscow.' She paused. 'But if they want you in there they'll find a way. They might slip something into your pocket, or leave something in your hotel room. I can't think why they'd think he was useful as a tool, though. And that's the only reason that they'd do it. No.' She held onto my arm a little tighter. 'I'm sure the embassy will find him now.'

We were back at the Metropol.

'There's a cinema here, if you want to watch a film,' she said.

'What?'

'No? You don't want to watch another film?' She laughed. 'Let's get something to eat, then.' She leaned back a little.

'You know, you could have a haircut. They have a hairdresser.'
She tugged a little at my hair.

I brushed it back with my hand. 'It's fashionable to have
it a bit longer.'

'Ah. My apologies.' She made her face serious, but her eyes
were still smiling.

'Come on, I'm starving.'

It felt almost natural now to have doormen and wide
carpeted stairs, to order food and have people bring it to you.
On this night there was a quartet playing at the back of the
room. Ursula sat down with a sigh.

'Lovely.'

I was happy that she wasn't discussing how worried she
was about Alan. I was happy that we didn't have to talk
about him, that we could spend time together without him.

She looked at the wine list. 'You know there is a cocktail
bar here that's open past midnight. It's hard currency, though.
You didn't bring much of that, did you?'

'No. I got into trouble with my boss when I went to
Bucharest. Somehow my guide managed to stick all of his
food and drink on my bill. I'm being punished, or proving
myself. One or the other.'

'Bucharest sounds lovely. What did you see?'

'I didn't have time to see much at all, just a couple of
museums. It is worth visiting. I'd like to have seen more of it.'

'You could go back.'

'I'm not sure I'd want that.' I thought about telling her
about Vasile, but the waiter came across, and Ursula ordered.

'Different food, this time. I think you'll like pelmeni.' She
stood and smoothed her dress. 'Excuse me.'

I lit a cigarette and sat back in my chair. The restaurant had
every table occupied, but some tables had only one or two
people. There was no doubling up tonight. I gazed around

the room, trying to guess nationalities, then I remembered Ursula's reaction and stopped. The quartet playing were in black tie, which surprised me, but most people were in simple Western clothes. One man on his own had brought a newspaper, and one woman was bending over a book, presumably as she waited between courses. And you could certainly wait here.

She lifted her head, as if she could feel me looking, and I quickly looked away. It was the same woman, again, but no purple hat this time. It was unsettling how she kept turning up. I'd seen her more than anyone, apart from Ursula and Alan.

Ursula returned and followed my gaze. 'Do you know, I've never been to a country where people read more than here. On the bus, on benches, while they eat, pushing prams. It's the best thing to come out of all this.' She gestured to the whole country. 'People are hungry to know things, for information.'

'The woman with the book, do you recognise her?' I asked.

Ursula shook her head.

'I'm sure she was here that first time we came, and I keep seeing her at the festival.'

'She's probably staying here.'

'But when we were here before, she was with the translators. I think she was with them at the festival too. She walks about with them, but then I saw her in the café alone.'

'Translators aren't allowed to mix with people attending the festival unless Inturist have arranged it. If they have to speak to foreigners, they have to fill out pages and pages on everything that was said. They don't get to eat alone in the Metropol, that's for sure.'

'Maybe it just looked like she was with them. I must have been mistaken.'

'Maybe.' Ursula began to rearrange her cutlery. She clearly didn't think there was anything to it. 'So, how do you feel about your meeting with Lenin in the morning?'

'I'm excited.' I paused when our wine arrived, then poured it for both of us. 'It's something I've heard about for such a long time.'

She leaned in. 'I knew someone who lived next to the factory where they touch him up.'

'Touch him up?'

'He's been dead for fifty-one years. Bits are going to fall off and need touching up.'

'I'm not sure about that. The body of Jeremy Bentham is still sitting in a London university, and he died in the 1830s.'

Ursula watched the first course arrive with horror. 'I'm not sure I want to eat now.' Then she smiled. 'I'm joking. It takes more than a body to put me off. They did up Stalin too, but then they decided against it and buried him.'

'They were both there, side by side, in Lenin's mausoleum?'

'Yes. After everything he did.'

I examined my soup. Vegetable and lumps of beef. I hadn't done very well with the beef here to date, it was far too fatty.

'Is this a beef soup?'

'Rassolnik. Try it.'

'Is it beef, though?'

'It's pickled cucumber soup, but it usually has beef or fish or something else. Don't worry, the beef isn't always bad. It might be better today.'

It was.

'Did Alan tell you why the meals take so long?'

'No.'

'Every single ingredient has to be weighed. The waiters take the order, the cooks get chits for the ingredients, the ingredients get weighed and measured and swapped for the chits. It's unbelievable. All to stop the kitchen staff sneaking out slivers of food, while entire cows get diverted.'

She pointed to the entrance. A young man stood there in a brown shirt with the widest lapels I'd seen yet in Moscow, and a woman next to him in a pink poncho with pink trousers.

'You remember what I said about those Russians who come to Helsinki?' She put her spoon down. 'Let's watch how they deal with this. All the tables are occupied, but they wouldn't want to share.'

I held my breath as the waiter spoke to them, and then approached the woman reading. She gave him something, and stood up to leave, taking her purple hat from the chair beside her.

Ursula tutted. 'I was looking forward to an argument.'

As the woman walked out, I saw the title, *High-Rise*. That was the new J.G. Ballard novel but I was sure it wasn't out yet. It wasn't in the library, anyway. I thought she gave me a little smile before she left.

'FISHERMAN' ADDITIONAL REPORT: FOR ADDITION TO WALKER FILE

There have been three attempts by friendly assets to gain the attention of the subject on behalf of our counterparts (after the first overt approach, more subtle ways were attempted: attractive agents were directed to drop items in the Beriozka and to be waiting in the corridor between the Metropol restaurant and bathroom). The overt approach was discarded under his seat. Neither covert approach seemed to register with the subject who was with URSULA KOSKINEN on the first occasion and returning to her on the second. Both assets have proved successful in the past and it can only be assumed that the subject's intense interest in KOSKINEN renders them, in effect, invisible to him.

The physical reactions of the subject to KOSKINEN's company (maintaining eye contact, constant companionship and attentiveness) confirm to our observers that he has no similar interest in men, so there are no plans to repeat this kind of approach.

It is known that he was made anxious about approaches to his hotel room in Bucharest (both by telephone and by knocking). While there are reasons why we do not want to escalate any underlying anxiety, these will not be conveyed to our counterparts.

We were informed by 'Nadenka' that Walker would be amenable to an approach as he agreed to this in the past, and is expecting to take an unknown item back to London. However, after the first attempt at contact failed he has shown no interest in looking for any contact who is to supply this item, and it must be considered that he has forgotten the agreement or we have been misled regarding his enthusiasm and compliance.

It is known that the subject will be attending a tour in Red Square on Saturday morning, a rare time to approach him alone. However, whoever does approach him will no longer be bound to our counterparts' plans as these are regarded as having failed, and we are free to pursue our own longer term project.

CHAPTER 23

My breakfast was delivered early so I wouldn't be late for Lenin, but I found I had already been used as breakfast myself. The open window had allowed in at least one mosquito which had fed on my ankle in three places. I scratched it until I couldn't bear it any more, then dressed.

There was already a queue stretching from Red Square, but I knew I didn't have to stand at the end. I found my Inturist guide at the side of the large red building, the Historical Museum, with a group of half-a-dozen people in the cool morning sun. Italian and Spanish, from the sound of it. Alan wasn't around, and the boring Terence, whom I hadn't met yet, didn't turn up, so I was the only British person. As Westerners, we were allowed to join the line at the police barrier where women had to hand over their handbags, and shoppers their goods. It was also where the single line became double, as those waiting were put into pairs.

I stood next to a Spanish woman, a guard moving us so that I was on the right, and looked forward at the queue. It was quiet considering there were so many people. Soldiers paraded the line, making sure that people did not smoke and took their hands from their pockets. As they got closer, men were told to remove their hats. I started to get nervous.

I had an overwhelming urge to scratch the bites on my ankle. I lifted one foot to rub my shoe against the itch, but it made it worse.

I looked up at the dark surround of the mausoleum, strange letters picked out in purple. Nearly there. I searched for where the sound of boots on stone was coming from, and saw soldiers marching towards the mausoleum. The clock struck the hour and the sentries who had stood so still left and were replaced by two more.

We passed the sentries with bayonets on their rifles, and stepped into the coolness of the tomb and its black marble walls. We turned left, passed a guard, then right, passed another guard, and then I stumbled into the person in front of me who had stopped suddenly. The nearest guard grabbed my arm. I put my hands up in surrender and apology, and carefully followed the person in front of me down a short flight of stairs. I was feeling disorientated, turned about until I'd forgotten which way I'd come, as if I was in a dark labyrinth. The pressure of remaining quiet, the bayonets, the subdued lighting were all making me feel quite claustrophobic.

After two flights of stairs down there was another right turn, and in front of me was the glass case. Lenin. He lay with four more guards at each corner, each with his bayonet gleaming, almost obscuring him. I wondered how long they had to stand here. Did they ever think they saw him move, just out of the corner of an eye?

We arrived at more stairs, this time going up where we could walk along a short balcony, past Lenin's feet. No lingering, the pace was constant, and all of a sudden we were back down the stairs, then up the stairs and out. We were released into a walkway that ran along the wall of the Kremlin, shaded by short fir trees.

That was it. That was Lenin.

I thought of his waxy hands and shuddered. Then I thoroughly scratched my ankle.

The Inturist guide was still with us, shepherding us to the Kremlin walls to see pictures of people I failed to recognise, but were important to look at it seemed. I caught a glimpse of Stalin, whom I did recognise, but he wasn't one of the ones she named. Speaking in English, Spanish and Italian meant that she tried not to say much at all, but there was one final recommendation.

'If you walk back to where we met and turn left, you will find the Tomb of the Unknown Soldier with the Eternal Flame in the Alexandrovsky Gardens. Please pay your respects there for the Soviet sacrifice in the war. The Historical Museum is also open until five o'clock.'

She repeated this in Italian, and then in Spanish which led to the Spaniards complaining. She returned to English.

'Of course, there is a Spanish film showing this afternoon which you might want to see.'

I smiled at the Spaniards to convey that I would be seeing their film, and then headed down to the garden entrance. I was intrigued about the Tomb of the Unknown Soldier, the place where the note had said I should meet someone.

The tomb wasn't far from the gate to the gardens, a large slab of granite with a helmet on top, but also flowers. A couple, just married, were standing in front of the metal star on the ground where a flame flickered from the centre. She wore a white dress and he wore a soldier's uniform, and they posed with sad half-smiles for another soldier taking a photo. I watched them leave and another couple approached.

I walked on, slowly doubling back on myself, and never left the gardens. This was the open space I could see from the hotel restaurant which ran along the wall of the Kremlin. It was criss-crossed by paths, a strange white Greek portico on one side, an obelisk on the other. I wandered over to a raised, circular bed of grass, and sat on one of the benches. One man opposite was reading a book. Another, a couple of benches over, held up a thin newspaper. A young woman walked slowly around the grass, her eyes fixed so firmly on her shiny red boots that she nearly fell over a low, granite wall. She smiled to herself, and carried on.

People were coming and going all the time, and it was quieter than I would have thought. Small children walked calmly, holding the hands of old ladies; older children didn't look around and fidget. I leaned back and crossed my legs thinking that I should have got an ice cream.

I liked Moscow. I liked having spare money for ice cream, I liked skipping queues and going to the best hotels and restaurants. I didn't mind rude staff and the odd dodgy course. I was important here in a way I would never be in England.

A woman walked away from the obelisk with a large black dog panting beside her. I looked up at her. She wasn't wearing her purple hat today. When she smiled I smiled back. She sat next to me, and her dog sat too.

'I recognise you from the festival, don't I?' she said.

'I am with the festival, yes. Small world, I suppose, us festival people. I've seen you in the Metropol too.'

She nodded. 'That's right. I saw you last night with your striking wife.'

'Oh, not my wife. A colleague. A reviewer, like me.'

The woman bowed her head. 'I'm sorry if I offended you.'

'Not at all. She's gorgeous.' I flushed. 'Just not my wife.' I fidgeted and made moves to leave.

'Please stay,' she said. 'I've upset you.'

'No, I embarrassed myself.' I settled back. 'You're not a reviewer are you?'

'No.'

'A translator?'

'I do work as one, but I'm more of a consultant to these translators. I have experience of British culture, so I can explain some of the more subtle or obscure references.'

'I didn't realise that they would employ British people like that. Do you speak Russian too?'

'Oh, yes. I live in Moscow.'

This was who I had been looking for. Someone I could talk to, interview, to get a sense of life in Moscow. She stroked her dog's head.

'That is a massive dog.'

'Do you like dogs?'

'Not really. I'm sure it's very nice, but I'm not keen on dogs generally.'

She shrugged. 'I'm just looking after it while my friend is away.'

In the distance a bell started to chime. It was noon and I was late.

'I'm so sorry, I have to run,' I said as I stood up, 'but I'd like to speak to you again, find out what Moscow is really like.'

'Of course. I'm sure we'll bump into each other again.' She held out her hand, 'Eva Mann.'

I shook it. 'Ted Walker. See you around.' I ran across the road when I saw a gap, and jogged back to the Natsional.

'Papers,' said the doorman.

I rummaged through my pockets, grumbling. 'You never asked before.'

He looked at the chit carefully before handing it back, and nodding. That was odd. I turned to look at him as I went down the corridor. He was still watching me. And I him.

They were waiting for me. Ursula looked nervous and Christopher looked annoyed. It was his day off, I supposed. I sat between them.

'Still got an appetite?' asked Ursula.

'Sorry?'

'After seeing the body.'

'Oh, Lenin, yes. It was all very tasteful, really.'

Christopher was eager to start. 'Ursula has ordered for you both. I don't have long.' He cleared his throat. 'We have found Alan. He hasn't been able to give me permission to talk to you, and you're not related, so I'm going to have to give you a very brief summary of the facts.'

'Hasn't been able to give permission?' Ursula repeated.

Christopher sighed, and looked outside as he spoke. 'He was taken into hospital in the early hours of Saturday morning. It seems the dezhurnaya, the floor attendant, heard a crash and went to check on him.'

He was lying. Or was repeating something he didn't believe? I looked at Ursula. She was frowning.

'He has been on a drip since. They have ruled out serious conditions, the heart or a stroke, but the doctors have prevented me from speaking to him as he is too unwell. They say.'

Ursula gripped my hand harder.

'Did you see him at all?' I asked.

'I saw him through glass. He recognised me and lifted his hand.'

Ursula said, 'So, that's a good sign?'

'Yes,' Christopher said, uncertainly. 'We'd prefer to speak to him directly, but they have told me to come back tomorrow.'

'What do you think happened?' I said.

'I couldn't say.' He shuffled his cutlery, and sipped from a glass of water. 'I was wondering, when I saw you at the Metropol on Friday night, which restaurant did you go to?'

Ursula clasped her hands together. 'We went to our usual restaurant as Ted only had vouchers. We couldn't go to the cash bar, and the restaurant was emptier than you suggested.'

Christopher half-smiled and nodded. 'I see.'

'Was there a danger in there?' asked Ursula. 'Did something happen in the restaurant?'

He sat back and shifted the cutlery again. 'I'm sure not. Anyway, we have found him, and that's good. After I see him tomorrow I will let you know the latest.' He pushed his chair back, nodded, and left as our soup arrived.

We both looked at the soup, and then each other.

'Didn't we all eat the same at the Metropol?' I asked.

Ursula nodded. 'I ordered the same for everyone.'

I picked up my spoon. 'Well, we've eaten there again, and we're all right. So, I'm sure it's fine.' I put my spoon back next to the bowl. 'I don't think I'm hungry.'

Ursula stared into her soup, shook herself and began to eat. 'Come on,' she said. 'We can't starve. Alan will be fine and so will we.'

'Do you contact each other between festivals? I mean, do you know where he lives?'

'The embassy would deal with all that, contacting his office.'

'And his wife. He never mentions her. Will you write to her?'

'I got the impression that she wouldn't approve of him being friends with someone like me.'

If he had to leave Moscow she wouldn't ever know what happened to him. If it was bad he wouldn't ever come back. 'How do you know each other will be here each year?'

'I get my magazine to contact his magazine.' She smiled. 'They've never asked why.'

We'd both given up halfway through the soup.

'Are you all right to go and see the films we planned?'

'Yes.' She pushed her bowl away. 'I don't think I'll be going out to eat, though. I need some time. Will you come with me to the Beriozka?'

Now I understood why she liked to have someone with her, watching the people around her.

'Of course. You have to keep the herring stocked up.'

CHAPTER 24

As Ursula did her shopping I looked at the ikons, matryoshka dolls and lace. I wondered whether I should buy something to take home. I moved to the guidebook section and decided on *Москва Moscow*, which now even I knew was just Moscow written twice. I liked the photos and decided I should go to a gallery or museum before I left. That had been the best part of Bucharest, even though it had never crossed my mind to visit a museum in London. The book, a bottle of wine, and I'd settle down after a quick dinner to write up my review notes. They'd become a bit sparse and I was worried my memories of the films were starting to merge into each other.

Ursula paid up, let me carry her bag, and we walked back to the Natsional, arm-in-arm. The sun was setting behind us.

'It feels like the end of a film,' said Ursula.

It did feel like the end of something. I couldn't think what to say. We'd barely spoken since we'd seen Christopher.

In the lobby I gave her the bag with her food in, and took mine to the café. I ordered wine with pelmeni, the small meat dumplings fried with butter, and took my notebook from my pocket. Tonight I would eat and work. Tonight I would earn my money.

Just as my food arrived, someone sat at my table. I made a big deal of closing my notebook.

'Are you eating here, Christopher?'

'I wanted to speak to you alone,' he said, leaning close to me. 'Your friend — what exactly is her relationship with Alan?'

'Platonic. They're both married.'

He raised his eyebrows, but didn't point out that meant nothing. 'For how long has this been going on?'

I was confused. 'You know Alan, don't you?'

'I just want to know what they told you.'

'This is their fifth festival together. Alan came alone to one before that.'

'All right.' Christopher looked around. 'So, there is nothing really between them to exploit, except a long friendship. They are just always together. And now you. Think back to Friday at the Metropol. Was there anyone in the restaurant who seemed to be paying particular attention to you as a group?'

I thought back. 'No.'

'Or Alan as an individual? Did anyone leave the room after him when he went to the toilet, or did anyone speak to him as you were leaving?'

'I can't think of anything.' I wasn't sure about the way he was looking at me. 'Why?'

He rubbed his chin and sat back. I waited for him to speak, eating my pelmeni before they got cold. He thought Alan had been approached in the Metropol, but why would that put him in hospital? And, if he hadn't had contact with anyone there . . .

'Do you think I did something to him? Or Ursula?'

He said nothing.

I put my fork down. 'Why would either of us do that? I've

only known him a few days, and Ursula has been his friend over years. What exactly happened to him?'

Christopher leaned back in. 'Apart from Alan and Ursula, who else have you been spending time with?'

'No one. There's only one other British reporter and Alan can't bear him. Terence. I haven't even met him. Then there are the Americans who are so paranoid that they only talk to other Americans. That's what Alan said. I haven't met them either. I don't speak any other languages, so that's been it. Alan and Ursula.'

'Alan and Ursula.'

'Yes.'

I decided to leave it there, carry on eating and let him talk if he wanted to. He leaned back and watched me eat. I concentrated, but still managed to drip some melted butter on my trousers. Another stain. I looked at the circle bleeding outwards and mentally gave away another handful of pounds for a new pair. It wasn't rational, but I blamed him for that.

He spoke quietly, looking at his fingernails. 'I walked down Manezhnaya to meet you and Ursula earlier.'

I shrugged.

'It's the road that runs past the Alexander Gardens.'

I swallowed. 'Alexandrovsky Gardens, I think you'll find.' I don't know what made me say that. He was just annoying me.

He nodded, but didn't speak.

'So?' He didn't look at me. I thought back to the gardens, the wall, the bench. 'Are you asking me about what I did? About the woman I was talking to?'

Now he made eye contact. 'Can you tell me who that was?'

'I can tell you what that was. That was none of your business.' I pushed the rest of my food away. 'I've done what I was told. I haven't had to resist women throwing themselves at me,

I haven't spoken to any Russians, I haven't exchanged money on a street corner, I haven't bought any ikons. I haven't done anything to be questioned like this.' I pushed my notebook and guidebook into the carrier bag with the wine and stood up to leave. Christopher put a hand on my sleeve.

'You are the reason that Alan didn't follow my instructions. You are the one who made him go to the wrong restaurant. If you would like some advice, Ted, I would spend less time with foreigners and more time with the British people who have been vetted as film festival attendees.'

I shook his hand off. 'I would be spending time with Alan if I could. And the person I was seen speaking to, Eva Mann, is English and she is connected to the festival.'

'Is she?'

I was thrown by that. 'She sounds very English.'

'What role does she have at the festival?'

'She's a consultant translator.'

'She's not.' He raised his eyebrows. 'The Russians don't employ consultant translators. They have entire universities set up for the study of languages. They travel abroad, they study hard, they train them up at the Illusion cinema. They get seven roubles a film, or more. It's a competitive business, and they do not like outsiders. Think about what you know about the Soviets, and don't accept what people tell you.'

I sat down, my bag on my lap. 'So, what is her role, then?'

He pressed his finger on the table. 'Never mind her role. Your role, Ted, is to stay away from her. Spend time with Terence while Alan is indisposed.'

'What about Ursula?'

'Ursula is not my concern. The British are my concern, people like you and me. I only want to make sure that you are safe, but I can't be everywhere. I know this is all new and strange, and how liberating that can feel. But you are responsible for the decisions you make here, so, please, make good choices.'

We looked at each other. I could sense he wanted me to agree with him so he could feel reassured and walk away. I knew he wanted me to see what we had in common, us British men, but I could only see the differences. I said nothing.

He stood up. 'Watch your back, Ted.'

He left me in the bar. I had wanted to walk out and leave him sitting there. He wanted me to abandon Ursula, but she was my concern, whatever he said. I wasn't like Christopher and I never wanted to be.

I wasn't in the mood to sit quietly in my room, so I decided to have a walk before I went upstairs. The streets were quiet again. No drunken gangs of teenagers. No skinheads. Not like London.

I walked through the underpass where there were a couple of stalls, and I was approached by a short, dark-haired man.

'Ikons?' he said.

I shook my head and picked up speed. It was my first approach and, although I'd been expecting it since I arrived, I was unsettled. Had I walked away fast enough? Was he following me? I half ran up the cobbled slope to Red Square, the wine banging against my leg, and then slowed before a guard could shout at me. Were there too many police here, too many soldiers? I noticed them around the Kremlin, but it was the centre of a city. I suppose they didn't worry me, so it hadn't felt too many. Now that someone had come up to me, tried to involve me in something dangerous, it looked as if there were far too many of them. I blamed Christopher for this too, making me feel guilty for no reason.

I arrived at the Kremlin just before the hour struck on the tower clock, and saw the exchange of sentries again. The river created a large dark space in the distance where there were no buildings, and I felt anxious about walking further and traced my steps back towards the Natsional. I thought I saw Christopher in conversation with a man on a corner, but I wasn't sure.

I wondered what he believed had happened to Alan. At least I could be sure that he wouldn't talk to Ursula about Alan without me. She was Alan's oldest and closest friend here, but she wasn't British. I wondered what had really happened to Alan to prompt all of this. And while I also wondered what Terence was like, I knew I wouldn't exchange time I could spend with Ursula for anyone else.

'FISHERMAN' ADDITIONAL REPORT: FOR ADDITION TO WALKER FILE

Background Report on the Recent Professionalisation of Journalism in Britain

In Britain, mass education raises two issues related to journalism. First, it removes some of the autonomy and influence of educators: by making journalism an academic subject which can be tested, it allows the state to supervise the key subjects and approaches of new entrants to the industry. Second, it inevitably ensures that new entrants are more middle class than those accepted through traditional apprenticeships.

Professionalisation, using the universities to exclude, rather than educate, is already underway. However, there is much we can do to further the advancement of individuals whose lives have not benefited from the rigidity of the establishment and feel no natural ties to its maintenance. Early work in this field has shown that valid concerns voiced by government services, regarding those who might be seen as our fellow travellers, have not resulted in those journalists being barred from employment, or even becoming editors themselves. Even unsympathetic editors can usually be relied on to be driven by the desire for the story, whatever its origins.

CHAPTER 25

I regretted the wine when I woke up at ten o'clock. It hadn't resulted in a thoughtful summary of the films I'd seen, but a scrawling rant which seemed to be largely about Christopher. I threw it away. No one had woken me. I'd missed the start of this morning's film, but they served breakfast in the restaurant until eleven, so I had a quick wash and left my key with the attendant. Day or night, it was the same woman sitting there. When did she sleep?

Ursula was in the seat she'd been in yesterday, staring out of the window. Her face was drawn, the dark hollows under her eyes deeper. The cutlery on her plate signalled that she had finished eating, but she'd left a lot of food.

She must have seen my reflection because she turned suddenly.

'Ted, you're here!'

She held a hand out to me, which I took and then awkwardly dropped so I could sit down.

'Are you all right?' she said. 'You don't look very well.'

'Too much wine. I couldn't sleep so I kept drinking, but I feel like I drank more than one bottle. I forgot to order a call or a breakfast.'

She nodded. 'I did order breakfast, but it didn't come. Or I didn't hear the door.' She looked distractedly out of the window again. 'I thought you might have gone without me, but I knew you wouldn't. Not unless you really couldn't help it.' She fiddled with her napkin. 'Just leave me a note, or something. Just so I know. Have you heard anything from Christopher?'

'No.' If I told her about being warned off spending time with her, it wasn't going to make her feel better

I ordered coffee and bread with butter, wishing that toast was on the menu. There's something comforting about the idea of toast, especially when you can't have it.

'Still fancy seeing the afternoon film,' I asked, 'the Czech comedy?'

'Yes. Christopher will know where to find us, if he has anything to say.' She reached for my hand. 'Are you worried about Alan?'

'I'm sure Alan is fine. I'd just like to know what happened.'

She picked up her coffee with both hands, sighing. I saw the coffee ripple.

I said, 'If he has to stay in hospital or something, I can get Christopher to give him my address and yours. Or I can take your address, and let you know. I know that you didn't have contact between festivals, but I don't have anyone who would mind if I got letters from abroad.' I thought of that Barry, and frowned. 'If I get the letter at all. My fellow lodger likes to open my post and only hands it over if I ask for it. If I'm not expecting something I might never know. Maybe I'll give you my work address instead.'

'Why do you stay in that house?'

'I don't know. It's handy for work. I need to move.'

'Ah,' she said, half-standing, 'it's Christopher.'

He sat down next to me at the table, palms on his thighs. 'I don't have long, but I wanted to let you know that Alan is being flown home.'

Ursula clenched her fists. 'Is he dying?'

'No, nothing like that. We're sure he'll be fine in the long run. We do, however, suspect that he has ingested a substance which made him ill.'

'Someone did it on purpose?' I said.

'Of course not,' said Ursula.

'We can't say,' he said, but he kept looking at Ursula.

'On Friday, when he was with us?' she asked.

Christopher looked at his nails. 'We know that he ate with you both on Friday night, returned to his room at eleven o'clock, and two hours later he collapsed. There was no food or drink in his room. The British doctors attached to the embassy can't see any underlying physical reason for his symptoms, so we're just going to be cautious and get him back home.'

'Is he speaking, has he said anything?' I asked.

Christopher looked at me. 'Yes, he is speaking. He doesn't remember anything after he got back to the room.'

'Why would someone do this?' said Ursula.

'It could be completely innocent, an unknown reaction to something he is unfamiliar with.' He clenched his hands together. 'It could be that he consumed something meant for someone else. We don't like to speculate.'

I raised my eyebrows. He had no problem with speculating about me the previous night. Ursula frowned at me.

'What?'

'Nothing,' I said. 'I think it all sounds like a bit of an over-reaction, that's all. I mean, he's not young, is he?'

'He's fifty-seven.'

'Exactly.'

'Ted. Why would you say that?' Ursula shook her head.

Christopher said, 'Exactly what is the cut-off past which we shouldn't concern ourselves with people being ill and just put it down to incapacitation by old age?'

'That's not what I meant.'

'Let's just focus on Alan,' said Ursula. 'Can I do anything? Do you need someone to pack up his room?'

'Thank you, Ursula, but that is all in hand. Until we know the root of the problem, we'll be taking precautions with his possessions. I can, of course, verbally convey any messages you'd like to send.'

'Tell him that I hope he feels better very soon, and I hope to see him at another festival.' She covered her face and started crying. 'I won't, will I? I won't ever see him again.'

I turned away from her despair. Christopher looked like he was waiting for me to speak.

'Just tell him that I hope he gets better too.'

He spoke quietly. 'Is that all you want to say?'

'I'm not good at this.'

He put his head near my ear. 'I showed you where I worked from the bridge. Should you feel the desire to say more, I am available for a chat. Any time. They know how to contact me.'

I whispered back, 'I don't know anything.'

It was silent. Ursula was staring as if she'd never seen me before.

'What is going on?'

Christopher leaned back, one finger on his mouth. I opened my hands.

'Nothing.'

She pushed her chair back and walked away.

I pointed at Christopher. 'Why did you do that? You've made her think I'm involved in this.'

He folded his arms. 'Are you? I don't like coincidences, Ted. Those two, they've been coming here for years, and then you turn up and something happens to Alan. That's one thing, but you're seen with Eva Mann, of all people, and here we are.'

'I don't know a thing about Eva Mann. I had a short chat with her about translators which was entirely relevant to why I'm here.' I was missing something important, I suspected. 'Why, though? Why would I want to hurt Alan?'

'If I knew that, Ted, we wouldn't be talking about this here. Stick with people you know to be official festival British attendees and we won't have any more problems. Try to remember what you're here for. It is not to make friends.'

He carefully pushed his chair back, and then slid it under the table again. He was going to do it again, walk out on me. I wasn't going to watch him this time. I hunched over my coffee and lit a cigarette. The coffee was cold. I drank it anyway, ordered more and watched the grey shapes of Moscow walk along the roads in the slight drizzle that speckled the window.

Was it strange that I hadn't been approached by a Russian? I hadn't expected to be. I had assumed those were extreme situations that I was being warned about. And Eva Mann — well, there was nothing to that, whether or not Christopher believed she was British enough. Ursula wasn't remotely British, and my favourite person here, so I wasn't going to be taking his advice on that. And there was no reason why anyone here would approach me. I'd been mistaken. I wasn't anyone, not here, not at home. Nowhere. I wasn't going to abandon Ursula. She might abandon *me* after this, though.

I got ready to walk over to the Rossiya and knocked on Ursula's door to see if she wanted to come. There was no answer. I tried to ask her attendant where she was but was waved away. She'd probably gone over without me. I didn't believe that, but I wanted to.

Outside, the drizzle was a little heavier than it had looked. My sock was going to be soaked again, and the embarrassing squelch would follow, but I was going to be down to mere pennies soon enough. I would have to live with it.

Dark clothed Russians walked, head down, while the occasional umbrella singled out a foreigner, someone who didn't belong. London was full of people from every continent, but you couldn't pick them out in the same way.

The more I thought about it, the more annoyed I got with Christopher. He'd taken a couple of unconnected events and put me in the middle of them on a hunch. I was still preoccupied when I entered the lobby of the Rossiya, and bumped into a man in a grey jacket standing just inside.

'Sorry,' I said. He ignored me and turned away. 'Fine. I'm not sorry.' He didn't respond to that either.

I stamped up the stairs to the cinema and slumped into a seat near the back. I couldn't see Ursula, I was damp, and I was not in the mood for a comedy. I kept my hands in my pockets and scowled at the screen.

CHAPTER 26

The film had made me laugh, despite my resisting it, and Christopher had faded to the back of my mind as an upper-class idiot. Ursula just needed a little time alone, then she'd be back. She knew me.

I decided to stay for the evening film too, and back in the usual café I found an empty seat on a table of Chinese people. I relaxed and enjoyed my blini and tea with lemon. I noticed the group of translators walk past the window and remembered that tomorrow was the day for the Romanian film and, maybe, Ingrid acting as a translator. I wasn't confident that I'd find the right woman and solve the mystery, but I was still curious.

My table companions left, and a couple of Spanish or Portuguese-speaking men took their seats. South American, maybe? There were films from Peru and Venezuela. Could be from there. I was back to guessing nationalities to stop me thinking about Alan. Then the fourth seat was taken by a tall, thin man with heavy stubble. I started a little as he pushed his hand towards me. It was cold when I shook it.

'Tovarisch Terence,' he said. He looked even more serious than Christopher.

'Tovarisch?'

'It means comrade. It's a joke. I'm not a communist. It relies on the context for humour.'

'Yes.' I tried to smile. I wasn't sure that was how the Russians used 'comrade' but I felt it could lead to a long and boring discussion. 'I'm Ted.'

'Yes. No Alan tonight?' He looked around, as if checking.

'No. I think he's unwell.'

He nodded. 'Yes. I heard that too. And that black woman?'

I wiped my mouth. 'If you know Alan's name, you probably know her name.' I wondered if Christopher had set this up. 'Are you watching the next film?'

'Yes. Shall we go in together? We could discuss it after.'

'No, I have plans tonight.' I stood up. 'Maybe I'll see you tomorrow.'

He stood too. 'You wouldn't want to have a meal later?'

'No, sorry. Plans.'

Finally I got to walk out on someone, but I didn't have anywhere to go. I'd promised myself that I would wait until the morning to try to contact Ursula, and it was too early to go to my room for the night. I left the hotel and wandered down to the river thinking, if I timed it right, I could slip into the film without him seeing me. I had wanted to see it, but didn't want to sit anywhere near him, even wearing headphones. I didn't generally make snap judgements about people, but there was something unsavoury about him.

It had worked. I had watched the film, made a few notes for the look of things, and darted out the second the credits came up. I still wasn't hungry yet, so I walked around the wall of the Kremlin and along the street I'd taken with Ursula. Shops stayed open later here, yet only the Beriozkas seemed to be open at this time. I went inside, bought a peace offering bottle of wine for Ursula, one for myself to help me sleep, and headed back to the hotel. Outside the Beriozka, I thought I saw the same man that I'd bumped into earlier at the Rossiya, but I wasn't sure.

I slowed my pace to see if I could catch sight of his face so I would recognise him next time. Maybe he'd walk past me. I passed an open door to a kind of bar that I'd seen before and stopped, as if I was considering going in. A few men stood around eating, but most seemed to down their vodkas and walk straight out. In the corner I saw Christopher and Terence in conversation. Christopher looked towards me and I walked on. The man in the jacket was standing at the corner ahead of me, lighting a cigarette. I could smell it was one of those Russian ones.

I could hear running behind me, and someone grabbed my shoulder. Terence was panting heavily.

'Ted, I thought you'd gone home. Join us for a drink in the pivnaya.'

'Thanks, but I'm off to bed.' I shrugged my shoulder from his hand and my bottles clinked together.

Terence looked at the bag. 'I see.'

I sighed and walked on. The man in the jacket had gone.

I walked into the Natsional, one eye on the doorman, but wasn't asked for my papers this time. I was still sure he was watching me. I plodded up the stairs, then crept back down a couple of steps to see if he was still looking. He wasn't. He was outside, talking to a man in a grey jacket.

I ran up the stairs to Ursula's room and knocked on the door. And knocked again.

She opened it, her eyes swollen, her blue shawl around her shoulders.

'Are you ill?' I asked.

She shook her head, and glanced at the attendant.

'Can I come in? Just quickly.'

She opened the door and I slipped past her, the bottles knocking against the door frame.

'I'm not drinking tonight,' she said.

I looked at her open cases, full of clothes, and waited for her to speak.

'What do you want?'

'I wanted to see how you were. Are you leaving?'

'Yes.'

'I wasn't involved with anything, I promise.'

She sat in the chair by the window, her bare feet tucked under her.

'I like Alan. I like you. I'm being followed in the street, Christopher is trying to pair me up with Terence, and I don't know what's going on.'

She looked out into the darkness. The red stars on the Kremlin towers, the headlights of cars, the heavy swoosh of the street washing machine — I don't think she noticed any of it.

'Is there anything I can do for you?'

She cleared her throat. 'No. It's over. I'm going home.'

'I brought you a bottle of wine. You could take it with you.'

'No, thank you. I don't feel safe eating or drinking anything here now.'

'Have you seen Alan? Did he say something?'

She looked at me. 'I'm not saying it was you. I'm saying that it all coincides with you.'

The same as Christopher. Had I actually done something?

She stood up and gestured to the door. 'I need to finish packing.'

'I'm sorry, Ursula.'

She had already turned back to the window.

The attendant on Ursula's floor watched me walk away

from her room, and my attendant watched me approach for my key.

'Dokumenty,' she said.

'What?'

'Dokumenty.'

'I've been here for days. I gave you the key this morning. You know who I am.'

'Dokumenty.'

I got my chit from my pocket and waved it at her. She held out her hand until I gave it to her, and she inspected it. I shifted my bag to the other hand. Finally she returned it with my key and I opened my door. Back pressed against the wood, I felt tearful. I should eat before I started drinking, but I didn't have much of an appetite.

I put the bag on the floor and went to the bedroom to take my jacket off. There was a plain brown booklet on the bed. I picked it up. *The Wolf Sleigh* by E. V. Mann.

I stormed out of my room and up to the attendant. 'Who left this on my bed?'

'Ne ponimayu.' She shook her head.

'This,' I pointed to it, 'who put it,' I pointed to my door, 'there?'

'Ne ponimayu.' There was a slight smile.

'Fine,' I said, 'I'll ask at the embassy.'

She nodded, and went back to staring into the distance.

Back in the room I tore the booklet into tiny pieces and lay on the bed, wondering how everything had gone so wrong. Had Alan eaten something meant for someone else? Why was Christopher trying to blame it on me? And why had Ursula believed him so quickly?

I'd had enough of today. I turned the light off and tried to sleep, before remembering that I hadn't ordered my breakfast. I forced myself up and wrote down every breakfast option on a bit of paper; bread, butter, soft eggs, hard eggs, ham, cheese, orange juice, mineral water, black coffee, coffee with cream, tea and yoghurt. I handed it to the attendant with a straight face. She glanced at it and nodded.

I went back to bed and looked through the photos in my Moscow guide until I fell asleep.

CHAPTER 27

I didn't quite get what I'd asked for. Just tea, white bread, butter and jam. I ate it, but I was still hungry. I half-thought about giving the festival a miss today and staying in bed, but of all the questions I had, this was the only one which might be answered: was Ingrid going to be a translator at the Romanian film?

I stretched out on the bed. I was feeling a bit better than yesterday, a bit less paranoid. Every other man had a grey jacket on, for God's sake. And Ursula had to make her own decisions. One more week and the festival would be over and I'd be looking at my last night. My pockets were feeling light, so it was probably a good thing to spend time alone. I'd just use the vouchers, go to the films, study what I could of Moscow and that was it. Before the film I would go to the Tretyakov Art Gallery that I'd seen in *Москва Moscow* and most articles on Moscow. Smith had not been glowing about this place, but I'd never been to a gallery in a state of dizzy chaos. His description just made me want to go more.

After getting directions and a sketched map from the reception desk, I walked to the museum. It took me on my usual route, past the Kremlin and the Rossiya, but then across the river. The buildings felt more human-sized, as if people could actually live here. Two or three storeys high, the line of buildings was broken up by the occasional tower and plenty of trees in small parks. Where the buildings did rise to four or five levels, they were brief interruptions in the skyline. The weather was good again, and the sun brightened the worn paint and made the windows shine. One building with a large number 19 had an archway and, although it felt like an official building, the two plaster faces on either side suggested that it was a place of quiet beauty.

On the left the street opened up to another green space with a round, glassed Metro station. I was starting to recognise these without understanding the individual Russian symbols. This meant I had taken the wrong road from the river, but as long as it was Novokuznetskaya Metro station, the map would still work. The woman on reception had given me directions for taking the Metro as well as walking. I walked on until the crossroads and turned right.

Now that I had gone a little wrong, I paid more attention to the people around me than the buildings. I realised that I was always watching out for a foreign coat or pair of shoes, someone who might be able to help, but I didn't see anyone like that until I turned up another road to the right and found the gallery. There were Inturist guides here with small groups of Westerners, and another gang of Pioneer children in red scarves. I didn't think I'd seen any children who weren't wearing that uniform, other than the very young ones in the park. I watched them march in silence behind a woman up to the pointed white entrance that looked like a church door, then followed them in.

The large coatroom only had a few coats and bags, but I had nothing to leave there. In the winter I could imagine it was packed.

I wondered around the large rooms, having little idea where I was heading, and found Smith to be right in saying the gallery was a little chaotic. Also, I couldn't seem to get out of the nineteenth century. I consulted *Smith's Moscow* again, asked for directions from a passing Inturist guide to Andrei Rublev – ground floor, rooms 38 and 39, on the right at the back. But, no, I couldn't go right, I had to do an entire circuit of the ground floor to get there, but, really, I should start upstairs at room 1 and see the upper floor first.

Once alone, I sneaked down the corridor on the right. This took me past rooms 40 to 52, which held their collection of realist paintings, lots of greys and browns and people mowing. Smith didn't recommend anything modern and Stalinist, but I wasn't sure about Rublev either once I got to room 38. 'Trinity' was much brighter and more beautiful than the reproduction in *Москва Moscow*, but the necks of the figures were weirdly bent in a way which made them look as though they'd been hanged. I thought there were people covered in sheets behind them until I realised they were wings. The figures all had the same shapes, the same draping, the same circular haloes. I walked around the room, trying to be moved by their age and importance, but they were too angular and odd.

There was a familiar voice from behind me.

'Have you been offered any ikons yet?'

I turned. It was that woman, Eva Mann. She wore the same brown dress as before with a cream jacket, but no hat. Maybe she'd lost it.

'Yes, I have, in a subway.'

She nodded. 'They're all fake, of course. I've been watching you look at these ikons. You don't seem impressed by Rublev.'

'I'm not. They feel forced somehow.'

'Shall I explain how you should read an ikon?'

'Please.'

'In traditional Western art the vanishing point is at the back of the picture space, but in these it is between us and the painting,' she put her hand out, 'here. It draws us into the other world, the sacred space between us and the image. Reversing the perspective pulls us in but a knowledge of perspective, ironically, pushes us out.' She led me to another ikon. 'This is the Ascension. The hovering figure of Jesus doesn't make sense on a literal level, and its understanding of chronology is not ours, but look at the use of circles. The earth is square and heaven is circular. An image of equality,' she smiled, 'that some places on earth are trying to replicate.'

I took a step closer. It was making a difference to know the ideas behind the images.

'The Soviets are the ones to have popularised the ikon. We worked out how to remove the soot and dirt after years of neglect and sent ikons to exhibitions all over the world. Of course, some people believed that they should be left in the monasteries and churches, but they had no idea what condition they had been left in. The Soviets regard museums as being as culturally important as churches, but accessible to everyone, like our metro stations.' She gestured around the room. 'These were all blackened and half-forgotten until the State took over, and then after they were cleaned they went to South Kensington in the 1920s, Boston in the 1930s, and so on. The tour included some of Rublev's ikons from the iconostasis in the Dormition Cathedral.' She noticed my face. 'Do you know what an iconostasis is?'

'Yes,' I said. 'I saw one in Bucharest. I was just wondering why you said "we". Are you Russian?'

'Ah.' She smiled. 'I thought you'd been warned about me. Does it make you feel uncomfortable?'

'No. I'm just surprised.' I thought of my conversation

with Christopher. 'Someone warned me off you, but I didn't understand why.'

'I moved here some time ago, and there are some people at the embassy who think that makes me some kind of traitor. Really, it makes me a free woman, making my own decisions, but they're not keen on that either. Would you like to carry on this conversation over a drink?'

I nodded. 'My guidebook says that they serve orange crush and ice cream in the courtyard.'

She patted my hand. There was something about Russia that encouraged women to pat my hand.

'Let me take you to a stolovoya.'

My feet were hurting a little. 'Does it have chairs?'

'Of course, it's not a pivnaya. A stolovoya serves simple meals, but I was thinking maybe cognac or wine. You're not hungry yet, are you?'

I was, but I said no.

She led me out of the gallery, and right, which I was pretty sure headed back towards the river but I'd taken a rounda-bout route and I wasn't quite sure. A couple of turns, and we were in a small café-type place. As she ordered wine, I jiggled my coins, trying to remember how much I had left.

'It is my pleasure to get this,' she said. 'You are a guest in Russia.'

'Thank you. I am running a bit short of cash.'

'In Britain, when I left, people used to hide the fact that they didn't have money. It's good to see that things change. There's no shame in poverty, just in the system that creates it.' She poured the wine. 'Didn't I see you at the showing of *Girl from Hanoi*? I thought it was the best film I had seen in months.'

'I did like that a lot, yes.'

'Will you write about it? You do write for a magazine, yes?'

'I will write about it. Whether they'll publish it or not, I'm not sure.' I shrugged.

'Why wouldn't they?'

I didn't answer.

'Propaganda?' She tutted. 'Same as ever, eh? If you could choose, what would you like to write about? Art, maybe?'

I hesitated. 'I'd like to report news, rather than films. Films are interesting, but they are temporary. Very few are important in a way that lasts.'

'The news could be seen as temporary too.'

'It could, but it builds on the previous news and becomes history. It feels a part of something bigger.'

'That is true.' She sat back as if waiting for me to speak. 'Do you work here?'

'Everyone works in the Soviet Union. I work at the Foreign Language Publishing House, Novosti. We work on guidebooks, among other things. It's good work. I enjoy it very much.'

'And what is it like to live in Moscow?'

'It can be hard.' She looked pensive. 'But I find it's worth the effort. I have no regrets.'

I looked around. I hadn't noticed the kind of hardship I'd seen in London recently. The electricity didn't cut out, the streets were clean, there were no kids without shoes urinating in the gutter.

'Sometimes you just don't belong to the place you were born,' she continued. 'It's odd that the kind of person who has benefited most from the class system takes criticism of it so personally.'

'Do you know anyone who works at the embassy? Like Christopher?'

'I've heard of him.' She looked at her tiny gold watch. 'We'd better be heading back if you wanted to catch the last film today.'

I must have missed her paying. I felt nicely numbed, not drunk, and hoped I would stay awake for the film. I should have eaten something. We walked out together.

'I was wondering if we could have a longer talk. I'd like to know more about what it's like to live here.'

'You'd like to know more, or you'd like to write about Moscow? I've read articles which are very rude.'

'Why would I be rude? I'm just interested.'

When she took my arm, I was aware of how much shorter she was than Ursula. She led me down streets lit gold by the sun. I listened to her talk. She didn't need any responses, and it was hypnotic, just one foot after another and the flow of words above the background noise of the cars.

'I should be taking notes,' I said, but to myself.

'We can talk again, properly.'

We reached the river and turned right.

'I have a river cruise booked for Saturday,' I said.

She pointed out the embassy on the other side of the road, then we were on a bridge and it all felt familiar. We stopped at the viewing point from where I'd seen Christopher, and I could see a group of women heading towards the entrance of the Rossiya. I was late.

'The translators are going in already,' I said. 'I still don't see her.' Eva was sitting next to me on the low wall which ran around the viewing point, looking at the hotel. 'Do you know one of them?'

'Not really. I was asked to see if I could find someone, to find something out. A man lost his sister and she might know what happened.'

'That's sad. What's her name?'

'Ingrid. It's not much to go on. I think she speaks Romanian and German.'

'And do you?'

I shook my head. It was starting to clear a little.

'How were you going to talk to her?' Eva laughed gently. 'In any case, you can't approach the translators. They aren't allowed to talk to any of the attendees.'

'Why?'

'I suppose it's to avoid any accusation of bribery should anything go wrong in a film showing. What if they'd been seen talking to the Japanese party and then an important word was mistranslated in a Chinese film? It's just better to keep everyone separate.' She looked back along the bridge. 'I suppose this is different, as you're not attached to any film studios. I could arrange for you to talk to Ingrid, if you like?'

'Could you?'

'Only if it would be helpful.'

'Yes, thank you. I would like to.'

'Come on,' she said. She didn't take my arm this time.

CHAPTER 28

I was happy to leave it all to Eva. She would probably be able to get further than I could, in any case.

That evening, I ate alone in the Natsional café with no interruptions, and had an early night after just one glass of wine. I felt much better in the morning.

I headed to the restaurant for breakfast. Ursula was already sitting there, surrounded by the four North Vietnamese women. Even sitting she towered over them and I wondered what Alan would make of the scene, these women protecting Ursula from my approach. She stared at me so I walked to an empty table where I couldn't make eye contact. I'd assumed she was long gone. Had she heard something about Alan? I wanted him to walk in more than anything.

I ordered eggs and bread and coffee and flicked through my notebook. By the time I had finished, all the women had left. My shoulders relaxed. I don't know why I felt guilty, but when everyone else believes you are it's infectious.

The drizzle had returned. I walked across Red Square, alert to groups of women. There were a lot of tanks parked up here today, and more soldiers than usual, which didn't help my paranoia. I went to the cinema early and took a seat at the back, out of sight.

The first film, *We All Loved Each Other So Much*, was one that I felt Alan would not approve of. Italians fighting the fascists was fine, but the only happy one was the communist who, of course, got the girl. I was a little tearful as I thought about the band of three reduced by circumstances to competition with each other, and Antonio ending up in hospital just made me think of Alan. There is always something about films which cover decades, lifetimes, which made me feel nostalgic for a future I hadn't had yet. It made no sense, but I desperately didn't want to look back on my life with regret.

I headed for the café. I would need to eat properly to manage all three films today. This was what I should have done every day. What kind of hardship was it to be fed and shown films?

Ursula was sitting in the café, still protected by the women, but it was my café too. I took a seat on the far side, away from the picture windows. I waited for my food, my eyes fixed on the wall. There was a waft of musty aftershave and Terence plumped himself down next to me. He'd had a shave. I wondered if he'd been to the barber in the hotel.

'Being a dedicated film reviewer today?' he said.

'Sorry?'

'I haven't seen you at many films.'

'I've been here.'

'There's a sense among some people here that film reviewing, criticism, is fun. I do hope you're not one of them.'

'I don't think so.'

'Film has a heritage as important as politics. It encapsulates societies and peoples. What more could you know about a country than what they want people to see?'

'Yes.'

'And a good film reviewer needs to know all about that society to understand what isn't being shown.'

Now I knew why Christopher wanted Terence to be my minder. A bit of lunchtime indoctrination. I listened as I ate. Finally, Terence excused himself and I wandered out to the lobby to have a cigarette, but it was sunny and warm so I went outside instead. I still noticed men in grey jackets. There was one in the phone booth, one in a cartoon-shaped black car, one in deep conversation with – oh God, Christopher.

I headed around the hotel towards the river side and bumped into the guard leading the translators back inside for the next film. I stood to one side, seeing Christopher waiting further up the line. I thought, I hope Ursula isn't watching this from inside, Christopher chasing me down, and then I saw Eva. She stepped out of the group to speak to me. The final guard said something to her, and she replied in a way which made him lower his eyes. She definitely wasn't a normal translator.

'Ted, I have arranged for Ingrid to meet us after the final film. Shall we meet at the Metropol?'

I had a few extra dinner vouchers, having missed some meals. If it was one meal, I could cover it. 'Yes. I'll meet you there at half past eight.'

She nodded, and I saw her glance at Christopher who was waiting until we finished talking. She nodded at him too, and he turned away. Her smile was wide, amused in a way which made me think she had met him before after all. She walked on and I waited for Christopher to come over. He was smiling as well. That was odd.

'Ted, can we have a word?'

'I have to get in for the next film.'

'I understand that. You're busy.' He was still smiling. 'Could we meet for dinner this evening?'

'I have plans.'

'Who with?'

'None of your business. And, to be honest, I'm angry that you set that bore on me.'

'Bore?'

'Terence. Being here isn't supposed to be some kind of punishment, you know.'

He put his hand out, as if to touch my elbow, and I stepped back.

'And everyone keeps patting me. What is that for?'

He folded his arms. 'Ted, I apologise if you feel Terence has been sent to talk to you on my behalf. I do think we should talk properly, clear the air. Do you have any free time tomorrow? I'd be happy to meet you for breakfast again, if that suits.'

'Yes, breakfast will be fine.' I felt magnanimous. He had something to say and I was allowing him to wait. It would eat me up to wait, but I had a feeling it would be worth it. I moved to go in.

'Just one thing,' he said. 'I'd like you to be careful when you speak to Eva Mann. I saw you just now and I know that she's good at getting very close to people. Whatever she promises you, she will want something in return.'

'Have you met her before?'

'No,' he hesitated, 'we've never formally met. I have heard a lot about her.' He cleared his throat. 'I'll see you tomorrow morning. Half eight?'

'That's fine.' Twelve hours apart.

I walked past the Lubyanka on my way to the Metropol. It wasn't as scary as the first time, as the setting sun made the windows bright orange. There were no shadows moving in the corners.

In the Metropol, Eva was waiting at a table next to a woman with dyed-auburn hair, an open bottle of wine and two glasses. I felt a jolt in my stomach. Ingrid was here. I would find out what Marku wanted to know about his sister, where Ana had gone.

Eva said, 'I hope you don't mind, but I ordered for us, Ted. The food can take a little while, and I'm sure you have places to be.'

'Thank you.'

I sat down at the table and got my first good look at Ingrid. I didn't recognise her. Even adding a few years to the picture I'd been shown, she was unfamiliar to me. I would never have picked her from a crowd.

Eva looked pleased with herself. The woman, this Ingrid, looked as if she'd rather be anywhere else.

'I'm going to translate.' Eva repeated everything in Russian. Ingrid asked something. Eva answered and Ingrid nodded. 'She just asked if you spoke any Russian.'

Ingrid was keeping her eyes down on the tablecloth. Her hands were clasped together, as if in prayer. She mumbled something.

'Ingrid regrets that she cannot stay for a meal as she has a prior appointment. She is happy to answer any questions. What would you like to know?'

I felt I was taking advantage. Her head bowed, Ingrid was as unhappy as I had ever seen anyone. Eva said something, and she lifted her face to me, still looking at the table. She was terrified. I would make it quick and let her get out of here.

'I heard of a girl that was taken from her family in Bucharest, Ana. She was ill and a German doctor said she'd take her for treatment in a German Sanatorium. They never saw her again. I wondered if you knew anything.'

Eva had been translating as I spoke. I had no idea how anyone could do that, although it happened daily at the festival.

211

In Ingrid's murmured answer I heard 'Rumyniya', 'Bukharest', 'Ana' and 'Marku'. I hadn't mentioned Marku. Maybe this was the right woman, drastically changed. Ingrid moved one hand to her palm, her feet and her side. Eva waited until she had finished to translate for me, but I was sure that she didn't translate everything. Ingrid had clearly said Nadia Osipova, the same name that Vasile hadn't wanted me to hear. Ingrid was telling the truth, but how accurate was the translation?

'Ingrid says she did help to collect a girl from Bucharest called Ana who was very ill. The priest had been petitioned by her brother, Marku, to find the best treatment and the Communist Party arranged for her to see specialists in the GDR. Sadly, Ana died on the way there. She doesn't know why the family were never contacted and told this.'

Ingrid was shaking. One hand fumbled onto the table and rested, clenched, by her empty plate.

'It just seems to be a terrible error. Ingrid is going to contact the authorities in Bucharest and make sure that the family is informed. Is there anything else you would like to know?'

'No. Thank you.'

Eva spoke to Ingrid. The tone sounded kind, but Ingrid's eyes filled with tears and her fingers slipped under the raised side of the plate.

She stood, nodded to me, and half-ran from the restaurant. On cue, our food arrived with more wine and vodka.

'Is she all right?' I asked.

Eva sighed. 'She has not had a good day at work, I'm sorry to say. She made a serious error in her translation and might lose her position.' She shrugged. 'Not much I can do. But you had your questions answered. What will you do with that information now?'

'Nothing, I suppose. It was just so that Marku could know what had happened to his sister. As long as he finds out, that's all I could do.' I sipped my wine. 'She didn't look how I expected.'

'No? She has aged?'

'I suppose.' I could see a small, folded piece of paper under the plate. Ingrid had left a note.

'It comes to us all.' Eva's mouth showed mock disapproval, and she laughed. 'Are you planning any more expeditions, or are you focusing on the films now?'

'Just the films, I think.'

'You've seen the winners already,' she said, slyly.

'Which films will win?'

'The Kurosawa from the first day, the Italian film you saw this morning and the Polish one from a couple of days ago.'

'Oh. How do you know?'

'I've been doing this a very long time. I can spot the winners. If you have notes on those three, you'll be fine.'

I wondered if I had made good notes on the Polish one. I remembered a grim tale of nineteenth century capitalism. I refused to look at the paper under the plate.

'They are repeated at other cinemas throughout the festival, if you do need to watch one again. Other than that, we have plenty to interest someone who would like to explore Moscow a little more. Have you heard about the Writers House of Creation? Or, if you like, I could arrange for you to meet a friend of mine, Svetlana. She's the director of the Central Cinema Studio, Mosfilm.'

I hid my shudder. It was tempting to get some insider knowledge, but all I could imagine was another painful interrogation of a shaking woman. And I couldn't stop thinking about the note. When Eva stood up, maybe went to the toilet, I could snatch the paper.

'I think I am going to go to all the films.' I paused. 'I have to behave myself and earn my money.'

'Is the embassy poking its nose in again?'

'Yes, Christopher is meeting me for breakfast.'

She waved her hand, dismissively. 'You could stand him up.'

Was everyone in Moscow going to try to persuade me to behave in a certain way? I missed Alan and Ursula, and their conversation which had never seemed to have an underlying purpose that I didn't understand.

'I was joking,' she said gently. 'I think you are feeling a bit battered today.'

'I am. There have been a lot of changes in such a short time. Is it always like this?'

'No. You're in the middle of a huge international festival in a city you're unfamiliar with. Everything is different. Is this your first festival?'

I nodded. I was exhausted.

'There you go, then. It's not Moscow. It could be New York or Cannes. You'll be more prepared next time.'

'I suppose.' I didn't even know what I was eating. 'Is this beef stroganoff?'

'Yes. It's a favourite of mine. You didn't mind going straight to the main course, did you?'

'No. It's a relief to not have to keep eating for hours.' I put my cutlery on the plate and sat back. She signalled and the waiter immediately cleared the plates. Eva signalled for them to take Ingrid's empty plate too. She picked up the paper as if she knew it was there, and put it in her pocket.

'Ingrid must have dropped this. I'll get it back to her. You should have an early night, Ted. These events are more tiring than you'd think. Let's have a toast, to friendship.'

We clinked small vodka glasses, and she downed hers. I copied, and managed not to choke.

'And good luck with Christopher tomorrow.'

She escorted me from the Metropol, and said goodnight before heading towards the Bolshoi. I stood there for a short while, looking at the statue of Karl Marx. I felt shaken. Was this onslaught of surveillance and persuasion what Marx had planned?

I walked back to the Natsional and watched everyone I passed with particular care until I felt a hand on my shoulder.

I snapped, 'Tell Christopher to get lost,' before turning to see Ingrid. I held a hand up. 'Sorry.'

She mimed handing me something and looked at me hopefully. 'My note?'

'I didn't get it. Eva has it.'

Her face fell and she nodded, took a small notebook and pen from a pocket and quickly wrote something before tearing the page out and handing it to me.

'Give Marku. Girl holy.' She crossed herself. 'Don't look. Holy girl leave safe.' She put a finger to her lips, and slowly walked towards Red Square.

When I got back to the room I looked at the paper: Erlöserbund Catholic Convent, Bonn. I would never remember that. I added the name to my notes on *Girl from Hanoi*, as if it was a reference to the film, and then I tore the note into small pieces and flushed it away.

It took me a long time to sleep. I wished that I hadn't waited to take the first note.

KGB Second Chief Directorate
2nd Department: British Commonwealth

'FISHERMAN' ADDITIONAL REPORT:
FOR ADDITION TO WALKER FILE

The intervention of 'Ingrid', approaching the subject and exchanging words with him, caught us by surprise. There is an investigation into how this was allowed to happen. Her knowledge of English may be greater than we thought, or she tried to convey a message in German or Romanian, which is unlikely. The note which was intercepted was in grammatically correct English, so there may be an English speaker involved in this as well: 'Meet me in front of the Bolshoi'. The translating group will be the first to be questioned.

Despite the translation limiting the impact of her narrative, 'Ingrid' did mention the name 'Nadia Osipova', despite having been told not to, and conveyed a number of relevant body parts through hand signals. The subject watched this with interest, but little apparent understanding of the condition it referred to.

The subject's apparent interest in Lobnoye Mesto ('The Place of Skulls', looking at the site, leaving the Smith guide open at this page) didn't result in anything after three days' observation. No one waited there for a noticeable time, or left any kind of object or message for collection.

Walker's file contains precise descriptions of his movements on each day, but there have only been repeated visits to an ice-cream stall on Red Square, other than the three hotels: Natsional, Rossiya, Metropol.

Walker is displaying increased levels of anxiety, looking around himself more often and critically evaluating faces. This may be partly connected with the successful removal from his circle of the man who was tasked with looking after him, and he became more dependent on the woman. The woman has been affected more than the subject by the removal of Sullivan. She has not removed herself from the scene as we wished, but she has distanced herself from Walker. The subject remains enamoured as well as confused. This may still work in our favour.

It is felt that directly acting to remove the woman would be too obvious as a technique, and the British Embassy are already overly interested in what is happening around the subject. This was a positive move for us when it caused a split between the subject and the woman, but it seems as if their position is shortly to be reversed just as we are starting to make progress. The threat remains that, if this woman were to warn him off any specific people he is speaking to, he would want to please her.

His increasing awareness of, and emotional reactions to, meaningless encounters mean that it is best that we remove the subject from the hotel and allow him to settle in a more private place before any suggestions are made.

As so much is being concealed from the subject, it has been decided that the best approach is to tell him the appropriate amount of truth, when he asks. This will allow him to feel both valued and trusted, feelings which should be reciprocated given his relative isolation in both London and Moscow.

CHAPTER 29

I met Christopher in the restaurant. He was early. No surprise there. He looked pleased to see me. That was a surprise. That made me nervous.

He shook my hand and waited for me to sit before he did. Then he waited for me to order breakfast. He had coffee. He leaned towards me.

'Mr Walker, we have some very good news about Alan.'

'He's all right?'

'He is, yes. The doctors in Britain have managed to diagnose him successfully and he should respond very well to treatment.'

'Treatment for what?'

'It seems that Alan has been suffering from stomach ulcers for some time. Probably all that rich eating and drinking that goes with your business.' He smiled. I didn't. 'And, um, it turned into peritonitis while he was here. He had been ignoring the symptoms.'

'Huh,' I said, 'so I didn't poison him?'

'Ted—'

'Really? You're not even going to apologise?'

'I—'

'Have you even told Ursula?'

'I wanted to talk to you first. Of course, I am distraught that I gave anyone the impression that you were under any kind of suspicion. However, I don't believe that I precisely suggested you were involved.'

He didn't look distraught, but he was using the gentle tone he'd previously only used with Ursula.

'I would like to offer my full and unreserved apology for any upset I caused, especially between you and Mrs Koskinen.'

I'd have preferred him to say 'I'm sorry', rather than that insincere legal phrase.

'I know you had been very close.'

There was something in his eyes then which angered me again.

'And are you going to apologise for having me followed?'

He frowned. 'Hold on. We haven't.'

'Oh, don't give me that. All those men in grey jackets, wherever I go?'

'Ted, I can only apologise for things I am responsible for. I, and the embassy more widely, are not responsible for anything like that.'

My coffee and bread arrived. I didn't touch them.

Christopher looked over my shoulder. 'Excuse me one moment, I'm just going to have a word with Ursula. I'll be back shortly.'

I didn't watch him. I just looked at the steam twisting from my coffee. I had clearly lost my mind, seeing all those men following me when they weren't. Why had I said that to Christopher, made that stupid accusation, right after he'd been convinced that I was innocent? I could hear his voice, slow and pleasant, as he talked to Ursula. My eyes felt heavy and I closed them. It was ruined, and it couldn't get better, but it was nice to be in the clear.

I heard someone walk to my side, and I opened my eyes.

Ursula opened her arms. I stood up and let her apologise soundlessly, her palms flat on my shoulder blades. She said sorry, although it was never her fault. Christopher had done this. Posh, arrogant, 'oh, do forgive me' Christopher. I gave her a little pat on the back. She let go and I left the hotel.

I walked for a long time. It took me a while to work out what I was escaping – pity. Ursula had looked at me with pity. The interest and vague amusement had gone and any time we had left together was spoiled. I was alternately furious and miserable.

I found myself in a park, bought an ice cream and watched old men play dominoes at tables under the trees. I would have thought they'd play chess here. The Russians liked chess, didn't they? I finished the ice cream, stretched back on a bench and watched the few high clouds scoot across the sky. What now? I felt as if I had given up, but I wasn't sure what I'd given up on. I was bunking off, alone, and everything was possible if only I had more coins in my pocket.

Probably I should have gone to the festival. Probably I should have eaten more than ice cream. Probably I should have been thinking about the future and bonding with colleagues and making international connections to take back to Mr Benstrup.

I bought another ice cream, and walked along the river trying not to stare at the sunbathers.

I hadn't spoken to anyone by the time I returned to the hotel in the early evening. My glum floor attendant handed me a letter with the embassy mark on it as I collected my key. I ran a bath and sat in it until it got cold, and then I dressed. I remembered the letter and opened it.

Christopher was worried. He left his number at the top

of the letter. He had arranged for Ursula to attend the English-speaking river cruise, so we could spend some time together before leaving Moscow. He hoped, he believed, he thought—.

I put the letter in the bin, picked up *Smith's Moscow* and went downstairs to the café. I ordered soup and blinis and a bottle of red with my voucher, and sat in the corner. My aim was to look unapproachable as I didn't trust myself to say anything at all. I held Smith to my face and flicked through the pages I hadn't read. Theatre, ballet, comedy and variety, concerts, cinema, television, dancing, sports – none of it interested me. Then, right at the back, I saw the section on how to get home. I could get a refund if I left early. All I had to do was give Inturist two days' notice that I was leaving. Maybe they could get me on an earlier plane and I could go on Saturday, rather than waiting until Wednesday.

The Inturist office closed at ten o'clock. I had plenty of time. I settled down to eat. The soup was especially tasty, and I felt as if I was finally getting the full experience with wine — taste, smell, appearance. I even swirled it in the glass. I expect Christopher did that with every bottle. I expect Christopher had someone else to do that for him. Smug idiot. No wonder his wife had left Moscow, and him.

An American couple joined my table and I pretended I couldn't speak English, French or German. They gave up trying languages, and I listened in to their conversation. Carrie and Mike were annoying the woman in ways she couldn't stop discussing. The man was more conciliatory. Maybe he fancied Carrie. Maybe Mike was his brother. Being multilingual must have some interesting perks, but I found it difficult not to look at the people I was listening to and they soon left to get to the Bolshoi on time. I decided that I should learn another language. It was the easiest way to spy on people.

As it was late, I didn't have to wait at the Inturist counter. I explained when I wanted to leave, and how (thanks to Smith) I would like the refund as a credit memo, and not roubles, to exchange in London. If I'd been given roubles I couldn't take them out of the country and Mr Benstrup would have had something to say about that.

The woman smiled and said the paperwork would be ready in the morning, with confirmation of my new flight details. I felt relieved. This was a strange place, or the British had made it one for me, and ten days here was plenty. I ordered my breakfast, looked out of the window at the red stars and shadows, and closed the curtains on all of it.

I thought about Mr Benstrup as I brushed my teeth. I hadn't exactly decided what I was going to say to him about this. I could say that I, too, had fallen ill. Not with peritonitis, but food poisoning could work. Or I could not tell him anything, go back to Harwich and come clean to my mother about how I had failed to keep my promise. I might get sacked and then have to go back anyway and live with that failure on a daily basis. I looked at the scar on my hand, and sighed. I was not a good fit with the world of fishing, but how many times could someone run away? I had run once, from Harwich to London. Did I get a second chance at this? I knew I should stay, but I just couldn't be around Ursula and know that it was different and it didn't have to be.

I was running back home. To which home, I wasn't sure. It didn't matter.

Even though everything was up in the air, and I had no idea what would come next, I felt quite calm. Somehow I knew it wasn't up to me any more.

CHAPTER 30

After breakfast I went down to the Inturist desk. It was a different woman who asked me to sit down. She introduced herself as Sasha.

'You want to leave early?' she said.

'Yes.'

'Is there a problem with the hotel?'

'No, the hotel is lovely. I need to get home to see my parents.'

'Why?'

'That's a personal issue.'

She nodded, and slid a piece of paper towards me. 'This is your bill.'

I looked at it and for a moment I couldn't breathe. I cleared my throat. 'There's some mistake. It was all paid in advance through Inturist.'

'No. It needs to be paid before you leave.'

My heart was beating fast. 'It was paid in London at the Inturist bureau. All in advance. Look.' I took the meal vouchers from my pocket and saw how my hands shook. 'I got vouchers for my meals. I wanted a refund because it's paid.'

She took the vouchers from me and flicked through

them. 'Unfortunately, we had a report that a guest had meal vouchers stolen while in the hotel.' She opened a drawer and dropped them in. 'How would you like to pay?'

'This is just a mistake.' I tapped my leg. 'I arrived on the 9th and was sent to the Inturist hotel next door, before they sent me here. The paperwork must still be with them.'

'No, I don't think so.'

'Can you ask them?'

She flicked her fingers. 'I asked. They don't have it. What proof do you have?'

None. I had no proof. Suzanne had paid. I just had the tickets, the itinerary, the visa. None of was in the form of a receipt. I had nothing else.

'You will have to telephone my office in London. They dealt with the payment.'

'And they can confirm that you have to leave early?'

'No, they can't confirm that. They can confirm the receipt details.'

She stood up to dismiss me. 'I will see what I can do. Come back at noon.'

'Can I have the vouchers back?'

'No. There will be an investigation. Come back at noon.'

When I stood up I felt dizzy, holding onto furniture on my way from the office. I was probably going to miss the river cruise, but not eating was more of a problem. I wondered whether I should pack now before they stopped me returning to my room, but felt some fresh air was urgent.

I stumbled as I passed the doorman, and stood on the pavement while streams of grey people passed me. I walked through the underpass and headed for Alexandrovsky Gardens. I was going to lose my job, that was almost certain, but I didn't want to end up in some kind of Russian debtors' prison first. If they couldn't sort it out I would have to swallow my pride and involve the embassy. I didn't look forward to seeing Christopher's smug face when I begged him for help.

People around me, people who belonged here, sat on the benches and read, or walked through the gardens. The Kremlin's high wall reassured them all that the whole state was behind them, or it would reassure me if I lived here. All I had was the embassy, an enclave of public schoolboys across the river who made assumptions and sweeping apologies which meant nothing.

I had time to walk around, but I just sat in the sunshine, arms crossed to stop the shaking, and watched people. Men walked purposefully with copies of Pravda, or in groups more slowly, their wide trousers looking like nothing like flares. An occasional woman in a bright summer dress was outnumbered by older women in dark blouses and stiff skirts.

Across the road I saw Christopher hurrying towards the Natsional and calmly thought, he's going to sort out this mess for me. The least he could do. Strangely, I felt at the absolute heart of Moscow in that moment. People paraded for me to watch them, the embassy sent its most annoying man to fire-fight while the sun shone only on me.

And yet, I had no faith that I was ever going to get home again.

I waited in the Inturist office for Sasha to return. I had been wrong about Christopher. He wasn't here sorting it all out. How would he have known if I didn't tell him?

I sat, head in my hands, the noise of the hotel continuing around me. Americans, Vietnamese, Italians all carrying on their holiday or business. I heard high heeled shoes and heavy boots on the hard floor.

'Mr Walker.' Sasha was back. 'We have telephoned your office in London, but there is no answer.'

'That can't be the right number, then. Someone has to be there. Can I try?'

'No. You say that you cannot pay for the room and tour you have already had, so I don't think you can pay for a telephone call also.'

I sat back. 'So, what happens now?'

'You will be taken to the Lubyanka until this is resolved.'

There was the sound of heavy boots again on marble. I turned to see two police officers behind me, both staring straight ahead.

'Sasha, please, this is just a mistake. It will all be sorted out.'

'I'm sure you're right, Mr Walker.'

One officer put a hand under my armpit to force me to stand. The other gripped my upper arm and we started walking to the entrance.

'Sasha, please keep calling London. And phone the embassy for me, please.'

'Very good, Mr Walker.'

We were in the lobby. Guests stared and staff didn't look at all. The doorman touched his cap as we exited the doors, as if we were off to the Bolshoi.

The first officer said something in Russian and I shrugged my shoulders. He pulled me to the left and I could see the black car waiting for us, one man at the wheel and another holding the door open. Four policemen to escort me to the Lubyanka. I was being taken to a cell in the KGB headquarters. I felt laughter bubbling with the utter disbelief in my stomach. I should have finished *Darkness at Noon*. Did he escape at the end? Maybe someone would take a photo for the British newspapers, so they would know what had happened to me. At least I didn't have handcuffs on.

'Ted?'

Oh, not Ursula, I thought, I don't want her to see this, but it was Eva, looking bewildered.

'What's going on?'

'There's some problem with my pre-paid hotel, so I'm being taken to the Lubyanka.' It was as normal as I could make it sound, but for some reason I was starting to find it hilarious and I couldn't stop smiling. 'I'm sure the embassy will sort it out. They are going to inform them for me.'

She didn't bother talking with me after that. She questioned the two officers either side of me. The second one, who still held my arm, let up a little, and they both exchanged what sounded like angry words with Eva. She looked at them, eyes flashing, and I began to think of her as my hero. Then the first officer pushed me into the car, and they sat either side of me. She had failed, I thought, but then she got in the front passenger seat. The car sped off, leaving the fourth officer on the pavement.

It wasn't a long journey. As we passed the Metropol I felt sad that I wouldn't go back there, and then we were at the Lubyanka but not going in one of the front doors. The car drove around and parked at the back, at the large door with a guard on either side. Like Lenin's tomb. I started to shake as I was pushed from the car but, joyously, I saw that Eva was coming in too.

'Won't you get in trouble?' I asked her.

'No, don't worry. We are all equal in the Soviet Union, and I am as important as anyone in this building.'

I hoped she was right.

She argued up the stairs, she argued in the waiting room where I had been placed on a wooden chair. I just watched her, seeing the dark blue shapes of the policemen come and go around her. Finally she came back to me. Her hair was starting to escape from its bun, and her cheeks were flushed with rage or excitement.

'Let's go,' she said.

'What?'

'The politsiya have agreed to release you into my custody while this is resolved.'

'Are you arresting me?'

She looked confused. 'They say you can stay with me for now. As a guest.'

'Aren't the embassy sending anyone?'

‘She looked around. 'It doesn't seem so, no. You're welcome to wait for them, if that's what you'd prefer. You'll have to go in a cell until they turn up. I couldn't say how long that would be.'

I didn't want to go in a cell. All I had was Eva. I stood up and looked at the remaining officer in the waiting room. He looked at me with an odd expression. For a second it was almost pity, but for whom, himself or me, I didn't know, and then his face was blank again and he turned away.

Eva was waiting for me in the doorway. I followed her down the stairs, and back out to the same car which only had the driver now.

She said, 'Kursky vokzal.'

‘I'm not sure that this is a good idea for you,' I said.

She patted my knee. We pulled up at a train station where she sat me in the buffet with a coffee and went off to get tickets. I hadn't finished when she called me over to catch the train. She got on but I hesitated.

'Where are we going?'

'We're going to take the train to Saltykovskaya, to my dacha. It's like a summer house. Very simple, but it will be good for you to get out of Moscow for a while. You don't look well, Ted.'

I was sure I didn't look good. I barely knew my name. She held her hand out. I took it and stepped on the train.

'That's right. We'll work it out. Don't worry. They are going to send your things on, but it will only be for a day or two.'

I nodded. 'Eva, I don't have any money to pay for this. I can't even afford the ticket for the train.'

'You are a guest, and in Russia the guest is honoured. Please relax. It won't take long to get there. Half an hour, that's all.'

I watched her face as the train pulled away. She was happy. I hoped she would stay that way.

CHAPTER 31

I didn't relax on the journey, half expecting to be pulled off the train by soldiers and beaten, like in a film about the Second World War. It was strange how suddenly the grey buildings of the outskirts ended and became forests and villages until I remembered that I had experienced exactly the reverse on the way in. We arrived in Saltykovskaya and I followed Eva onto the open, concrete platform.

'This way,' she said. I looked around. There was a stall with some vegetables, some structures that I hoped were sheds and not dachas, and a few old women in black, their heads covered with muted scarves.

We walked along a road, going south, I thought, and I reached into my pocket for my cigarettes.

'Oh no.'

'What is it?'

'My duty-free cigarettes. I left them in the room with all my clothes, and notes, everything.'

'How many cigarettes do you have left?'

'Three.'

She checked her watch. 'They will bring all of your things here by four o'clock. Can you pace yourself till then?'

'Yes. They're going to bring my things? The KGB?'

'Of course.'

'Am I under arrest?'

'More like under investigation. But you paid for the hotel, didn't you? So, you'll be fine.'

She carried on walking. There were a few houses as we walked, and lots of trees. I assumed they were 'houses', but many were one-storey barns with rotten roofs and some were made from sheets of corrugated iron. A summer house in England would just be a fancy shed in the garden, not somewhere you could sleep.

We walked on. The sun was shining and I wasn't in prison. Small mercies.

After twenty minutes we arrived at a much busier road and had to wait to cross it. Lorries thundered by and a bus.

Eva looked at me. 'I prefer the train, but there are buses into the city from here, too. It's well connected.'

If you had money, yes.

We managed to cross over to a small shop at the side of the road, and Eva told me to wait outside. I turned my face from the dust spun up by wheels and tried to control my breathing. Eva came back out and we walked west for another five minutes before she stopped and dug around in her pocket for the keys to a huge pair of gates. She pushed them both open, wide enough so that a car could drive through, and gestured to the house. And it was a house. Two storeys, wooden and it didn't look like it was crumbling away. It even had curtains.

'Look round the back,' she said.

I passed the house and, through the trees, I could see a lake.

'It's called Silver Pond,' she said.

'It's big for a pond, isn't it?'

'When we say "lake", we mean somewhere like Lake

Baikal. That's nearly four hundred miles long. This is a baby, so it's a pond.'

'If you had somewhere like this, why would anyone live in Moscow?'

Eva laughed and swept green leaves from a pair of wooden chairs, a small table between them.

'It must have been windy the last couple of days,' she said. 'I can grow my dahlias, gladioli and marigolds, but in the winter it gets very cold. And winter starts in September and doesn't end until May. So, we make the most of our summer. Lots of people commute from their dachas in the summer, some just come out at the weekend. My vegetable patch is over there,' she pointed. 'The people who run the shop look after it during the week. It's good to grow your own food.'

I stretched my legs out. 'It feels like an entirely different place. A different country.'

She smiled. 'I'll make some tea.'

It was almost unnaturally peaceful here, with just the rumble of traffic on the other side of the house. Birds flew in and out of the birch trees which framed the garden down to the water. Bees dipped into groups of flowers that were embedded into long grass. I didn't think I'd seen a bee in the city, but I supposed there must have been some. There were fruit trees near the house. I saw apples on one, and thought that the other was cherry. I could have been in England, I thought, and shivered as a cloud passed the sun.

Eva brought a teapot and tea-cups on a tray. I was in England.

'How long do you think it will take to sort everything out?' I asked.

'Oh, not long.'

'Am I under house arrest?'

She laughed. 'No! You haven't got any money to go anywhere else, though, do you?'

'No. That must be why they let me leave.'

She passed across a pair of scissors with one of those strange pyramids of milk I'd seen in the Beriozka brochure.

'I always spill it everywhere,' she said.

'Did you just get this from the shop?' I said as I struggled to hold it steady and cut it cleanly.

'Yes. I told them to bring round my friend's dog as well. You remember, the one I was looking after? She's been staying there while I'm at work.'

I tried to relax. That massive dog. The carton opened and I poured it into a small jug on the tray before adding some to both tea-cups.

'It that all right? About the dog?'

'Of course.'

'You're not scared?'

'No.' The dog would know, dogs can smell it, but Eva didn't need to know.

We sat silently for a while. I glanced at her now and then, but her face didn't reveal anything.

'Aren't you expected at work?' I asked.

'I've gone through most of the English translations with the official group,' she said, 'and it's Friday. I never start any new work on a Friday.'

'So you won't be going back to the festival at all?'

She looked at me slyly from the corner of her eye. 'Are you worried that no one will know where you are?'

Yes. 'Not exactly.' Yes. 'It's just Ursula. She's already had Alan disappear, and now I've gone.'

She turned to me. 'What did happen to Alan?'

'Oh, a stomach ulcer. Peritonitis.'

She laughed quietly. 'And I'll bet the British Embassy thought it was a poisoning or some such nonsense.'

'They did. They accused me of doing it.'

She looked genuinely surprised, her mouth open, but her eyes were still smiling. 'You?'

I nodded.

'You see, Ted, that is the problem with the upper classes. They believe their education was so perfect that they can't possibly jump to the wrong conclusions. And they wouldn't dream of blaming someone of their own class.' She smiled. 'Peritonitis. That's painful. Poor Alan.'

What could she tell about me from my voice? She clearly still had a good ear for accents.

'Where are you from?'

'All over. My parents were great travellers and we never settled in one place for long.'

'But you lived in Britain, somewhere?'

'Somewhere.'

She was smiling, enjoying the evasion.

'Why did you come here?'

'I just followed my heart.'

'How long have you been in Moscow, Eva?'

'Oh, a lifetime.'

'How long is a lifetime?'

She assessed me before saying anything. 'What answer would make you feel comfortable?'

I thought about it. 'More than five years, less than twenty.'

'Why?'

'It just wouldn't make sense to be so at home here if it was less than that, and you've kept too much knowledge of Britain and Britishness. Unless you are studying it. For work.'

'You're a bright boy, Ted. I don't think you've been allowed a chance to really stretch that brain of yours.' She pushed herself up and beckoned me. 'Come and have a look at my pond.'

We walked towards the water and I had the strangest feeling, as if she was going to push me in, but the edge of the water sloped up like a beach here. Somewhere you could beach a boat. The sun shone bright on the gentle waves and I squinted. The lake stretched so far that the houses on the other side looked tiny, and I saw little wooden docks with miniature rowing boats. It felt like money.

'How do people get one of these places?'

'As recognition for their work. And we really do value hard work in every area here. It's not just the kind of job which has status in Britain. Over there, there is a bus driver. There, a teacher. There, a journalist.' I couldn't see what she was pointing at.

There was an odd tone to her voice now.

'In the Soviet Union it's all about what you achieve, not what you are born with.' She turned. 'Oh, Vorona, you're here.' That massive black dog was standing behind us. She stroked the dog's muzzle and lifted a hand to a man standing up by the house who must have brought it over. He left without doing the same.

'Let me show you around the house, and I'll take Vorona for a walk while you settle in.'

CHAPTER 32

I sat on my bed. It was an attic room with wooden rafters, walls and floor. A tinderbox.

I had watched her walk out of the gate with that dog by her side. I doubted that dog belonged to anyone else; it was alert to her every movement. She was hiding more than the dog, though, I was sure. But now I was hungry.

I went back to the kitchen, basic but fully fitted, and helped myself to the white bread and jam that she'd left out for my lunch. The milk she may have put in her pocket at the shop, but she had not been carrying a loaf of bread. It was fresh. Where had it come from?

I took my uneven sandwich with me as I walked around the cabin-like lower floor. There was a sofa, a chair by the back window, a swept fireplace and a small sideboard. Apart from the clock on the wall, the only ornamentation was a black-framed picture of a young man, maybe eighteen, nineteen. She had left me a pair of cotton shorts with the towel on my bed, 'in case you want to go swimming in Silver Pond'. I did have the urge to go swimming and not come back.

The door opened and I jumped. Eva came back in with the dog and a string bag full of food.

'I thought you might be having a nap,' she said. 'You must feel exhausted by all the changes today.'

'I'm too tense to sleep.' There was no point pretending this was normal.

She unpacked her bag. 'I'm going to make lamb shashlik for dinner. They don't take long, but I want to marinate them first. Why don't you go for a swim and they should be well on the way.'

'All right.'

The dog watched me leave the room. As I got changed I could hear her talking in Russian to the dog. I hoped it was to the dog.

I felt naked as I went back downstairs, but she was busy and didn't look at me.

'See you in a while,' she said. The dog just watched.

I wandered down to the bottom of the garden and paddled in the water. It was a sunny afternoon and the water wasn't cold, but it wasn't quite warm either. It would have been easier to jump from one of the little docks, but I edged my way into the water and began to swim. The Lido at Dovercourt came back to me, and the relative freshness of this water made a nice contrast. As I swam, I weighed my options.

Swim to the other side of the lake and do a runner in my wet shorts? No.

Maybe I had enough money to get a bus back to Moscow. Travel was cheap here. I could just walk into the embassy. In my shorts. And see Christopher's face. No.

They wouldn't let me back into the Natsional. I could go to the Rossiya and find Ursula, or wait for her to walk past me on Red Square, if they wouldn't let me in there. Possible. But not in shorts.

I could wait here and see what happened. I had the sense that Eva wanted something from me in return for all this. And, really, it was a holiday. No one expected me back until the night of the 23rd and this was the 19th. I could always say no. I could always, as with Vasile, say yes and mean no. I liked this option best.

In the middle of the lake I stopped to tread water. I could see my limits, yet I could also see where I was heading.

I'd seen shashlik on a few menus, but I hadn't ordered any. If Eva's were anything to go by, I'd been missing out. We ate outside, like a picnic, with some good red wine and vodka to follow. I was happy. My possessions had arrived while I was out so my suitcase, my cigarettes and passport (which I'd forgotten about) were all here.

A racket began in the taller trees along the lake, and we both looked up.

'Starlings,' said Eva, 'all bluster and noise.'

'I saw starlings in Bucharest. I hadn't realised that you got them outside Britain.'

'Ah, we have tigers, leopards, bears *and* starlings, sparrows, nightingales. There's even a kingfisher on this lake.' She smiled. 'Best of both worlds. I have a book on birds, if you'd like to look at it.'

'I might. Thank you.'

'Did you spend much time on the Stour Estuary?'

She knew where I was from. I kept my hands steady. 'No. Not much.'

'What do your parents do?'

'My father is a fisherman. Goes out for cod, pink shrimp, oysters, with whoever needs an extra pair of hands.'

'He doesn't have his own boat?'

'Not any more.' I swallowed. 'My mother stays at home. A bit of sewing, knitting, that kind of thing.'

She said, 'Good, decent work.'

I was blinking and hoping she kept her eyes fixed on the water beyond. I don't think she looked, but she probably heard the lump in my throat in the way I spoke. I gulped some wine.

She went inside, telling the dog to stay, and came back with the picture frame from inside.

'My son,' she said. 'I haven't seen him for—' she paused '—ten years.'

'What's his name?'

'Alexander.' She took it back inside and I knew it was time to change the subject before we both started bawling.

'Where is your friend?'

She looked confused.

'Who owns the dog?'

'Ah, Lubya. She is far away at the moment. She used to be a cosmonaut, and now she trains cosmonauts.'

I laughed in surprise. 'Does she?'

'Yes. Is it funny?'

'It was unexpected. So, she's been to space?'

She shrugged. 'That is what they do.'

She looked so cross with me that I started laughing and couldn't stop.

'What?'

'I'm sorry. It's just if I knew someone who had been to space it would be the first thing I said to anyone. And the dog as well. I'd say, hello, I'm Ted and this is a cosmonaut's space dog. And you're just shrugging it off.'

She smiled.

'You must know a lot of amazing people for that to be nothing.'

She refilled our glasses and offered a toast. 'To space.'

I clinked.

'I don't think you'll meet Lubya. Not unless you're here for rather longer than I expect.'

'How long do you expect?'

'Two or three days, I think.' She nodded to herself. 'You can stand it for that long, can't you?'

'Yes. Do you know, has anyone got through to the office?' I half-wanted them to know where I was, and half-wanted them to think I was still at the festival.

'I'm not sure yet. It might drag on until Monday. I assume they don't work at the weekend?'

'No.'

'I'm sure it will be fine. We'll get along for a couple of days and you will have an adventure to talk about when you get back, or keep to yourself. Whichever feels best.' The wine was empty and she opened the vodka. 'I'll get bread to have with the vodka.'

I was drunk enough. With any luck I would sleep despite the light skies. I'd seen how thin the curtains were, but the curtains in my room at my parents' house were no thicker and I hadn't minded it then. There was something else which reminded me of home, and I was starting to think it was Eva. Maybe it was the sheer luxury of someone cooking for me, or just being interested in what I had to say.

She came back out with rye bread and a knife.

'What were you told about your predecessor at the magazine?'

'Nothing. I was just told there was someone who'd left suddenly.'

'He died, Ted. While he was abroad reporting on a festival. Joseph North.'

'How did he die?'

'Well, there's no official story. I heard it was an accident. The CIA are good at inventing new concoctions, but aren't as good at working out what they'll do to people.' She put the bread on the table and began to slice it. 'It's all been hushed up, but I think someone should have told you about him. Don't you?'

'Does Mr Benstrup even know? Should I tell him?'

'That's up to you, but whatever you choose to say, you shouldn't mention me.' She sat down. 'Do you like your job, Ted?'

'Why do you ask?'

'You're not worried about what they're going to say, and you were going to leave without seeing the festival end. Don't you want to know who's going to win?' The vodka glugged loudly as she filled the small glasses.

'You told me who would win. And no, this isn't what I want to do.'

'What, then? What do you want, Ted?'

She was too eager, too keen to get that out of me. I smiled, and pointed at the vodka.

'Show me how to do this like a Russian.'

She blinked slowly and tilted her head. 'You drink the vodka and eat the bread. But first we toast.'

I clinked her glass.

'Rabochiye mira!'

We drank.

'What did I drink to?'

'Workers of the world, tovarishch.'

'Have I been signed up?'

'Do you want to be?'

CHAPTER 33

Did I want to be?

I didn't sleep well, but the sun was high when I eventually got up. Eva had left me a note next to a breakfast of bread, butter, jam and kefir.

'Please help yourself to tea or anything you would like. I will return after lunch.'

She had also left me the dog.

After breakfast, I changed into my shorts and took my towel down to the lake. I sat in the sun and watched the light bounce back from the water. I tried to remember when I had last been given time to just think. In Harwich I had worked in the holiday park in the summer and on the boats in the winter. In London I had weekends to myself, but this was a holiday. My first since I left school at fifteen, and I'd had to work through those anyway. Here I was free to think about what I wanted. If I knew what I wanted.

I heard a clatter of starlings behind me, and laid back on the sandy soil. The white-trunked birch trees were full of life and movement. It was probably true of the Stour as well, but when did I ever get the chance to soak that up? It was all cleaning chalets and throwing bloody, clammy fish into boxes, and cutting my hands on brutal bits of machinery. I inched into the water.

We'd been allowed to go to the Lido at the end of the season, and we had swum in the sea up the coast on late summer evenings. This water had neither chlorine nor the salty chill of the North Sea. It wasn't clear right to the bottom, but it was fresh and warm now that I'd adjusted. I floated on my back, my ears underwater, listening.

I knew Eva wanted something from me. I never knew I had anything to give, anything anyone wanted. It made me want to say yes without asking what it was.

Eva was back by the time I went inside. I had a bath while she got lunch ready. She appeared to have bought food from a café that she had wrapped in newspaper.

When I came down she was talking to the dog.

'She telling tales on me?' I asked.

'What tales could she tell?'

'She sat by the house while I was swimming but I was sure she had her eye on me.'

'How was the water?'

'Lovely, once you adjust. It's quite cold at first.'

'Every New Year's Eve people swim in the Moskva. We call them walruses. Maybe you'll work your way up to that. Shall we eat?'

We sat down and she uncovered the plate of blinis, sour cream and an open can of black caviar.

'Do you want to know where I have been?' she asked.

'Apart from shopping? I'd guess that you were looking in at the festival to see what people were saying.'

She nodded. 'How's your caviar?'

'Lovely. I had red before, but I prefer black.'

She was silent for a while. I knew she was waiting for me to ask, so I didn't.

Finally, she said, 'Do you know the names of those four Vietnamese women in the Natsional?'

'No. They don't speak English, so I never asked.'

'It's interesting. Ly, Phuong, Qui and Long. They mean Lion, Phoenix, Turtle and Dragon, representing the four sacred mythical creatures.'

'It that a political choice?'

'I don't think so. They were very informative. Between them they seem to know most things that are going on at the Rossiya. They are taking good care of Ursula, by the way. Christopher was harassing her and they got rid of him. He seemed to think that you were hiding in her room.'

'I would have thought he had information from inside the hotel.'

'I'm sure he does. He does like his hunches, whether they are correct or not.'

'Did you speak to Ursula yourself?'

'I didn't. I didn't speak to the Vietnamese women either, the translator of their films did.' She raised her eyebrow. 'I can't speak every language.'

'Any word on Alan?'

'Fully on the mend.'

'And what is Christopher doing?'

She smiled. 'Turning Moscow upside down, looking for you.'

'I have ruined his weekend.'

'Do you feel bad?'

'No. Alan getting sick was bad enough, but I still could have experienced the festival and made two good friends and written my report and taken away some great memories of Moscow.'

'I hope you can still take good memories with you.'

I swallowed and sat back. 'I can.'

'I have a typewriter here. You should use this time to write up your festival report.'

'Yes. Maybe.' I didn't want to think about work or Plumstead or my bedsit. It was all too small.

'I get the feeling, Ted, that things have changed for you. You don't want to be a film reviewer, you said that. So, how are you going to get what you really want?'

I looked towards the lake. 'I don't know.'

'Maybe we should think about that together.'

'Maybe. Eva, what's your view on translation? Is it about conveying the spirit of the film or the literal words?'

'It's more than that. It's about understanding the cultures of both the place the film was made and the place it is being seen and finding a way to communicate between both of those cultures. A literal translation often makes no narrative sense as the spirit of the film is lost, but then if one tries to convey the spirit of the film it becomes an entirely different film. To some extent a film or a book is always altered by the person who translates it. But finding a way for two peoples to communicate and understand each other, that's what I think translation is for.'

She was surprisingly passionate about this. Any doubts I had that she worked as a translator had been set to rest. That didn't mean that she *only* worked as one, though.

I sat in front of the grey Olympia Traveller De Luxe with its smell of fresh ink ribbon and oiled parts.

'Isn't this new?'

'Of course. They are made in Yugoslavia. I use it for my work in English, the translations. For Russian, I have a different one, obviously.'

I nodded. A review of the festival.

'Have you read a festival review before?'

'Yes. In the library.'

'Can you remember how they are structured?'

I looked at her. 'No.'

'Just write down what you want to say, and I'll get you some examples.' She paused in the doorway. 'I read your article on Mircea Drăgan. You write well. You can do this.'

Then she was gone, and I realised that no one had ever said that to me before, not since I left school anyway. She came back with her bag.

'I'm going into work to find some magazines for you. Shall I take the dog?'

I looked at her. 'She's fine. You can leave her here.'

She lifted a bag. 'I'm going to take your shoes. It's not to stop you leaving, it's just I think your soles need replacing.' She looked into the bag. 'I might get them polished too.'

'Thank you. That's very kind.'

Eva left and the dog lay down at my feet. I flicked through my film notes, and remembered what Eva had said about the winners: *Dersu Uzala* by Akira Kurosawa; *The Promised Land* by Andrzej Wajda; *We All Loved Each Other So Much* by Ettore Scola. I would never think of Kurosawa without thinking of Alan, and the thought of the Scola film still made me well up.

They had bonded, Alan and Ursula, over pressure from something happening to them. The phone calls, maybe, I wasn't sure, but it felt like more than that. If I gave in to Eva, wasn't that letting them down and saying there was nothing to fight against here? And Ingrid, poor, shaking Ingrid — what had scared her so much?

I rubbed my lips. The dog raised her head to look at me, and then sat up to look out of the window. I looked too, but I couldn't see what she could. Was there someone out there? Had Eva left someone to watch me while she was away? I pulled my shirt over my fingertips and rubbed at the typewriter where I thought I might have touched it, and then realised how ridiculous that was.

The dog was still looking. Something was there. I pushed the chair back and ran through the back door, right down to the water. Panting, I turned around. There was nothing. The dog was still inside, watching me now. I walked back to the table and then looked around the room. I went through the chest, but there was just a hairbrush and an empty notepad and pen. I listened out for any car pulling in, and then went to Eva's bedroom opposite mine. The door had never been open when I'd gone to my room or to the bathroom. I opened it quietly and looked in. It was the same as mine, bed by the window and chest of drawers. There was a pair of slippers by the bed and a dressing gown draped over the end. I wasn't going to look in her drawers and there was nowhere else to search.

I went back to the table.

'Don't tell Eva,' I said to the dog.

The dog lay back down and I started to type my review. I started with *Girl from Hanoi*, partly so I didn't have to think too much about Alan and Ursula and partly because I wanted to know whether Eva would say anything. If she didn't say I should cut it, then it might mean that she didn't have my interests at heart. And if she did, I would take it from there.

CHAPTER 34

I typed two pages, half a page on each film, and then I went for another swim. I had more to say than I realised and while swimming I thought of more I could add. When I got back to the house Eva was there. She gave me the old festival reviews to read while she made dinner, and I made notes on my pages about what to cut and what to add.

'Tell me about meeting Mircea Drăgan,' she shouted from the kitchen.

'I would, but I don't think I did meet him. I think it was someone pretending to be him.'

She looked around the doorway, her hands covered in flour. 'Why is that?'

I was struck by how much she reminded me of my mother, apron and floured hands.

'It was just a feeling I got. He seemed anxious to please Vasile, and I didn't think an award-winning director would be so deferential. He also didn't physically match the way Alan described the real one.'

'Did you say anything to this Vasile?'

'No. He would never have admitted it. He was on a big sales job for Romania and old Vlad. I couldn't trust anything he said.'

'Did you tell anyone that you didn't think it was the director?'

'No. If I'd told my boss he'd have been even angrier about the bill.'

'What was wrong with the bill?'

'Vasile had put all of his drinks on my bill, and ordered the most expensive wines in Romania.'

'You could tell them, the Secu. They would be interested. They'd probably refund your whole bill and Mr Benstrup would be happier.'

The Secu? That suggested a familiarity that made me uncomfortable. 'No. I won't be telling the Securitate anything.'

'Ah, they're full of great stories. The US diplomat, did you hear about his shoes?'

'No.'

'He sent them to be resoled and the Secu put a bug in the heel. Then one of them seduced his wife.'

I shuddered. She smiled and went back to the chicken breasts. I had eaten chicken Kiev in the restaurants, and I was glad she'd picked this to cook. I didn't feel guilty for not helping. I could sense that something was coming. The tension in her shoulders showed that she was working up to it as she talked it over with the dog. If I'd had just a few words of Russian I could have been spying on her. That was what she was, I was pretty certain. The only question was, what did she want from me?

She shouted through, 'I left your shoes at the bottom of the stairs, if you need them.'

'With or without a bug?'

'Oh, I didn't request a bug.'

Over dinner she told me more about Bucharest, the coal pollution and disasters which were kept secret from the population, the disappeared people. We'd finished eating before she finally spoke about anything of consequence to me.

'Do you want to know why I invited you to stay, Ted?'

I tensed my hands. This was it.

'I miss my son. I miss England. You remind me of both, and I am glad that we could spend this time together.'

Son and parent. No, that wasn't it.

'I think there's a way we can help each other. Everything that I would like to do for Alexander, I can do for you instead.'

I waited.

'I think, during your time in Moscow, you've come to a realisation. The people who say that they're on your side aren't always. As we both know him, let's take Christopher as an example. He will never have to worry about money. If he loses one job, he'll have three more to choose from. Family money, class connections, nothing will ever not work in his favour. You, on the other hand, are living week to week. If you have a debt it becomes an insurmountable burden. It never goes down. A lot of this is assumption, so correct me if I'm wrong, but I don't believe that your parents can give you any assistance.'

'No, that's true.'

'Now, think about how easy that was to say here, and how hard it would be in some places in England. The British behave as if poverty is a character failing. The country has to limit their electricity, but those with money get around that. If the rubbish isn't collected, they can pay someone to make that go away too. What I want to do, what we all want to do here, is to level that playing field for people like you, Ted.'

I wanted to believe her. I really wanted to. It all sounded right.

'You've had a bit of time here to think about things calmly.

You know that all you have had is breathing space and choices. The leisure that money and security can bring.'

'I'm not staying here. I don't want to live here. Life isn't as easy as you are making out, and people aren't as happy as you pretend.' I thought of the angry waitresses, the sullen hotel floor attendants, the way no one quite looked you in the eye.

'I'm not asking you to stay. Your flight is booked for Monday.'

I felt deflated. Only two more days. I nearly asked if I could stay longer, the festival went on until Wednesday, but of course I couldn't. This was her home. She had a job which wasn't looking after me.

'Do you mean you're offering me money?'

'Not exactly. I read through your review, and I've made some suggestions on it. Generally you have shown a good sense of which stories should and shouldn't be told. You didn't tell anyone about the fake director or the grasping Vasile.'

'I told you.'

'Because you knew you could trust me.'

Did I? 'What are you offering?'

'You've probably been looking at routes into journalism. There are two options for postgraduate diplomas in news-paper journalism. The London School of Journalism, or City University who will open their Department of Journalism next year.'

'Postgraduate courses? I don't have any qualifications.'

'We will be able to give you certificates noting your O Levels, A Levels and a degree in English Literature. Or politics. Whichever you prefer. It will be from one of the smaller, newer universities. You didn't get a first, I'm afraid.' She smiled.

I drank some wine.

'At twenty-two, you are just the right age for this to work.'

'But why? What is in it for you?'

'First, I can help you achieve what you deserve. Second, there are certain stories which we would have an opinion on which we could explain to you. You would never be under any obligation to follow our line, just be a friendly ear. We may be able to give you stories that are being suppressed. But you can be certain that our focus will always be on the working men and women of Britain.'

'But I wouldn't be told to write anything?'

'Never. Let's take a walk down to the lake.' The dog followed her, as always. 'Third is a personal reason.' She put a hand on my arm to stop me. 'One day I might want to return to Britain. I want to see my son and I want to see the England where I grew up. You could help me with that.'

We continued walking.

'They're going to suspect something like this, aren't they? Christopher and the rest of them.'

Eva shrugged. 'They can't prove anything, as long as you don't tell them, and we have all the contacts you might need. You don't have to say anything now. You have until Monday to decide. I won't say any more about it, but I will answer all your questions fully and honestly until that happens.'

We reached the water's edge and stood there silently. The water moved, the birds fluttered in and out of the trees and the clouds sped on.

'Is that your dog?'

'Yes.'

'Do you know a Lubya who is a cosmonaut?'

'I do.'

'Where did you buy the food we've eaten here?'

'In a special elite food shop. I got permission because you

are a guest in my country, and all guests are privileged here.'

There was a glint in her eye, as if she was waiting for me to ask a specific question.

'What did you think of the review?'

'A little stilted. You need more practice, and I would cut the section on *Girl from Hanoi*. It won't be published, so sometimes it's best to make these decisions ourselves. I am pleased you saw it and liked it. If you want more writing practice, you could write up your time in Romania.'

Ana, Marku and Vasile. And Ingrid.

'I'd be happy to read it over and give you some pointers. Translating goes hand in hand with editing.'

'Did you tell me the truth about what happened to Ana?'

'Yes, I was told she died. It's not something which I enjoyed telling you. Did Ingrid tell you something different?'

'No. You know what she said. You translated it.'

Eva smiled.

'Will Ingrid get in trouble?'

'Do you think she should?'

I spoke without thinking. 'No. I am not sure that she was responsible.'

'Because she's only a translator?' said Eva, but she had turned her face to the dog and I couldn't see her expression.

I thought of another question. 'Do I get a code name?'

She looked up and laughed. 'You have one already.'

I wasn't sure if that was a joke, but her smile was wide and I smiled too. That look in her eye faded and I suspected I had lost a chance to know what I needed to know. She took my arm and we walked along the water's edge, past other houses, through their trees and under their sky.

I felt she had answered all my questions truthfully, but still had the sense that I had forgotten to ask the big question.

'Have you read *Darkness at Noon*, Ted?'

'Some of it. I never got to the end.'

'Do you remember the bit about Cell 14? The worst, more dangerous place that anyone could be sent, the threat that made everyone break down and confess?'

'No.'

'It wasn't real. It didn't exist. It's the most important thing to take from that book. The threats people hold over us are most often imagined. We even create them for ourselves.' She sighed. 'I love England, and this place reminds me of it.'

I knew what she meant. It was calm and green, but only on the surface.

'There's a place on the east coast that faces west. That's where I think of, sometimes.'

It sounded familiar. 'I think I've been there.'

'Oh, I doubt that,' she said. Her hand tightened a little on my arm, then relaxed. 'Let's go inside.'

'FISHERMAN' BACKGROUND REPORTS:
FOR ADDITION TO WALKER FILE

Suzanne Prout – Plumstead Train Station

17.16 18th July

Early 20s, navy blue cord trousers, pale blue blouse and denim jacket over her arm. Small patent leather handbag.
I started a conversation with this subject on the platform at Plumstead Train Station as she travelled home after work. She tightened the hold on her handbag as I approached, and remained tense throughout. She refused to discuss where she worked or anyone she worked with. I took the same train. She alighted at Charlton and I stayed on until Maze Hill.

Dorothy Cunningham – 159 Griffin Road, Plumstead

14.27 20th July

Late 40s, answered the door wearing a stained housecoat, unbrushed curly, brown hair, bare legs and brown slippers.
Having failed to ascertain a time when the house was

unoccupied, I assumed the role of someone looking for a lodging house. She happily told me that Ted was a 'right weirdo, never here' and 'that Barry was a nosy bastard' (no surnames offered for either lodger). She wouldn't mind getting rid of either of them. She seemed to be attracted to me, so I played on this. I asked if I could have a look around Ted's room, as it sounded as if he might be leaving soon.

She said, 'It's the one at the front, my best room. But I don't have a spare key. I did, but I can't find it. I'll have to get a locksmith, and you know how much those buggers charge.'

We chatted for a while longer, and she invited me in for a cup of tea. I asked if I could call back later with some fish and chips, and she agreed.

I brought fish and chips and two bottles of wine and returned at 17.46. We heard Barry come in at 18.12 and the footsteps in his room were clear as he moved around. After we had eaten she drank most of the two bottles and had fallen asleep by 21.57. I conducted a search of her living room and bedroom, but there was nothing of interest. I wiped over all handles and hard surfaces which had been touched before putting on the gloves.

I waited until 00.04 and, as I hadn't heard any noise from Barry's room for over an hour, I went upstairs intending to pick the lock of the target's room. On reaching the landing, and having made no noise, I was surprised by Barry opening his door allowing the light from his room to illuminate the landing. From his expression I do not believe that it was a deliberate interception, but he had seen my face. I had to react quickly and left the residence at 00.11.

CHAPTER 35

I woke with the feeling that I'd forgotten something, then I remembered my conversation with Eva. Had I decided? No, I had until Monday. Nothing was fixed.

Wainwright's list of checks for a society kept popping into my head. Are the shops empty, transport links broken, the utilities not functioning, are there too many police evident? Do people look tired and hungry? To my lengthened list, I would now add, are people too scared to look you in the eye?

I heaved my legs over the side of the bed and put my head in my hands. If I accepted Eva's offer, I could train properly as a journalist, but someone in Russia would always hold something over me. Yet Eva seemed to care about getting me home, and that was enough for me to think about agreeing for now.

She was frying bacon in the kitchen. 'I've been thinking, Ted. You need a bit of practice, and we are always in need of articles for our newspapers. You have the review to take back for your magazine, but how about you write an article on visiting Moscow for us?'

I leaned against the cupboards. Had she seen the notes that I had made? 'Vasile asked me to write an article on the Romanian tourist industry.'

'Did you?'

'No.'

'Why not?'

'I didn't trust him. He told me, rather than asked me, and he expected me to do it for free.'

'I can pay you. I have contacts who would be interested. Let me think over what we can offer you, while we eat.' She got two plates out. 'Go outside. I'll bring it.'

I walked outside, the wind blowing my hair into my eyes. I never had got a haircut. One of the chairs had been blown to the far side of the garden. As I picked it up I wondered how a heavy wooden chair could be moved like that.

Eva brought the eggs and bacon out, went back in and returned with cups of coffee.

'You don't think it's too windy?' I said.

'I love the wind. Everything goes a little mad, unpredictable.'

She pointed at the dog who was alert, head up, sniffing at all the little signs coming her way. She jumped and skittered around the garden.

I ate the food quickly, but the wind had taken all the heat from the coffee by the time I drank it.

Eva watched the dog playing with the blowing leaves. 'Ted, do you owe money?'

'Why do you say that?'

'It seems to be a concern of yours, but not for yourself. I would guess that you have a debt you want to pay off.'

She was exactly right, but had she really got that from small hints? But then, no one could have told her.

'I do owe some money, yes.'

'And how much do you need?'

'I have £79 saved. I owe £140. I thought I'd be able to keep the price of food down, but it's difficult as there's nowhere to cook where I live.'

'And that £61 would leave you with a clean slate? Nothing owed, nothing saved?'

I nodded. 'I should never have taken the money. My mum had always said that when my dad sold the boat they'd put that money with their savings and visit her sister in Sydney. They haven't seen each other since 1957. Do you know how the prices have dropped in the last few years?'

'I heard.'

'Going to visit became a real possibility. My mum wanted to go over for spring there, which is autumn here. I persuaded her to lend me £140 without telling Dad and swore I'd get it back to her in six months. That would be August, next month, so they could fly in September. She'd paid the deposit and everything, but whatever I seem to do, the amount I've saved goes down. And I'm living in a terrible bedsit with a terrible landlady and a man who steals my post, and I'm rotten at my job but I can't leave it.'

Eva leaned forward, her hands clasped in front of her. 'What we can do, Ted, is pay you £20 for an article on visiting Moscow. I will translate it and it will be published in Russian. You can choose whether it goes under your transliterated name or a Russian version of Edward Walker.'

'What would the Russian version be?'

'How about Edik Khodunki?'

'All right. I'm glad that isn't actually my name.'

'And I can add £50 to that as a refund from the Natsional who would like to apologise for taking your food vouchers and making a terrible error with your booking payment.'

'They admitted it?'

'Of course.'

'You had all that food ready for me. I was starting to think you'd arranged it with the hotel.'

'Why would I do that? I didn't have to bring you here to

talk. I could have invited you to dinner again.' She looked amused. 'I may know cosmonauts, but I don't have any real power.'

I didn't believe that one bit. But still, to pay my parents back and have nearly ten pounds left over sounded good to me.

'The other option is that you go back to the Natsional, finish watching the films and pretend none of this happened. It is entirely up to you.'

'Can I think about that too?'

'Of course. Are you going swimming?'

'Yes, I think so. I'll just let my breakfast digest.'

'If you'd like to challenge me later, I can tell you that I am good at dominoes, draughts and chess. Perfect for a Sunday afternoon.'

'I think I'll choose draughts.'

There were leaves all over the grass, but the wind had calmed and the dog came to lie by Eva's feet. She murmured in Russian to her, and watched me light a cigarette from the corner of her eye.

'You are good at not asking questions, but as a journalist you will need to push a bit harder, you know.'

'I know. I don't have to write a review of you as well, do I?'

'Ha, no.' Eva stroked the dog with her foot. 'That wouldn't be a good idea. I am sure that you will find lots to write about because one thing you are is observant.'

I held my breath. She did know me. She knew much more about me than my parents, or anyone else had for years.

'You have noticed a lot of small things that others haven't. With a little training you will notice even more. I wanted to be a journalist for a while. I like spotting connections and unravelling coincidences. I want to know everything.'

'Me too. Now more than ever.'

'Good. I think you needed Moscow, Ted.'

She was right. I had needed all of this to shake myself from the pit I was in. I had nothing before, but now I had a shot at it all.

She went out for a few hours. I swam, I typed up my tourist view of Moscow, and had a bath. She was back and had made dinner by the time I came down and as we ate we played draughts. She beat me again and again.

'Another loss, another shot of vodka,' she said.

I downed my penalty and ate my bread. 'Maybe I'd have had a better chance with chess.'

'No one can beat me at chess,' she said. She sipped her wine, the vodka glass untouched. 'Have you decided what to do?'

'I wrote a piece on Moscow.'

'I noticed the typewriter had moved. I'm glad.'

'And I would like the chance to train as a journalist.'

'So, you'd like the certificates?'

I began to doubt myself again.

'Ted, I wouldn't have offered this if I didn't think you were capable. You write well and you are observant, and you care about what you observe. What you might have missed by not going to university is the discipline of applying yourself to research and deadlines, but these apply in your work life. The only thing that concerns me is that people like you get the same run at life as those who are less capable and, yet, more successful as a result of the efforts of other people. And their money, of course.'

'And I'll be free to write what I like?'

'Not necessarily. You will either be employed by a newspaper, who will want you to write certain things in a certain way, or you can be a freelance investigative journalist. The latter means that you will be free to write what you want.'

'Then, yes. Yes, please.'

She smiled, poured me another vodka and we toasted my decision.

'Eva, you said my name could be more than one thing. Can you tell me what variations of Nadia are?'

She stroked the dog before answering. 'There's Nadusha. That's quite common.'

'What about Nadenka?'

'Yes. That could be a form of Nadia, too. Is this about someone you know?'

'Maybe. It could be someone you know too.'

She held my gaze.

'Nadenka Benstrup. She's Nadia Osipova, isn't she?'

She leaned forward, lowering her voice. 'I wouldn't let her know that you've discovered this. We remain uncertain about what happened to Joseph North and why.'

'Why was I given the job? Did they only want me to act as a courier?'

'I wouldn't worry about any of that, Ted. However it started, you've proved to be much more interesting.'

She held her glass up for a toast and we drank together. I felt informed for the first time since I'd started the job. Everything was falling into place.

I was being collected in the morning. I had packed my bag and put the cash inside my book when Eva knocked on my door.

'Our last night, and I have one favour to ask of you, Ted. A personal favour. My son, Alexander, has a friend in England who passes messages to him for me. I don't want to put this in the post. You understand how it is. Could you hand deliver this for me?'

I took the envelope from Eva. 'Of course.'

'I have put it in an envelope within another. If you could write your parents' names and address on the outer envelope, no one will pay any attention when you go through customs.'

I turned the envelope in my hands. 'So, this is illegal?'

She moved her head from side to side. 'It is discouraged.' She held a finger to her lips and I nodded, but I didn't know why. She also handed me a folded piece of paper. 'Take this too. Write it inside a cigarette packet and leave the paper here. I still have connections in England, I told you that. This is the address of someone I know who runs a boarding house. When you leave your job, when you start studying, you'll need to be in the centre of things. It's near the British Museum and only £6 a week.'

I took the paper. 'That's less than I pay now.'

'I'm sure there will be plenty of options, but just in case you need it,' she said. 'Even if you gave up work and went on the dole until your course started, you would still have £5 for living expenses.'

The dole. That's not something I had ever considered. But why not?

She placed a hand on mine. 'And, Ted, when the time is ready for me to come home, back to England, will you help me?'

'If I can, I will.' I knew that I would. I might not trust her, but I owed Eva.

CHAPTER 36

After a last quick early swim and breakfast, a black car pulled into the driveway beside the house. I picked up my suitcase and followed Eva out to the car. Her dog sat and waited by the back door. Eva said something to the driver, and he pulled out of the driveway. I caught a glimpse of his face in the rear-view mirror. He adjusted it.

My heart began to beat faster. His hair, the grey jacket. This was the man who had been following me. My eyes dropped to my newly polished shoes.

Eva was talking and I tried to follow what she was saying. Maybe this is what I should have asked that afternoon when she was being honest – have you been following me? But maybe she had already been honest about it. She'd said that I already had a codename, and I could have been wrong to take it as a joke.

'Are you anxious about seeing Christopher?' she said, a hand on mine.

'I think I'm just a bit car sick.'

'Yes, you don't look well.'

She put the back of her hand to my forehead and spoke to the driver. He opened the glovebox and I put my hand on the door handle thinking, that must be where he keeps his gun.

When he slowed down, should I try to leap from the car?

He passed back a small, glass bottle and Eva tipped out two tablets and showed me the label.

'Aspirin.'

I couldn't read it. It was in Russian. She emptied them into my hand. I touched their chalky surface and imagined how they would stick in my dry throat.

'I don't think I can take these without water.'

Eva spoke to the driver again. For the first time, he spoke back. I could only catch one word, repeated: 'polkovnik'. His hand went back to the glove box, and the car swerved to the left. Eva barked something, and he straightened up. In his hand was a pocket-sized bottle of vodka. Eva said something that sounded like a rebuke, and he put it away and shrugged his shoulders. 'Polkovnik.'

'We'll get you some water,' Eva said.

I tried to forget it was Eva who had been following me, or someone close to her. I kept my gaze fixed on the passing trees, then blocks of flats, big mansion buildings, parks, statues, and there was the river. We passed the British embassy, crossed the bridge, and the driver pulled up outside the Rossiya. Eva spoke to him again and he got out of the car. I could see Christopher waiting outside another large, black car. He took a couple of steps towards us, and then waited, watching the driver at the kiosk outside the hotel.

'Just one moment,' said Eva, her hand on my arm.

The man in the grey jacket came back from the kiosk with a bottle of clear liquid. He opened Eva's door, handed it to her and she handed it to me.

'For the aspirin.' She untwisted the cap.

I unclenched my hand. The sweat had created a white mush in the centre of my palm. I picked off what I could and glugged the sugary drink. I had expected water.

'All right,' she said. 'We'll be in touch, Ted. You probably won't want to tell anyone about what we talked about. It will be easier for you that way.' She patted my hand one last time and gestured for me to leave the car.

'Goodbye,' I said. I got out, the driver handed me my suitcase while avoiding my gaze, and I walked over to Christopher. Behind him, I saw Ursula inside the hotel, one hand up to the glass. I lifted a hand to her, and let it fall.

'Ted,' Christopher said, 'good to have you back with us. I'm afraid that your flight leaves soon, so we'll have to talk on the way to the airport.' He took my suitcase, placed it in the boot of his car, and got in the back with me.

I looked around for Eva, but her car had gone. I couldn't see Ursula either. I put my head back on the head rest, closed my eyes and exhaled.

'Am I really leaving?'

'Yes, but we need to have a bit of a debrief first. Can you tell me what has happened since Friday?'

'The hotel gave me a massive bill because they said I hadn't paid. I got arrested and Eva rescued me.'

'Why didn't you call me straight away?'

I opened my eyes and looked at him. 'The hotel said they'd call you.'

He shifted and looked towards his driver.

'We've had a few issues, but you still should have contacted me the second there was a problem at the hotel. I must say, you don't look well, Ted. Have you been given anything odd to eat or drink?'

'I just feel a bit sick today. Car sick. Nerves. I don't know.'

'So, what happened after Eva collected you?'

'She took me to a dacha in Saltykovskaya, next to a lake. I swam, she cooked, we talked. It was good. I had a nice time.'

Christopher sighed. There was something about his

expression, that slight sneer, that made me lift my head and sit up a bit straighter.

'Right. That all sounds very pleasant. Did Mrs Mann offer you anything else? Assistance or information or something like that?'

'We talked for hours. I suppose that could count as offering information.'

He flashed a fake smile. I was annoying him. I was glad.

'Did she give you anything to take back to Britain?'

'Like what?'

'I don't know. Anything.'

I pretended to think. 'No. No, I can't think of anything apart from some nice memories. Eva fixed my shoes, too.'

'You can't think — Ted, this is a serious matter. From the perspective of the embassy, you have been abducted by a Russian and kept away from your rights as a British citizen. This is not the time to conceal information, no matter how much you dislike me personally.'

'I don't dislike you, Christopher.' I smiled at him.

'That's very reassuring.'

So posh, so assured, so confident. I looked at his fitted suit, his polished shoes and thought, I'm really not on the same side as you. I never will be.

'Could you tell me what you believe Mrs Mann's interest in you was?'

'I think that Eva is just interested in people. She saw that I needed help and she helped.'

'I hear that she was there at the exact moment of your arrest. You didn't find this suspicious?'

'Not really. She lives in Moscow, and she works in Moscow.'

'Ted, I really feel that you should think about whether coincidences like that are truly coincidental or whether they could be stage managed to provide a sense of a link between you and this stranger.'

'Coincidences are very strange,' I said. 'There is this man I keep bumping into which is very suspicious.'

Christopher looked concerned. 'What is his name?'

'Mr Attridge.'

Christopher turned away from me and looked out of his window. He clenched his hands. I smiled, and then saw the driver watching me in the rear-view mirror. I was feeling better now.

Christopher said nothing else until we pulled up outside Sheremetyevo. The driver got out of the car, and took my suitcase from the boot.

'If you remember anything on the aeroplane, it would be very useful if you could tell Mr Attridge when you arrive at Heathrow. Our relationship is clearly too damaged for you to trust me, but there are other people you can speak to.'

'I'll bear that in mind.'

He took a plane ticket from his inner pocket and a letter. 'You have your passport, customs declaration and exit visa, I understand. This letter is from Mrs Koskinen. Ursula. I was going to escort you in, but my driver can do that, if you like.'

'I'll be fine. Thank you.' I took the letter and put it in my inside pocket, next to Eva's. 'You should have been the one to have told me about Joseph North.'

'It wasn't for me to say, I'm afraid.'

The driver opened my door.

'Be careful, Mr Walker,' Christopher said. 'We really do have your best interests at heart.'

I closed the door and took my suitcase from the driver. Like the other, he avoided eye contact.

I walked into the terminal, presented my papers and went through to departures. I found a buffet, ordered a coffee and sat down for a cigarette. I watched the people around me, how they talked to each other, any slight physical contact. When I had finished I walked around, and tried to let my thoughts settle. One thought wouldn't.

I stopped a tired-looking woman in uniform.

'Excuse me. What is polkovnik?' I asked.

She looked around and answered quietly, 'A Polkovnik would be a Colonel. Is there something I can help you with? Are you looking for someone in particular?'

'No, thank you.'

She nodded and walked away. I strolled across to the plate windows and looked at the planes. Well, I couldn't pretend that I didn't already suspect that Eva was KGB.

I wandered away to find the duty free. I had nine quid, after all.

KGB Second Chief Directorate
2nd Department: British Commonwealth

'FISHERMAN' FINAL REPORT:
FOR ADDITION TO WALKER FILE

22nd July 1975

As previously discussed, I have expressed the belief that recent changes in our approach to targets should be influenced by a growing understanding of the relationship between the British 'working' classes and 'upper' classes (inadequate, but generally accepted terms often used within Britain to distinguish those with and without social privileges).

Our work in the preceding years has not taken into account the great shift in social awareness in Britain. Trade Unions are having an impact in their attempt to gain better conditions for physically demanding work within the population. The working classes are pushing for change, and we need to help them achieve a similar parity to that which we have now gained. The tram driver is no lesser a citizen than the politician, and never should be.

In earlier times targets such as 'Mädchen' and 'Söhnchen' had the potential to succeed politically within the British political system, the former because he had potential and the latter because the British have a baffling yet ongoing tolerance for objectionable rich men. 'Otto' was indeed successful in recruiting many young men from privileged backgrounds to serve the Soviets. But what of the time and money invested and wasted on all those other public school boys who achieved nothing? Who, recruited by 'Klaus', 'Hans' or 'Uwe', achieved anything but a drinking habit and a sexually transmitted disease? The exposure of the 'Cambridge ring' (as the British call them) has meant that the upper classes closed rank and more diligently patrolled their well-off young.

Acquiring more information directly from Britain suggests we need changes to our approach. The workers may not have access to sensitive information in the traditional way, but they do have access to more forms of information and new ways of getting it. Knowledge is harder to restrict to those born in a particular class, and technological advances will make this even more egalitarian. Our problem has always been how to find individuals to target? The benefit of the university referral method is that politics can be openly discussed, and the referrer soon falls out of contact with the referee. It is difficult to find working class people on a similar cusp of change. But it is possible.

This brings us to the latest target, Walker (codename 'Fisherman'). Out of interest, we attempted the same dangle as used previously with the story booklet. This was immediately rejected. It may have worked previously not because the target, Hughes (codename 'Wolfcub'), was more thoughtful, but trained and experienced in analysis, owing to her upbringing. She was also easy to remove from the Moscow situation owing to her social position and obligations. Given a little longer, more could have been achieved. This situation remains unresolved. [See update on 'Wolfcub'.]

 It should be noted that with Walker, the traditional provocation with an attractive female 'Swallow' in Bucharest was not effective, and we had no reason to attempt a provocation with a male 'Raven'. We have noticed this in other cases as well, but not all. The declining success of this technique cannot be due to Britain becoming more prudish, so it may be that the warnings giving by the British service are more effective. At least they still work on the Americans.

Walker required a much fuller understanding of his personality and background once it became clear that he was indeed committed to following up the idea seeded in Bucharest (see Internal Service reports). We then deployed 'Kingfisher' to explore his childhood and present situation (notes attached). An examination of the bin in the target's hotel room proved very useful, signalling a great dislike for the embassy employee detailed to his care. (Additionally, using an operative who does not instantly register in interactions as 'Russian' has been very useful. To date, the British have proven very reluctant to extend their warnings to interacting with other 'Britons' or those who might appear/sound British, although this could now change.)

Surveillance audio tapes from within the Natsional, Metropol and Rossiya cafés and restaurants, led to interesting information which added to our picture of Walker (transcripts in file). The discussion revealing his dissatisfaction with his job and living conditions raised further movements on our part, which worked well with his desire to break into journalism. We were also able to make an early assessment of the relationships he formed with Alan Sullivan and Ursula Koskinen, and early intervention disrupted this with great success. As was reported, the British had made use of Sullivan in other roles and his constant appearance at Walker's side made things very difficult. Koskinen was less of a threat as she was already anxious about spending time in Moscow and relies on support. This can be followed up (see transcript for details regarding her family), but it is unlikely to be fruitful. However, as we know, relationships are currency. The transcripts provided allowed us to establish where Walker's greatest self-doubt could be exploited in order to encourage his reliance on other sources.

With the background and audio information, as well as the earlier reports from Bucharest, we were able to approach Walker in a specific way which addresses our concerns about the changes within British journalism. The final elements of this were put into place at the house of — Nosovikhinskoye Shosse, Balashikha, Moscow Oblast (see transcripts). Walker had debts which had strained his relationship with his parents, no close friends, an unsatisfying job and no opportunities to improve his position, all due to the financial position of his parents and his class. By offering him a way forward (a satisfying job, solvency and a chance to become the person he desired to be) he will have a loyalty to those who put arrangements in place which allow him to move forwards.

We did not directly discuss politics, but the conversation makes clear that the working classes are already politicised in every aspect of British society. We just need to get better at seeing where they are ready for change. This current target also makes a habit of reading all newspapers and, as a result, has a strong interest in the way they are written as well as a strong distrust of what they say. It can be assumed that he is attracted to the role of 'journalist' as a way of exercising power over others, for being 'heard' instead of forgotten.

In the past there has been a sweetness to turning the cream of British society against their makers. This form of 'traitor' has particular resonance in the newspapers, although we know that the treachery goes much deeper and much higher than them. 'Fisherman', as a journalist, will be a perfect tool to spread information, if and when we choose to employ him in that capacity. It may be that his malleability suggests other uses, with the potential for moves into political or foreign reporting. He has no reason to feel loyal to his country which failed to educate him properly. At the same time, his frustration at having to wait to be recognised as a fully functioning adult in the corrupt British system could also mean that he should be receptive to stories which reflect this. His country failed him, but we must protect him and ensure his reputation remains intact.

Separately, although the information gained was useful, we must alert Bucharest to get rid of 'Starling' in whichever way they see fit. Now that 'Ingrid' has revealed where the afflicted Romanian woman, Ana Boldea, is being held, arrangements need to be made to access and move her to another institution.

Nadia Osipova ('Nadenka') was making some complaints about the loss of her asset. After being assured that her husband, Benstrup, would receive a letter telling him where to look in his house to find the cause of his illness, she has agreed to cut links with Walker and will hire another 'critic' willing to travel. Arrangements have been made to add financial incentives to her co-operation.

Finally, the incident in London last night will need further investigation. For now, 'Kingfisher' is detained.

ALL WALKER FILES TO BE COPIED TO <u>First Chief Directorate: Information Service (Special Service I)</u> AND CROSS REFERENCED WITH REYNOLDS.

END

KGB First Chief Directorate
Information Service (Special Service I).

'WOLFCUB' INTERIM REPORT: FOR ADDITION TO REYNOLDS FILE

Martha Reynolds [married name Hughes] update 5 August
1975
For cross-referencing with Walker file

The actions of 'Wolfcub' after her return to Britain were
not what we anticipated. Having applied to the University
of Essex, an ineffective approach served not only to get a
refusal but also resulted in her returning to familiar terri-
tory. She changed her mind about studying Politics, and
returned to Classics, picking up her degree in the second
year at Birkbeck. She is expected to graduate in July 1976.

'Wolfcub' does not respond well to changes within
friendships. If she is to be approached again, it must be
by someone whom she already knows or believes to be
working for us.

She has maintained contacts with friends and family
working within the area of state secrets, but there is no
reason to expect that she would willingly provide information on them in the future. It was discovered that enquiries
had been made in relation to her future after graduation
in the sphere of government, specifically working as a
government researcher. She has been heard to refer to

this as being a 'glorified secretary', so we await her career decisions to see whether they may be useful.

We know that 'Wolfcub' maintains an interest in the USSR due to the books she borrows from the public library, which are unconnected to the degree-related books she borrows from the university library. She has not sought out any dissidents or disinformation. She remains interested in people as individuals, and resists stereotypes. She also maintains an insubordinate streak (two warnings from the Vice-chancellor's office), and shows no sign of behaving in a manner appropriate to her class and upbringing.

LONDON

CHAPTER 37

I had time on the aeroplane to consider exactly what I had agreed to. I would get the certificates I needed to achieve what I wanted. I would be given information. I would, essentially, be gifted my future and, in return, I would have an obligation to consider information that I was given. Still undecided on whether I was actually going to do this, I was hard pressed to find a downside as I sipped my wine and looked out over the clouds. They couldn't make me write anything that I didn't think there was a market for. Their material would be biased, I was sure, but I'd read enough versions of the same newspaper story to know that there was no truth, only interpretations of it.

The only thing left was the whole idea of being loyal to my country. There was no round platform in Trafalgar Square for the execution of traitors, because the establishment wouldn't want to remind people that they didn't have to agree with the way things were run. They relied on people being passive, and I could be loyal, struggle on and let down my parents, but I needed something to change. If I could help Eva reunite with her son, I would. She'd looked after me and given me the space to make decisions. I knew there would be strings.

There was just the man in the grey jacket who had clearly

been following me for her. Maybe that was the question I should have asked her, but I didn't think so.

The pilot announced that we had left Soviet airspace and there was a cheer from the back of the aeroplane. I put my head back and tried to sleep. The letter that Christopher had given me from Ursula remained unopened. The information from Ingrid on the lost sister stayed in my film notes, but I had no idea how I would get the information to Marku, somewhere in Bucharest. If I phoned Mihaela she would be investigated for having links with Westerners. I didn't trust Vasile, or any of them, to tell Marku. It felt unfair that I had found out the facts when it wasn't possible to tell the man who needed to know.

But maybe this was my story. If I could find it all out and get it published in a newspaper, wouldn't Marku find out too?

A grim-faced Mr Attridge was waiting for me at arrivals, arms crossed.

'Mr Walker.' He uncrossed his arms and put his hands in his pockets. 'I'll drive you into London, if that suits.'

'That suits me fine.'

We walked outside and a police officer, standing by a black Triumph, moved away.

'Is he making sure you don't get towed?' I asked.

Mr Attridge didn't answer. We got in and he said nothing until we were on the A4.

'Can you tell me what happened in Moscow, Mr Walker?'

'You know what happened.'

'I'd like to hear it from you.'

'I went to the film festival for a few days, spoke to a few people, and was arrested for non-payment of a bill which had been paid, and spent a few days at a dacha.'

'Do you know that foreigners are not allowed to stay at the houses or apartments of any Russians?'

'No, but she's not Russian, is she?'

'She's not British. Didn't I tell you that anyone who approached you would want something from you?'

'You said to watch out for Russians. What is she, then?'

He sighed. 'What is it that you think she wanted?'

'Company. She seemed lonely.'

Mr Attridge stared at me, and then braked hard before he nearly hit the car in front which was slowing down. We had already reached the turning for the South Circular.

Richmond, Putney, Clapham.

'What did she offer you, Mr Walker?'

'Lamb kebabs. Chicken Kiev.'

'This is not a joke. This is the security of the country.'

'Vodka.'

'Mr Walker, please.'

'You know what I brought back. I was searched. They went through everything.'

'We don't know what you brought back in your head,' he muttered.

Or my pockets, I thought. My book was not touched, or my inside pocket, just the luggage.

Dulwich, Forest Hill, Lee.

'Last chance, Mr Walker.'

'There's nothing to say. I didn't trust the embassy to help me, and they didn't even turn up. I had to trust her.'

He pulled up suddenly opposite the Royal Artillery Barracks. A car behind beeped and drove around. Cars using their horns. It seemed quite alien.

He tapped on the wheel and looked straight ahead. 'I take it that you know how to get home from here.'

'I do.' I opened the door.

'We will have no choice but to find out what happened through other means, Mr Walker. It won't be easy for you.'

'Is that a threat?'

'We have just driven past HMP Wandsworth and HMP Brixton. I could have left you outside there, saved us all some time, but we're good at the long game. If you change your mind, you have my number.'

I slammed the door closed. His number was floating around Bucharest. I lit a cigarette and crossed the road. Nightingale Road, and then Plumstead Common Road and I'd nearly be home. I looked behind me at the open fields and smiled. It wasn't so bad here. It was nice to be back.

When I saw the policeman standing outside my house, my stomach dropped. Mr Attridge had meant it. I was going to be persecuted before I was prosecuted. I stopped, but he'd seen me, so I continued up to the door.

'Can I help you, sir?'

'I live here.'

He took a small notebook from his pocket. 'Name, please.'

'Ted Walker. I'm in C, the room at the front.'

He wrote something down. 'Wait here, please.'

This was something else. I put my suitcase down and waited for him to return, but it was a different man, this one in a suit.

'Mr Walker?'

'Yes.'

'Detective Inspector Haverly. Come inside, please.'

I followed him into the hallway and the first officer went back out to the doorstep.

'What's going on?'

'Can I ask you where you were last night?'

'Moscow.'

'Moscow? What were you doing there?'

'I was covering a film festival. Do you want to see my aeroplane ticket? I just flew in this morning.'

'Please.'

I took my ticket and passport from my inside pocket and passed them to him.

'Thank you, sir.'

'Can I know what happened now?'

'I'm sorry to tell you that your fellow lodger, Mr Shepworth, was murdered last night.'

'Who is Mr Shepworth? Do you mean Barry?'

'Yes, Barry Shepworth. I take it that you weren't close.'

'No, not at all.' Barry had been murdered. 'Is Mrs Cunningham all right?'

'She is helping with our enquiries.'

'You don't think she killed him?' I laughed, and then made my face serious again.

'Your landlady had a friend staying but she is proving reluctant to give us any details about him. Can't give us a surname, or much to go on. You don't happen to know anything about him, do you? A,' he checked his notes, 'Vic, or Victor?'

'No. I didn't know she had any friends at all. I never saw anyone.'

If I'd been here, I'd be top suspect. If I'd been here, it might have been me who was killed. I leaned back against the banisters. DI Haverly looked at me sympathetically.

'I know it's a lot to take in, sir. We'd be very grateful if you could come to the station and give us a statement. Just anything you know about Mr Shepworth and Mrs Cunningham.'

'Of course.'

'And I'm afraid that you'll have to find somewhere to stay for a couple of days until we finish up here.'

'Could I get some things from my room first?'

'Yes, of course. I'll escort you up, but please don't touch anything on the landing.'

I carried my suitcase up the stairs. Now I could smell the iron stickiness of blood.

'You will have to be careful where you put your feet.'

I was very careful. It must have been a knife, there was so much blood.

DI Haverly held my suitcase as I unlocked my door, and handed it back to me as he waited outside.

I emptied the last of my clothes into my suitcase, a couple of books and the money from the bottom drawer. An overcoat over my arm, and that was it. I didn't need to come back, if I chose not to.

I went to lock the door and Haverly coughed.

'If you wouldn't mind, sir, we'd like you to keep that door open. Just so we can check that the intruder didn't come through here.'

I gave him the key and carefully followed him back outside.

'I'll arrange for someone to collect you for that statement, then you'll be free to go.'

Go where, though?

HARWICH

CHAPTER 38

It was late Monday evening by the time that I got to Harwich Town station. I walked down to the quay, thinking of all the times as a boy that I'd dreamed of being on one of the ferries that sailed out of the Stour to more exciting lands. The Mayflower which sailed to America had been built here, but now it was mostly journeys to Holland, Denmark, Germany or Sweden. That had seemed exotic enough back then. Now I looked across the water to Shotley and took a deep breath. Time to go home.

'Teddy!'

Mum was in her dressing gown, her rollers in, having her last cup of tea before bed.

'Why didn't you tell us you were coming? You're not in trouble, are you? Don't you have work to go to? Dad has to get up for the tide, so I won't wake him. He'll get such a surprise tomorrow. Let me put the kettle on.'

As she clattered around the kitchen I took the money from my case and the book, and laid everything I owed her on the table.

She brought in my tea, and put it next to the money. 'I'm just making you some toast. You can have beans on it, if you like.'

'Just toast is fine, Mum.'

Then she saw the notes. 'Oh Teddy, you did it.' She threw her arms around me. Just before she turned back to the kitchen I saw she was crying. She took her time over the toast.

I'd done it. It was worth it.

I told her about my work, how I had a couple of days off, and she beamed. Then I said I'd have to move, my landlady had got in a bit of trouble, and she berated this woman she'd never met. She got out the Qantas brochures from the travel agent and we looked at the pictures together. Then she slipped some money from the pocket of her house coat, hanging on the back of the chair.

'I want you to have this, Teddy. I did a thing, answered lots of questions, and they gave me £5. I couldn't believe it. I didn't tell your father, but I saved it for you.'

'Spend it on yourself, Mum.'

'I'd rather you took it.' She looked at the pile of notes again. 'I can't believe it. I'm going to see my sister. I'm going to Australia.' Her eyes filled with tears again.

I wondered whether she had ever told my Dad that they would lose the deposit and have to keep saving up.

Back in my old room with the window open I could hear men leaving the pub at the end of the road. I settled down in my bed as I had done only months earlier. It wasn't a muted dark, like it had been by the lake; the orange streetlights strained through the curtains. I tried to get my head around waking outside Moscow and ending up here. And knowing that Barry was dead.

I couldn't work out why Barry would be killed. Could he have done something to the man staying with Mrs Cunningham? He was annoying, but not to the point of murder. Then again, I wouldn't miss Barry one bit.

When it got to late morning, I waited on the quay for Dad's boat to come in, just as I had done when I was too young to go with him. He saw me in the distance and held his hand up. I waved. He was shouting something, but I couldn't hear what it was until he got closer.

'Go get some overalls on, you can help us unload!'

'No thanks!'

'Oh, you're in your good London clothes, are you?'

'That's right!'

He said something to the other two men on the boat and they laughed. I watched them bring the boat right up and tip the fish into plastic boxes ready on the quay. I smoked while I watched them work. Occasionally my dad looked around to see if I was still there, gave a dramatic shake of the head and a big grin.

When he'd finished he stripped off his overalls, and came over. Gulls screamed in the air around our heads.

'No more fish for me,' I said.

'Ah, well, you don't know what you're missing. It was a beautiful morning out there on the water. I suppose you're only just up?'

'With the racket those gulls make?'

He laughed. 'Fancy a pint before we go back?'

I followed him up Eastgate Street. He ordered two pints of bitter, and we sat down next to the window.

'When are you off, lad?'

'Tomorrow morning, I think.' Even as I said it, I wasn't sure that was true. I was feeling anxious about going back. I didn't want to tell him about Barry, though. He'd only worry. 'I have to sort out somewhere new to live.'

'A flying visit.'

I lit a cigarette.

'Give me one, Teddy, and don't tell your mother.'

I gave him the last one and put the empty cigarette packet in my pocket.

'How are you finding that there London?'

'I like it. I like working in an office.' I wasn't sure how much to say. The longer I spent away from Moscow, the more unlikely everything seemed. 'I might see if I can train as a journalist, get a better job.'

'You always did like to be indoors. I never understood it.'

'We can't all be out on the sea. There'd be no fish left.'

'There's not many left as it is.' His head sank.

I'd started him off again.

He took a deep breath and put a brave face on. 'But we'll be off to the other side of the world, and your mother says I have to retire, sign up for my pension and get a bus pass.'

'There's nothing wrong with that. Think of all the things you can do with your time.'

He looked at me and I knew, there was nothing he liked better than going out on the boats.

'You'll have to get yourself a little rod and stool,' I said, 'go up the estuary and catch some different fish. Or get a pair of binoculars and look for sea monsters from the quay.'

'Maybe. Maybe.' He finished his pint. 'Another? Seeing as you're off again.'

'Go on, then,' I said, and downed the rest of my pint. It would be so easy to stay. The house would be empty while they were away, and maybe there was more work in Harwich now. It was easy being here in lots of ways. Easier than anything in London. Then I heard him talking about me to Eric behind the bar and I realised that, for the first time ever, he was proud of me. I hadn't crawled back when things got hard, I hadn't messed it up. I was doing all right and he could see that. I had to go back and prove it was true.

It was Tuesday night that it all hit me. I sat on my small bed with the orange light seeping through the curtains and realised, Barry's death wasn't a coincidence. What had happened to him had to be connected to what I'd agreed in that small house surrounded by birds outside Moscow, even if I couldn't understand how. If I did this, if I worked with the Russians, I'd belong to them. There would never be any getting away from it.

I slid onto the floor and wrapped my blankets around me. I lit a cigarette. What happened if I pretended none of it had happened? They already had me. I had smuggled a ring and I had left the festival to spend time with a KGB Colonel. I groaned as I realised that Alan's illness might also be my fault. Not directly, but still. And if I stayed here, then what? Signing on, maybe night school. Would that ever be enough to leave again?

I stubbed out my cigarette and lit another. If I didn't go back, my parents, who had looked at me with such pride, would never feel that way again. If I went back they could go off to Australia and be proud of me, their son who had made it in London. I couldn't tell them that I had failed. I couldn't tell them I messed up and the Russians paid off my debt. I'd taken the money. Worse, I'd given it to my parents and made them complicit.

I would live with my decisions. I had to.

I slipped back into the routine of home, and Mum had been so pleased to have me there while Dad was working that it was easy to put it off going back. It was Wednesday evening by the time I got the empty cigarette packet out of my pocket.

The phone box still smelt like a toilet, but some of the graffiti was new. My first attempt at dialling was a wrong number. On the second attempt I got through.

'Hello. I was given this number by a friend who said you might have a spare room to let.'

The voice was high and clipped. 'Yes, I do. Would you like to come and see it tomorrow, around noon?'

She gave me the address and I wrote it inside the cigarette packet, next to the number. Montague Street. The closest tube was Russell Square, but there wasn't much in it with Holborn, she said. I counted my money in my head. After train fares, I had five pounds left over from Moscow, and now I also had the five pounds that Mum had given me. I hoped that I wouldn't need more than a week's money. I should have asked, but if I had to wait until I got paid on Friday, I'd work something out.

I walked back down the small streets I knew so well and realised that, in Moscow, this was the last day of the festival. I had been due on the aeroplane tonight, and back at work tomorrow morning. The thought of work made me anxious even though I had my review all typed out. I didn't know for sure who had won what, for a start. Then there was the idea that Christopher, somehow, could tell Mr Benstrup that I had left early. I did regret not asking Alan what magazine he worked for, so I could get a message to him and check he was all right. On the other hand, I didn't want to have to lie to Alan, and it would only make me think of Ursula.

I would have to ring the office first thing and let them know I was looking for somewhere to live. Hopefully they would have heard about the murder and not ask too many questions. And living in central London would be fun, whether I got on the course or not. I wouldn't see Julia again, but she'd never even notice I was gone.

The sun was setting, the gulls were crying, my mother was cooking, my dad would be dozing in the armchair, and I had somewhere else to live. Everything was how it should be for the first time since I'd left school.

All was right with the world, and it couldn't have been more wrong. It was a strange feeling.

LONDON

CHAPTER 39

Changing onto the Central Line at Liverpool Street, I was still thinking about the odd tone to Suzanne's voice when I phoned to tell her I'd be in the next day. I was soon distracted by the striking difference between people in London and Moscow. Had London become angrier while I was away? Men scowled at each other and teenagers smoked with quiet fury on the platform seats.

I sat very still on the tube, suitcase on my lap, worried about infuriating someone by accident, and was pleased to get off at Holborn. I hesitated in the entrance, studying the map on the wall to work out which of the two exits was mine. I checked again. Yes, Montague Street ran right down the side of the British Museum.

I headed out onto Southampton Row. People walked fast, even though it was well after nine, and I saw no children at all until I turned left and passed Bloomsbury Square Garden. Smartly dressed women in black walked prams along the paths. Were they nannies? This was a very different kind of London. Right onto Montague Street. I found number 49 and knocked.

A short woman with cropped grey hair opened the door with some force.

'Mr Walker?' I recognised her voice from the phone call.

'Hello, yes.'

She stood aside, and gestured for me to walk past her.

'I am Mrs Constance Macfarlane, widow. If you would like to go straight up the stairs. Third floor.'

I walked ahead of her. The stair carpets were a dark grey, but worn to cream threads in the middle of the tread. The brown walls were barely lit by the small lightbulbs hanging in the stairwell, and there were so many doors leading off the landings, that I felt disorientated by the time I reached the top floor.

She busied herself with a keyring and opened a door. Again, brown was dominant. Brown coverlet on the single bed, dark brown wardrobe and desk, an even darker brown wallpaper, but relieved by a high ceiling and cast-iron fireplace, both painted white. She walked over to the window and pulled the curtains open which introduced a little light.

'I have space for five guests on each of the top three floors. The ground floor contains my private rooms, but also contains the breakfast room. Breakfast is included every morning between seven and eight thirty.'

She opened a door and what I had thought was a cupboard was a small bathroom.

'Everyone has their own facilities.' She closed the door. 'My guests come here for privacy. It's very important to them. We will not see much of each other, Mr Walker. You can leave the rent in a box by the front door every Friday. The British Museum is opposite the front of the house.' She beckoned me to the window. 'These are private gardens.'

I looked out over an oblong of trees and grass.

'Does it suit?'

'Very much. I do need to ask how much you might need for a deposit.'

'All my guests are personal recommendations. That won't be necessary.'

'Do you know—'

'As I said, privacy is very, very important.'

I nodded. 'Which day could I move in?'

She looked at my suitcase which I was still lugging about everywhere. 'You look as if you've come prepared.'

'There was an incident at my previous lodgings. A man was killed and the police asked me to stay away for a couple of days. I am hoping that I can get back in today. I'm paid up until tomorrow.'

'Do you have the £6 you need for next week, should you move in here?'

'Yes, I do.'

'Then, as it's Friday tomorrow, I think you should settle in now, Mr Walker. Pay your rent every Friday and we won't have any issues. I would ask, though, that you don't offer the police your new address. If you could give the address of a friend, that would be preferable. Only if they ask, of course.' She smiled. 'Taxes. You know how it is.'

'All right. Thank you.'

'I'll leave you to get settled in.' She left the keys on the bedside table and pointed at a low cupboard under the window. 'You'll find a kettle and other items in there. No milk, I'm afraid, but I'm sure you are used to black tea by now.' She pointed at the desk. 'There is a letter for you that you might find interesting.'

She left, closing the door behind her.

I put my suitcase down and sat on the bed. There was something about her that reminded me of Eva.

Then again, central London. I bounced a little on the bed. New mattress. Free breakfast every day. I would have to pay to get to work, but no longer had to save for anything. This would work.

I opened the letter on the desk. It was a typed list of which films had won which awards. Eva had been spot on.

After an hour or two of just enjoying a choice of places to put my things, I thought I'd better show my face at the office. I also needed to find out which train I needed to take to be at work on time, now I was a commuter.

I found a train timetable at Charing Cross and studied it on my way to Plumstead. This was going to work. The clouds were thickening but the rain held off until I got in the office.

Suzanne looked surprised. 'I thought you weren't coming in today.'

'I think I found somewhere else to live.'

'I'll need your new address.'

'I'll give it to you when it's all sorted. I'm just staying with a friend in the meantime. But I have been working.' I handed her my typed festival review. There was a huge burst of coughing from Mr Benstrup's office. I looked at Suzanne and she shook her head.

'Doesn't sound good, does it? So, how was Moscow?'

'Great. Very interesting. I'll take this to him.' I waved the review, knocked and opened his door.

'Ted!' He was wheezing as he tried to stand, and failed. 'I thought you weren't coming in. Bad business about your friend, but a good job you weren't there, hey? Could have been you in that body bag.'

'Yes. I'm sorry I didn't come in, but it will take me time to settle somewhere else. I did type up the review for you on a friend's typewriter.'

'That's very good of you, Ted.'

'And I have a list of all the winners, for your records.'

'And how did you find Moscow?'

'I loved Moscow. It was full of new experiences.'

He winked. 'Didn't come back with a wife, did you?'

'No wife, no.'

'Listen Ted, you take the rest of the day off. Suzanne has a couple of films I'd like you to go and see next week and we can have a proper chat about Moscow tomorrow. And I need to talk to you about wages too.' He saw my face. 'Nothing bad! Suzanne will have a surprise in your wage packet tomorrow, but you get off now. Have a drink!'

'All right. Thank you, Mr Benstrup.'

I went back to Suzanne's desk. 'Why is he so happy?'

'The magazine has received some new orders, really big ones. I believe he was thinking it would have to close, and now it's all come good. You get an extra £2 a week.' She smiled, but her eyes were confused.

'That's good. I wonder why now.'

'Yes. I wondered that too.'

She looked towards Mr Benstrup's office, and then pulled me onto the landing, closing the door behind her.

'Listen Ted, I heard his wife telling him to give you the sack. He's resisting, but I'd look for another job, if I were you.'

I could feel my heart beating. Could it have been because I didn't go to that meeting, and I didn't bring anything back for her? I didn't want Suzanne to know and be disappointed in me.

'Mrs Benstrup? Why would she say that?'

'I don't know. I just thought you should know.'

'Thanks, Suzanne. I think you should remember this name, just in case. Nadia Osipova. It might come up.'

She nodded and went back into the office.

I walked down the stairs and thought about the mysterious Joseph North. I could have asked Suzanne why she never told me. It certainly explained why she was angry with me when

I didn't come back on time from Bucharest. I didn't hold it against her. I wasn't sure I would have done anything different if I had known. I needed the job, and they had needed me. But no longer. Nadenka, Nadia, didn't want me around here. I wondered what else Suzanne had overheard.

I could sense her watching me as I left the building, and when I looked back up through the rain I could see her face at the window. I waved and she waved back.

When I arrived back at Montague Street, the rain had soaked through everything, from my shirt to my shoes. I opened the door to see Mrs Macfarlane waiting for me. Had she changed her mind? I stood on the mat and dripped.

She said, 'I wondered if you would like a look at the garden, Mr Walker?'

I looked down at my clothes.

'You are already wet, after all. Take that umbrella.'

I took the umbrella and followed her through the back of the house. 'Breakfasts are in there.'

She pointed to a large dining room, set for a meal at multiple small tables. Two steps down and we were in the kitchen full of gleaming pots. Out the back door, down three more steps and she waited inside the door.

'At the bottom of our garden you'll find a small gate in the fence. Have a little walk around the communal private gardens, just to get your bearings.'

I thought about refusing, but didn't. I found the gate and stepped through. It was open with a few shrubs and lots of puddles on the sun-baked lawn. I took a few steps forward, the rain hammering on the umbrella above me. A man with a trilby pulled low appeared from behind one of the bushes and I jumped.

'Mr Walker?'

'Yes?'

He handed me a plastic bag and pointed at a window in a house opposite Mrs Macfarlane's.

'First floor, twelve windows from the right,' he said. 'Between 7pm and 8pm. Should you see a light on with the curtains open, maybe you would be so good as to have a little walk in this garden, Mr Walker.'

I tried not to smile. It was like a bad film. The rain was running off his brim so I could hardly see his face, let alone his expression.

'Who will I be meeting?'

He shook his head. 'No questions. I believe there is one more thing you need to do.'

There was. As I thought about it, he walked away.

At the door I shook the umbrella out, and went back inside. Mrs Macfarlane had gone. I put the umbrella back in the coat stand, and went to my room. The bag was thoroughly taped up, and I had to tear the plastic and stretch the tape to get the envelope out. Inside were certificates: O Level, A Level and Degree Level. Only a 2:2 in English Literature. I was strangely disappointed in myself for this, but fair enough. Two names and addresses for my references. Right at the bottom, there was a German-English dictionary.

Would I need that?

At the weekend I would find the address of the London School of Journalism and work out how to apply. After I got my extra two pounds in the morning and paid my rent, I would have twenty-six pounds and no debts. Maybe I would go to the British Museum.

I lay back on the bed and thought of the women who now had a say in my life. Eva Mann and Mrs Constance Macfarlane. I tried to think about what it was about one that reminded me of the other, but I couldn't pinpoint it. Two women who both felt they knew what was best for me. It was a relief to hand over responsibility, in a way.

Ursula's letter stayed sealed on the mantelpiece. One day, when I was ready to say no to all of this, I would open it and find out what she needed me to know. I would remember Ingrid's shaking hands. I would think clearly about why that Barry died in that place at that time. Until then, I didn't want to know.

Days after I got back, I opened my final packet of duty free cigarettes. There was a piece of paper curled up inside, covered with tiny pencilled words.

'If you find out anything about this person, tell me directly. Wait until you know how.' And a name and address. Hunstanon. I knew I'd been there. The place on the east coast that looked west.

KGB First Chief Directorate
Information Service (Special Service I).

'FISHERMAN' INTERIM REPORT: FOR ADDITION TO WALKER FILE

Letter from Ursula Koskinen to Walker – no stamp, hand delivered by Hughes. Koskinen was observed to handwrite this in the lobby of the Rossiya hotel on the morning of the 22 July. The letter is not dated.

'If you have agreed to anything, run. Break with them now and you might get away with it.

Be careful, please, but don't approach me if you see me again.'

As of 5th August, this remained unopened by Walker.

CHAPTER 40

One last thing to do, the man had said. Well, two.

The previous day I hadn't seen anyone else at breakfast before I went to work. I didn't mind. On Saturday I again breakfasted alone, then I finished my application to the London School of Journalism. I was excited about it, but I was waiting until I heard back to say anything to Mr Benstrup. Suzanne was still looking at me strangely, but she handed me my extra pay and said nothing.

I got ready to go out, and posted the application. I took the tube at Holborn, and changed at Notting Hill Gate. At Paddington I consulted my new *London A to Z*. I'd been flicking through it, recognising museum names and streets. I hadn't been to Parliament yet, or the palace. It had all seemed too far away in Plumstead. I felt the money in my pocket and wondered where I would go later. Maybe I could find out how to join the nearest library and spend the afternoon reading in a pub. Or maybe I should start thinking bigger.

I reached the right street, full of large houses with driveways. I searched for the right number, no car on this driveway, and knocked on the door. It was a big house, double fronted, the front garden neatly tended with bedding plants. Now that I was near the net curtains, I could see the room on the left was full of books. The room on the right had a dining table with flowers in a vase. A young woman with short black hair answered the door. I could hear music in the background, and I noticed the hallway contained two suitcases, airplane tags attached. One was open, its contents spilling out. I forced my eyes up. The woman was smiling.

'Hello.'

I swallowed. I didn't know what had made me nervous. 'Mrs Hughes?'

'No. There's no Mrs Hughes here.'

I took the envelope from my pocket and checked the name and address. She read it.

'Oh.' She went back inside and shouted, 'Martha! It's for you!'

Something was odd. Why didn't she know Martha's last name? I read the envelope as I listened to a quick tread on the stairs. Mrs Martha Hughes.

Another woman appeared in the doorway, her brown hair pulled back into a towel on top of her head, her feet bare.

'Hello,' Martha said. 'I'm sorry about the mess, I needed to wash my hair. We're just back from Paris.'

That name, Martha. I had heard it recently. I played for time.

'What's that song?'

She laughed. 'Young Americans. Harriet's new favourite.'

I nodded and her smile faded. I held onto the letter, but she held her hand out.

'Is that for me?'

I let it go and she read the envelope.

She laughed. 'Is it from Kit? He's the only one who would call me that.'

'Kit?'

'Sorry, Christopher, I mean. No one else uses my married

name. I changed it back. Well, I hadn't changed it at all really, being out of the country when people were calling me that.' Frowning, she turned the envelope and sniffed it. 'It smells of papirosy. It is from him, isn't it?'

'I don't know.'

I took a step back. This didn't feel right. She wasn't supposed to know Christopher from the embassy. She was supposed to know an Alexander.

'Have you brought it from Russia?' Her voice trembled and she cleared her throat. 'From Moscow?'

I stepped forward again and reached for the envelope, 'I don't think—'

She held it away from me, and I retreated.

'Who are you?'

'No one.'

She took a step towards me. 'What is your name? Do you know Christopher? Why were you in Russia? Why do you have this?'

I couldn't say anything. I knew now. That was the question I should have asked Eva: do you have a son called Alexander? But would I have done this anyway, if she'd said, 'no'? I think I would have.

The woman, Martha, was trembling all over now. The more she tried to hide it, lifting her chin up and pressing her lips together, the younger she looked. She pulled the towel from her head, let it drop and pushed her hair back.

'Is Kit all right? Who is this from?'

I took another step backward, towards the gate. She ripped the envelope open and I could see it was a postcard of the Kremlin. She read it aloud, her voice shaking. 'You look like an angel. I just can't help falling in love with you. I'm caught in a trap.' She sobbed, and turned inside. 'Harriet! Harriet, come here!'

They sounded like Elvis quotations but it made no sense to me. It did to her.

She staggered and held onto the door frame, crumpling the envelope. 'Who gave you this? Have you seen Ivan? Where is he?'

Harriet ran through the hall and put an arm around Martha's shoulders. She stared at me too.

'I don't know an Ivan. I'm sorry.' I fumbled the catch on the gate and opened it.

'You don't know an Ivan?'

She was shouting now, her tone desperate, and I was running as if she was chasing me.

'Do you know an Eva?'

I paused and turned around. They were still standing in the road, watching me. I kept running.

KGB First Chief Directorate
Information Service (Special Service I)

'WOLFCUB' INTERIM REPORT:
FOR ADDITION TO REYNOLDS FILE

For cross-referencing with 'Fisherman' file

Letter to Martha Reynolds delivered by Ted Walker on 7th August.
   Everything now in place.

ACKNOWLEDGEMENTS

This novel has depended on the helpfulness of many people. I am always grateful to Sue Dawes who takes my early drafts and gives them a good shake. Thanks also to Mark Hardie who read an early draft, and Bieke Dutoit who again shared her knowledge of Moscow and the Russian language (any errors are my own). I am also grateful to Moira Forsyth, whose sensitive editing adds depth and clarity, and to all those behind the scenes at Sandstone Press who work so hard on getting books out into the world.

I read so many interesting and useful texts when writing this novel, but I am particularly grateful to have read Elena Razlogova's articles on simultaneous translation and Soviet cinema. I have started to gather a collection of 1970s travel guides to Moscow to get a sense of tourism in the Cold War and have drawn on *Smith's Moscow*, among others. In thinking about how to represent the voices of the people who watched and noted everything, I was influenced by Gilles Perrault's novel, *Dossier 51*, as well as the two memoirs written by Katherine Verdery, *My Life as a Spy* and *Secrets and Truths*, which draw on her experience of reading through the secret files which had been kept about her time in Romania.

NOW READ MARTHA'S STORY...

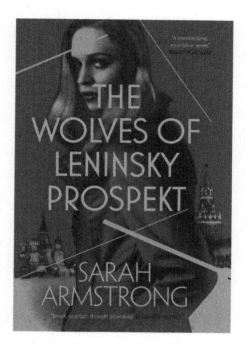

Rebellious Martha escapes bleak 1970s England for a fresh start in Moscow. She falls in love with the city but ignores the rules – dangerous, when every move is monitored and one mistake can cost everything.

'Armstrong evokes a Moscow that is both magical and oppressive, and has created a young heroine who is foolish, inquisitive and achingly lonely.'

HEATHER RICHARDSON

978-1-912240-71-5 – RRP £7.99

www.sandstonepress.com

f facebook.com/SandstonePress/

@SandstonePress